I0785410

# THUNDERSTRUCK

# Also By Shannon Delany

**13 to Life Series:**

*13 to Life*

*Secrets and Shadows*

*Bargains and Betrayals*

*Destiny and Deception*

*Rivals and Retribution*

**Weather Witch Series:**

*Weather Witch*

*Stormbringer*

*Thunderstruck*

**Classic Tales**

*Beastly Babes: Nine Classic Tales of Female Vampires*

**ShannonDelany.com**

# THUNDERSTRUCK

## A WEATHER WITCH NOVEL

# Shannon Delany

WOLF PRINT PRESS, LLC
New York
www.WolfPrintPress.com

For more, write: Wolf Print Press, LLC at PO Box 403, Otego, NY. 13825.

WOLF PRINT PRESS LLC
New York
www.WolfPrintPress.com

Delany, Shannon.
Thunderstruck: a Weather Witch novel/Shannon Delany.—1st ed. St. Martin's Press May 20, 2014
Ebook Edition ISBN 9781250018663

Delany, Shannon.
First Wolf Print Press, LLC trade printing: July 16, 2025
Print Edition ISBN: 978-1-962819-08-4
Ebook Edition ISBN: 978-1-962819-09-1

Cover design by Nazar with www.GetCovers.com

SECOND EDITION: July 2025

*Thunderstruck is dedicated to the bold and kind souls who continue to work on behalf of others, long after exhaustion's set in.*

# Foreword

In 2013 the *WEATHER WITCH* series debuted through St. Martin's Press (Macmillan). Every six months a new book released —just like the contract for the 13 TO LIFE series required. As a previous history teacher and lifelong student of history, I enjoyed reimagining America in her formative years—particularly America during that tenuous period between our Revolutionary and Civil Wars. To look back and say "Look how we've come" is comforting until you realize how easily democracy can be stolen away.

Within these covers are the original *THUNDERSTRUCK*, with only slight changes. Eventually I'll rework each book, but I felt it was vital that everyone could have the originals—especially this novel—which never released as a paperback due to an untimely death at the helm of the traditional publishing house it first called home. That death was followed by a new vision for the publisher —and steampunk wasn't a fit. As a result, *THUNDERSTRUCK* didn't receive the attention my previous books had from my publisher, readers complained they couldn't get a paperback and few owned e-readers, so (surprise, surprise) sales tanked. I fell into a depression and struggled to write. I re-entered the classroom, got my MA in Genocide Studies, and became a Library Director. Ghostwriting fell into my lap, my agent retired after winning back my fiction rights, and TAH-DAH: Here we are, circling back in a way suitable to those who recognize the ringing rhyme of history.

Although the books' covers are different (thanks to designer Nazar and project manager Carin at Getcovers), the books remain as close to the original size as possible so fans can purchase *THUNDERSTRUCK* to complete their collection, or buy a whole new set—their choice. The new and expanded editions should release in late 2026, and include extras like the updated the *13 TO LIFE* series books do. None of this would be possible without my fabulous formatter, tech (and amazing husband) Karl.

Shortly before Christmas of 1776, Thomas Paine published *The Crisis*, in which he wrote: "These are the times that try men's souls. The summer soldier and the sunshine patriot will, in this crisis, shrink from the service of their country; but he that stands by it now, deserves the love and thanks of man and woman." The fledgeling country was faltering and Paine wanted to inspire good people not to give up and not to give in. That, I think, is the true spirit of patriotism—to push always towards the dream of an America which is a beacon to those seeking freedom and equality and which, therefore, must be worthy of such seekers by truly offering freedom and equality to all.

*My love to each of you ever-working towards freedom for all and keeping the future in both heart and mind!*

*Shannon Delany*

# Prologue: 1844

Philadelphia

Light was fading from the sky when the first raindrops of a typical Philadelphia Tuesday evening began to dampen the tight salt-and-pepper curls covering John's head. Looking up, he squinted against the summoned rain clouds and wiped his palm across his forehead. He had fallen behind with his outside work—there could be no arguing that.

Philadelphia, like many cities in the young United States, had a regulated schedule of rainy and dry weather and of light and dark, all thanks to the Weather Witch at the city's Hub.

A few minutes remained before the drizzle became heavier and stuck his clothing to his skin, so he brushed his hands off and gathered the shovel and trowel from the narrow garden bed outside the Astraea estate's imposing wall. Throughout the city people would be hurrying indoors, servants closing windows, the wealthy members of the Hill settling down for an evening meal.

The clatter and hiss of a carriage's wheels skipping across damp cobblestones drew his gaze, and John watched a pair of pale horses pulling a fancy wagon down the street. The driver sat hunched, hat's brim pulled low over his eyes. The stormlit streetlights reflected off the barrel of a gun in his lap, and John squinted against the growing dark and damp to better see. Two men rode clinging to the back corners of the carriage, heads above its roof, hats forced low to battle the rising breeze.

The carriage paused at the nearest intersection and John glimpsed the rack on the wagon's back, usually where additional luggage was secured.

But not this evening.

This evening, rather than carpetbags or trunks, there was one long bundle tied tight with fabric and rope.

John recognized the thing by its shape and size, and when the carriage turned to take the road to the Below, he hurried inside the Astraea gates and into the nearest door. Inside the servants' quarters, he propped the shovel and trowel against a wall, paying no mind to the dirt that dropped off their edges, making a mess of the floor.

A quick right turn down the hall and he passed through another door, stumbling out the building's back and onto the darkening lawn. The grass slick beneath the worn soles of his shoes, still he made his way through the hedgemaze with practiced ease. He paused a moment at the edge of the Astraeas' expansive yard, perched on the highest of many slate steps, a dizzying distance above the faint and flickering lights of the city's most dangerous neighborhood—the Burn Quarter of the Below.

The only place the rival fire companies would rather see burn than saved—because even the most reprehensible gang members understood some people were irredeemable.

In the distance, John watched the carriage make its slow descent on the main road, weaving past neighborhoods of declining value on its way down the Hill.

His knees twinged in pain as he jogged down the long flight of steps, wiping his eyes and flicking water off his face as the storm overhead thickened. He splashed through deepening puddles, water soaking his feet and weighing down the hems of his pants legs.

The carriage turned. If they both continued on their paths they would meet in front of the alley, not far from the slate stairway's bottom step. John hurried, emerging from the alley just behind the carriage.

The carriage turned abruptly, rattling down the road leading to the water's edge, and John maintained his pace, eyes fixed on the object wrapped and still in the vehicle's rack. The horses snorted, bucking in their traces. No horse willingly neared briny water—not with the threat of hungry Merrow lurking by any salty shore.

The driver pulled the horses to a stop and lashed the reins down before sliding from his seat, gun gripped tightly in his hands.

The rain grew heavier; the images before John blurred and swam. His back pinned flat to the wall of the nearest building, he stayed under the roof's narrow overhang and in the thickest shadow possible, catching his breath and all the time thinking he should turn back.

Go home.

What was he but an old man with aching knees? What he'd done recently, helping Reanimate a wealthy woman who tried to take her own life, and now this—racing through the rain and shadows—such adventures belonged to younger men.

From the carriage's corners the men jumped down, handily untying the bundle hitched to the rack. They hurled it to the ground and it landed with a sickening *thud*.

Long, light-colored hair fell free of the fabric.

John stiffened.

It was a woman's body.

And she was handled with such indifference it was clear they had no interest in Reanimation.

But what they planned to do with her instead ...

He had no idea.

One door of the carriage swung open and a tall man stepped out—a man frequently featured in the city paper.

Councilman Loftkin.

"Keep watch," Loftkin told the driver.

The man shook his head, adjusting his hat's brim so water poured off it. "Ain't no one in his right mind coming outta his home on a Tuesday evening."

Sheltered in the shadows, and wicking up water, John would not disagree.

"Grab the girl." Loftkin pointed inside the carriage.

The men reached in and snared the last member of their party. There was cursing and shouting. It took both men, grunting, to drag a very-much-alive girl out and toss her to the rain-glossed ground.

John gasped, recognizing the girl, as well.

Cynda. She had worked in the Astraea household until young Lady Jordan was taken to be Made into a Weather Witch. With the family's subsequent fall from power, most servants moved to other households—Cynda determined to make a fresh start.

As one man unrolled the fabric from the corpse, the other hefted Cynda, forcing her to look Loftkin in the eye.

Behind the trio, the first man pulled a knife and went to work on the dead girl's body, contemplating his every cut as the driver stood silent nearby, watching.

Fighting the swimming sickness in his gut, John crept forward to better hear and see.

"You will stay the night here," Loftkin explained to Cynda. "In the morning you will scream, and, panicked, tell people Merrow attacked you and your friend."

Cynda shook her head miserably.

Grabbing her by the shoulders, Loftkin shook her until her head lolled. "You *will*."

"They'll never believe me ..."

The man with the knife stood, a strip of bloody fabric in his fist. Striding over, he thrust it into Cynda's shaking hand. "*Make them believe.*"

Loftkin stooped, his face and Cynda's nearly touching. "If you do not obey—do not *succeed*—I will arrange for you a meeting with the very same man your friend saw last. We shall see how it goes for *you*."

The men climbed back aboard the carriage, the driver turning the horses once more toward the Hill. Left by the mutilated corpse of her friend, Cynda sobbed, and John looked on, thunderstruck.

# Chapter One

*Aboard the Airship Artemesia*

Borne high above the world of the Grounded population, a breeze whisked around the brightly painted and carved body of the great airship *Artemesia*. It danced across her figurehead's wild feminine face, tracing along her shoulders and open arms to race up the broad balloon and painted wings at her back. Up the breeze scurried, cresting the great netted balloon to come Topside. Skimming the pockmarked surface of the deck, it teased around the hem of ship's Conductor Jordan Astraea's blue dress, leaving it fluttering in its wake. Jordan seemed not to notice, resting her head against the broad chest of the handsome blond sporting questionable-looking facial hair.

From beneath her skirt, two small noses poked out, and the Fennec foxes, Kit and Kaboodle, checked that the deck was clear of the *Tempest*'s rampaging cook.

Beside Jordan, a small girl knelt. Never relinquishing her grip on the pleated fabric of Jordan's skirts, she giggled, spotting the two furry troublemakers.

*Surreal.* That was the best way to describe Rowen Burchette's life: utterly and irrevocably surreal.

He stayed still, his arms wrapped around Jordan, his breathing shallow. Standing quiet as a man whose only goal was to hold a girl as long as he could now he'd found her.

His gaze took in Topside's sweeping rails, the glowing storm-lanterns topping each post, and the largest stormcell crystal he had ever seen mounted in wicked and reflective jags of wire—making the ship's heart and power source. *Non-human* power source, he mentally corrected. Because, central to every function of this airship was its Conductor, the very human Jordan Astraea.

"You came," Jordan whispered, her lips brushing the rough muslin of his shirt. Her breath warm, it pushed through the shirt's thin fabric, and Rowen stiffened, sucking in his breath.

The scent of her—like the smell of the forest on a cool summer morning—washed through him—and her hair, cut so strangely short, brushed the tip of his nose. He sighed.

This was it, then, he thought, *this* was rescue.

Rescue for her and—he closed his eyes tightly and pushed the memories of his recent losses away, stuffing them down—rescue for *him.*

The whirr of gears and the sound of wood and metal crunching against each other as something thumped to a stop nearby drew Rowen's attention. A set of three joined walls pierced the Topside floor, an elevator rising out of the heart of the large airship. Crushed together and wearing the blue and gold of the *Artemesia's* staff stood men dressed in sharp uniforms, their eyes sharper yet. Grasping thick loops of heavy rope connected to leather with strange metallic stitching, they carried collars and leads reminiscent to those used on hunting hounds.

Only stronger. Thicker.

*Fiercer.*

They eyed the *Artemesia*'s deck, covered with the mangled remnants of lightships plucked from the sky by the little girl's temper tantrum? Rowen considered but determined to keep his mouth shut about the possibility of so young and strong a Witch.

Torn from the air, the ships had gouged their way across the deck's boards, scattering debris behind them.

Among the wreckage lay the lightships' wounded and stunned riders: Wardens, Wraiths, and their prisoners turned accomplices.

Hats skittered and rolled across the deck, veils flapping from brims and unmasking Wraiths. Rowen shuddered, holding Jordan the smallest bit tighter. Every child heard tales of what was beneath the Wraith's veils, along with warnings of "I will sell you to the Wraiths for stew meat"—but the reality of tormented and puckered flesh was more than imagination might conjure.

The Wardens were oddity enough: tattoos boldly marking their faces and necks, permanent sepia-colored reminders of the brutal touch of the sky's cruel finger—what many called Lightning's Kiss. But being an oddity was worlds different from being a living horror.

The Wardens' tattoos looked like the strange burn that bloomed pink and frost-like across Jordan's left cheek and scrawled down her neck—running along her shoulder and disappearing beneath her gown. On Jordan it was beautiful.

On Jordan anything was beautiful, Rowen realized.

But the Wraiths ... Lightning had twisted them, their faces forever caught in a moment of torment no joy could erase. *There was a crooked man, who walked a crooked mile,* Rowen thought remembering the old nursery rhyme. Lightning's Kiss had shaped the Wraiths down to their long and pointed teeth—teeth that shook Rowen back to memory.

He swallowed hard. He'd seen such teeth on the Merrow who attacked Jonathan and him as their horses drank from a stream they'd thought safe from the ongoing Wildkin War.

Merrow murdered Jonathan and pushed Rowen to face his destiny alone.

From the ship's bow, a man wearing a hood and mask in the shape of a rhinoceros's head clapped his hands together, striding forward with a grace more suited to an elegant gentlemen than an entertainer. He commanded everyone's attention. Rowen knew him, masked or not.

The Wandering Wallace looked at the remnants of splintered lightships scattered about the deck and assessed the groaning Wraiths and Wardens working free of their destroyed vessels. He raised his head, saying through the open mouth of his heavy leather and brass mask, "I dare not say clap them in irons as that could create quite a shocking result, but," he instructed the gathered guardsmen, "secure them and take them below. Disperse them among rooms so they cannot plot. But do use nice rooms. They deserve to be treated more gently by us than by those previously controlling them."

The guards spread out from the elevator, picking paths through the smoldering wreckage, grabbing Wardens, Wraiths, and their more human-looking companions alike, looping the collars so snuggly around their necks Rowen thought more of a hangman's noose than a dog's leash. A few Weather Workers threatened, gnashing needle-like teeth as guards approached, but most were too stunned by what they had witnessed to resist a collar.

Rowen understood too well, his own shock only receding as he held Jordan close—her body a warm reality in a world that kept turning upside down before righting itself in strange new ways.

Willing as lambs, the Weather Workers were led to their fate below deck.

All but one.

A Wraith rolled up to its full height, tall and unnaturally slender, tufts of fine white hair dotting its wrinkled and dented scalp. Its cheeks creased in jagged furrows as thin lips pulled back from fangs. Glaring at the approaching guards, it gathered the moist air, pulling it free from the roiling nest of dark clouds surrounding the airship *Artemesia* and holding her aloft. Tugging the wisps together, it stirred them in the air and thickened them like a sauce reaching a boil. A hiss escaped its grim and grinning lips and it tightened the storm clouds, whipped the wind up with its will, forcing it all into a circling and screaming gale that tore around the Wraith, clawing its long, black coat. Mouth stretching wide, its lips curled at their ends, barely holding its cruel teeth back.

Any who somehow kept their hats during the earlier fight now clutched them to their heads, grimacing against the Wraith's whirlwind.

Jordan twitched in Rowen's grasp. The little girl with curls the color of platinum clutched Jordan's dress tighter, both girls turning their faces from the Weather Worker and squeezing their eyes closed.

Rowen adjusted his hold on Jordan, shielding her face from the snarling air while he squinted against it, mesmerized.

In the midst of the growing storm, the Wraith threw back its head and howled. A tornado twisted along its long body, thickest by its booted feet, and with a growl, the wind lifted the Wraith into the air.

The guards moved in, but the Wandering Wallace gave no new command—merely watched dishes and linens from the over-turned dining table scramble away, animated by the rush of air. Suspended above them, the Wraith spun once in midair, taking in the view and then, with the flash of a ruby ring, it vaulted into the thick cloud bank beyond, disappearing from sight.

The Wandering Wallace shrugged.

The tail of the Wraith's windstorm wrapped Rowen's trio even tighter, and he rewarded himself with the touch of Jordan's silky hair between his fingers. It should have been longer. This awkward hairstyle she sported was nearly boyish, as if by shearing off her dark locks she became someone else.

Someone *new*.

Old or new, scarred or flawless, with long hair or short, Witch or Grounded—to Rowen, Jordan was beautiful.

The realization gave him pause.

Jordan Astraea, wearing a lowborn's dress, her hair chopped short, her face scarred ... was beautiful. He had worked so hard to find her—to rescue her—and lost so much to win her. As changed as her physical appearance was, so equally was he changed.

Inside and out.

Perhaps she was changed as much as he. Was she the Storm-bringer? The one prophesied to unite them and end the conflict?

Or was she just the girl he flirted with—now battered and worn by being dragged so far from home?

The child at Jordan's feet shifted. In the crook of one tiny arm she held a flopping stuffed animal with long ears, horn buttons for eyes, and carefully stitched fingers. She looked up at Rowen, the strange power he'd seen in Jordan's face shimmering beneath her skin as well. "And who are you?" she asked.

He hesitated, unwilling to move away from Jordan as she slumped against him, hiccupping from time to time. But running his hand across her short and spiking hair he broke the spell between them.

She pulled away, meeting his eyes briefly before looking away. Before looking *down*.

He managed to keep one of his hands on her shoulder.

Rowen cleared his throat, darting a glance at the child. He skimmed his right hand down Jordan's arm, and sank into a crouch, face-to-face with the little girl, and carefully taking Jordan's hand in his. His gaze flicked from Jordan—stiff, still, and staring off into some place he wasn't welcomed—and then to the child.

Her face was bright as starlight.

She released Jordan's skirt, taking her free hand instead.

A smile twitched across Jordan's lips before fading and Rowen saw her squeeze the child's hand.

The girl tilted her head, addressing him again. "I'm Meggie. And just who are you?"

Rowen went the last distance, resting on his knees. Eye level with the diminutive blond angel, he tested his most winning smile. "Hello, Meggie. I am Rowen. It is both an honor and a pleasure to meet you."

He held his empty hand out to her, and they shook.

Meggie grinned. "Nice to meet you as well."

Rowen glanced up at Jordan, who, caught watching him, looked away again. "And you are whose darling daughter?"

Meggie opened her mouth, but a man swooped over and whisked her away, saying, "Your pardon, good sir."

Rowen popped to his feet, his eyebrows tugging together. He stared at the retreating man's back until he stopped—far from Rowen's reach. He stopped by a sturdily built woman, swinging Meggie in his arms while watching Rowen, eyes worried. Rowen's lips pressed together and he wiggled his jaw. "Who ... ?"

Jordan slipped her hand free of his and turned to focus on the workings of the ship.

"Jordan?" Rowen asked. "Who are these people?"

She sucked down a deep breath and stared at a large glass cylinder holding a clear liquid, white crystals floating near the top of the glass like finger-sized pieces of frost.

The creak of a board behind him made Rowen swing around, his reflexes sharper than ever.

A dark-haired young man stood there and Rowen stepped back, sucking in a breath at the sight of him. He was all at once perfect and ruined—his face a patchwork quilt, seamed together with thin white scars as if someone had cut him apart just to see how he might eventually heal. Frequently told he was handsome, Rowen knew he could not compare to this young man. Beneath the puckered skin his features were fine, perfectly symmetrical. Sharp cheekbones, dramatic eyes, and bold, arching eyebrows beat back the scars that dared try to overpower his natural beauty.

Jordan studied the intruder's face with an intensity matching

Rowen's own, as if she, too, had never seen his face, although it seemed she knew him.

"I, too, am filling in some blanks," the boy whispered, eyes searching Rowen's face as if he had a question he was not yet ready to ask aloud. "Caleb," he finally said in introduction before focusing on Jordan. "My dear," he said, reaching slender (and equally scarred) hands out to her, "might you enlighten us? Perhaps tell me enough that I might not spill the Maker's guts in front of his adorable daughter? As you thwarted my efforts once before?"

Rowen straightened. "The Maker's daughter?" His head snapped around to look at the man holding the little girl, the man standing as far as he could get from the rest of them. "He is the Maker—the one who Made you ..."

Words failed.

Jordan snorted and asked, "Into *this*?" The words hissed with venom.

Frustration built inside him and he took a step toward her, measuring the space between his breaths. Slowing his breathing, he steeled his demeanor. "Is he the one who did *this* to you?" He reached up to touch her cheek.

She stumbled backwards as if his touch would burn fierce as any fire.

His hand dropped away, fingers flexing at his side. "Please," he said, forcing his voice to stay as level, as controlled, as he could. It cracked, betraying him and he cleared his throat. "Please," he repeated. "Tell me, Jordan. Tell me so I can make him pay for what he's done to you." His hand moved to the pommel of his sword.

Observing him, Caleb ventured, "I might just come to like you...."

Jordan's gaze skimmed Caleb to rest on Rowen, and for a heartbeat her eyes snared his. Then they darted away again, flashing like the wings of a bluebird.

"Tell me, so I might make him pay for what he's done to *us*," Rowen corrected, the words staggering out.

She shook her head. "I want no violence."

Rowen stepped forward. "Jordan ..."

Caleb slid between them, his back to Rowen.

"Caleb," Jordan said with a welcoming sigh, and hearing that name—no, Rowen realized, not hearing *his* name—was a knife thrust between his ribs.

A knife aimed at his heart.

Caleb kept his back to Rowen, and whispered, "Oh, darling ..." Blocking much of Rowen's view, he slipped his hand up, resting it on the slope of her bare shoulder.

Jordan stood, motionless, her eyes locked on Caleb's. She did not resist his touch, did not flinch away as she did when Rowen touched her.

Rowen turned his head, looking at anything else on the raised dais—anything but the tender reunion before him featuring someone he never anticipated.

He expected there would be some change in Jordan. That she was thinner did not surprise him. That her hair was cut short—shocking, but it was not beyond understanding. That she did not wear a shawl, or gloves, or even shoes ... Strange, but surely there were logical reasons.

Even the scar on her cheek—even as startling as it was—it was simply physical and meant less than he'd ever believed it could.

Physical changes he grasped. She'd been imprisoned and Made a Witch.

But for her to find someone else while imprisoned (because Caleb was surely not a passenger on this liner if his rough clothing was any way to judge) was beyond comprehension. Beyond what Rowen could bear, being so close to success but suddenly so far away.

A guard pushed between them, reaching for Caleb, a collar and lead in one broad hand.

Jordan spun to face the interloper, shouting, "Don't you *touch* him!" Her hand shot up, sparks dancing like living lightning between the tips of her fingers.

"Leave that one be," the Wandering Wallace agreed.

Wide-eyed, the guard stepped back, checking the deck's surface one last time for any stragglers. He collared another Weather Worker, instantly crippling its powers, and rejoined his comrades by the elevator. Three groups of guards and their accompanying prisoners stood there, descending in shifts into the ship.

"I will not let them take you," Jordan assured Caleb.

Rowen's shoulders slumped but he straightened when a hand dropped onto his shoulder. Jerking around, hand tight on his sword's handle, he found himself nearly nose-to-nose with the red-headed captain of the ship he'd only recently come to consider a temporary home, the *Tempest*.

Nose-to-nose with Captain Elizabeth Victoria.

"Evie," he acknowledged.

She tipped her chin to one side, and eyes fixed on his, he suspected she fought the urge to look at Jordan and her companion. "Come along, Rowen," she said, her tone tight. "Let us give everyone time to get sorted out as we sort ourselves out. We have all just had quite a battle-filled reunion."

Rowen nodded, jaw clenched so hard his temples felt they'd pop. Evie was right—vexing as that was. Everyone was only coming to grips with what had just happened.

Weather Witches, Wraiths, and Wardens had dropped from the sky at nearly the same time the *Tempest* came alongside the *Artemesia* and—and what exactly had his group done other than shoot grappling hooks at a dinner table? They hadn't taken the *Artemesia* captive, nor had they fought for control of the ship. He dragged his feet across the deck following Evie.

It was all a bit less like a battle and more like a team quietly reuniting, their secret plan already underway.

*Philadelphia*

Lady Cynthia Astraea slid from her bed, bare feet touching down on a cool wooden floor that inspired her to move with haste across her chamber and to her armoire. More correctly: to Jordan's armoire. She had sold her own recently and had Jordan's brought to her room instead.

It was not as if Jordan needed it where she was.

The coolness of the thought gave her pause. Licking her lips, Lady Astraea leaned over before the nearby vanity, peering at herself. She had sold *her* vanity, and *her* armoire ...

Why was that again?

She reached into the pocket secreted away in the top of her shift and fished out a tiny blue crystal. It warmed at her touch. Her breathing calmed, her heartbeat steadied—small comforts when she forgot things as easily as she did now. She rolled her shoulders forward, peering into the mirror to find herself more clearly in her features.

How did that even make sense?

Thinking that made it seem there were times she didn't recognize herself in the features of her own face!

Her thumb rubbed across the stone's faceted sides, slipping down to one of its two points. It was a Herkimer diamond like any other ... and yet, somehow, not like any other.

Not at all.

She pressed one point into the pad of her thumb, trying to untangle the thought that tumbled and turned, sliding toward the darkness at the edges of her mind.

Her youngest daughter had been taken as a Witch. Her family had fallen from grace and she had started selling things—expensive things—to support some cause ... ?

The answer dodged out of her reach and her chest tightened. A fog seeped into her mind's eye, slowly filling her head. "No," she whispered, digging the tiny blue stone into her thumb so hard blood wept up around it. "No," she hissed as she saw her eyes shift and change in the mirror, growing catlike. Specks of gold and bronze colored her irises, making her eyes glitter with a foreign and icy glint.

The room—her bedchamber—faded, somehow becoming more distant, the edges of things growing fuzzy and indistinct. She felt further from herself ... no, further from her eyes and her nose and her mouth and her fingertips ... like she was being dragged down into dark waters without ever leaving her body. Her vision reduced to a single slit as if she peered out between shuttered windows, she thought different thoughts.

She saw different things.

No, she saw things *differently*.

She tucked the blue stormcell crystal into a drawer in her vanity, far in the back of it and underneath some old letters of Jordan's. Bothersome little thing, that touchstone. She placed it as far from sight and mind as she could, sucking her thumb until the taste of salt and iron was gone. She lounged a moment before the mirror of the less impressive vanity, then rolled her shoulders back and straightened her spine, raising her chin like a woman of good breeding should.

She rested her hand over the spot by her heart where the Reanimator had inserted her soul stone, letting out a sigh as she rose. A skip in her step, she bounded to the armoire, and flung its doors open.

A fine assortment of clothing awaited her. Metallic embroideries, glittering gemstone beads, pressed velvets and delicate lace. Yes, she had no qualms selling furniture, sets of silver, or an occasional necklace or brooch to funnel money to the rebels, especially when none of the items were her own. She grasped a fine gown with gold and silver birds stitched into its neckline, cuffs, and hem.

Lord Morgan Astraea looked askance at her when she first had it brought to the estate, but she held out her hand and alluded enough about the power of her appreciation that he paid for it himself. She had worn it to dinner with him that same evening and realized then she would need to handle him carefully.

She had been like him. Hopeful. Forgiving. Once. Nearly a hundred years ago. Right up until the time the God-fearing population of her town tied her to a stake for magicking up a flood that washed away their crops. It had been an accident.

Still they lit a fire under her—and not in the inspirational way one might have wished. Slow to catch, its tinder damp and flames smoky, in one last show of rebellion she demonstrated how best to make a fire and burn a Witch. The lightning she'd called burst through the crown of her head, poured from her eyes, mouth, and fingertips.

And laid all the spectators low.

It had certainly stung, but it was over quickly enough. And from what she knew from her short time playing at being Lady Astraea, no one had dared try to burn a Witch since.

Even the Grounded population could learn, ignorant as those without magick were.

Her room was dim, the candles yet unlit. Rain snapped against the shutters, slipped through the spaces between and slid down the rippled glass of her windows. The reflection from one outside lamp pierced the shuttered windows, its glow wavering on the floor, warming the slender space it marked. She focused on the soft light, encouraging it to brighten. She tugged all remaining warmth from the wood floor, packing it tighter and tighter together. Wisps of smoke curled up from it, carrying the faint scent of burning wood. Pressing one bare foot against the spot, she smothered the smoldering boards with her flesh. She grinned.

Fire no longer scared her.

Neither did the threat of death.

There was a knock at her door. Most likely the servant girl, Laura, come to peer in on her for the evening. The servants mostly left her be and seemed not to care when she dozed or woke. Except for Laura. For a servant, the girl was slow to respond and slower to obey. But, if Lady Marsham could train the population of an entire town to never again burn a Witch, surely she could teach one hesitant servant to step lively.

It merely took the right sort of persuasion. She rubbed her fingertips together and smiled as sparks bridged the spaces between them.

It was good to be alive.

Again.

# Chapter Two

Only the dead have seen the end of war.

—PLATO

*Aboard the Artemesia*

A group gathered by the fallen dining table, dishes and glassware shattered nearby and spread across the deck in glittering shards.

Only one chair remained upright from the supposed surprise attack. Rowen froze, seeing how it managed such a feat.

It was bolted to the floor.

He focused on it, staring at the belt lashed across the back of it and lying open and loose. Nearby a small, overturned table wobbled on its rounded edge, rolling with the gentle and somehow haunted movement of the ship. Leaping forward, Rowen righted it, only breathing again when it stood still and mercifully silent.

Evie brushed past him, sweeping garbage and clutter out of her way with a swing of her foot. Things grated and smeared across the floor beneath her boot's sole, becoming multicolored smudges and elongated puddles between the remnants of food and drink.

The smells of meat, wine, recently baked bread, sweat, and fear hung heavy, despite the movement of the air.

"A bit of help, please?" Evie asked. Moving to one end of the long table she looked at Rowen.

But Ginger Jack slipped around him and set something Rowen presumed came from one of their attacker's lightships. Striding to the table's far end, Ginger Jack grunted agreement and, smacking his palms down on its edge, asked, "Ready, gorgeous?"

Evie looked from Rowen to Jack. "Are you talking to me or the pretty boy?"

Jack snorted. "Nothing pretty about that boy from my vantage," Jack replied, adding a laugh.

"That's because you're short—you've got a bad angle," Rowen returned, his chin raising arrogantly.

"Bad angle. That *must* be the reason," Jack agreed as he and Evie reset the table.

"Must be," Evie agreed with a wink.

"I am very nearly as pretty as they come," Rowen added. "And I am man enough to admit it."

Jack chuckled. "Is he flirting with me, Evie?" he joked. "I'd hate to break his heart, but I have eyes for another," he admitted, "and not one of his gender," he clarified, a grin sliding across his face. "Even though he does *scream* like a girl ..."

Evie barked out a laugh. "True, true! Well, for the sake of that *other*," she said, "I do hope you have more than just *eyes* for her."

Jack's grin widened. "Oh, I do. I most certainly do," he promised.

Rowen rolled his eyes and rubbed his chin. It was disastrously stubbly again. When had he last shaved? Before they had docked in Bangor? No wonder Jordan was taken aback. A man must keep his appearance up whether aboard a pirate ship or a luxury liner if he wished to impress a lady, Witch or not. He brushed his hands down the front of his shirt and adjusted his collar. "You two seem quite comfortable—"

"In what way precisely?" Jack asked, stepping away from the table.

The flirting between the *Tempest*'s engineer and the ship's captain immediately stopped.

"In the way that you both seem quite at home considering we've barely been here half an hour—aboard a ship we wanted to wrest control of forcibly if need be."

"*If need be,*" Evie specified. Evie and Jack stripped off the tablecloth. "Where's that girl?" she asked, ignoring Rowen's implied question.

"The servant?"

"Yes," Evie said, kicking the stained fabric aside. "There is a severe need of linen laundering and I would suggest a thorough swabbing of this deck."

Jack shrugged. "Maybe she disappeared belowdecks?"

"Are you ignoring me?" Rowen mused aloud.

Evie shook her head at Jack and muttered, "Someone needs to do something around here. This is a liner of good repute. Airworthy and well-formed. It should be kept in top condition, whether under siege or not."

"You *are* ignoring me," Rowen said, incredulous. "Did you know the ship would be ours so easily?"

"There is no need to let standards slip," Jack agreed.

A grumble grew in Rowen's throat. "How long have you planned to take control of this ship?"

Evie gave a negligible shrug. "We never intended to take control of this ship ourselves. We were simply a means to achieving a goal obviously reached before someone with an itchy trigger finger harpooned a table full of food," she said. Her gaze fell on Jack.

"You said, *bring us alongside,* and I took the appropriate steps to bring us alongside."

Unimpressed, she turned her attention back to Rowen,

cocked a hip and raised an eyebrow. "I do believe you are assuming things again due to our occupation."

"Right," Rowen said, folding his arms over his chest. "Of course. Because of your occupation."

"We cannot help it if, subconsciously, you are still not keen on being allied with—"

"—*liberally aligned traders*," Rowen said, though he knew them for what they were: pirates.

She smiled. "Our intention was not to captain a second ship—captaining one is work enough. But we did need to get creative when you changed our timeline by being discovered in the Hill King's Cavern. We are used to traveling with wanted men, Rowen Burchette," Evie said, putting an emphasis on his surname, "but not someone wanted by so *many* different people for such high prices."

By the ship's controls, movement and discussion ceased. Out of the corner of his eye, Rowen noted Caleb and Jordan watching him from the corners of theirs.

Spotted in the open, the Fennec foxes were chased by a laughing Meggie.

Rowen lowered his voice. "It was never my desire to draw such attention—or trouble—to myself. You both know I have had only one goal since being taken forcibly by your crew in Holgate." He stared openly at Jordan, raising his volume, and said, "There was only one thing—one person, one goal—on my mind the entire time I was with you."

Jordan turned away, fiddling with the ship's controls.

"I did everything I could to reach that goal. I never intended to be kidnapped."

"You throw that in our faces all the time," Evie said, again winking at Ginger Jack, "as if it was a bad thing. Imagine how dull—how drab—the last few weeks of your life would have been without being a part of the *Tempest*'s crew."

"Drab," Rowen muttered, scrubbing a hand across his face. "I could do dull or drab. Both at the same time, in fact."

"Pish-posh," Evie scolded. "Adventure makes the man far more than any clothing does."

Rowen adjusted the cuffs of his sleeves. "That is a good thing, considering my current selection of clothing."

The Wandering Wallace approached, his slender form top-heavy beneath the rhinoceros's head he wore. No matter what face he hid his own behind, Rowen recognized him by his body language—his grace and poise. The Wandering Wallace had head-lined Jordan's disastrous birthday party. He moved like a prowling panther—elegant, sleek, and dangerous, his beautiful Oriental companion a shadow at his back.

"Wandering Wallace," Rowen greeted.

The Wandering Wallace had taught Rowen basic sleight of hand for Jordan's party—a skill that had come particularly in handy when Rowen slipped Jordan the birthday gift he'd commissioned for her: a brass heart pin engraved with the words *Be brave.*

*Be brave* were words he'd used to encourage her to try things beyond what she'd been taught was proper—like sneaking into Philadelphia's most dangerous (and exciting) neighborhood known as the Below. Like slipping out into the Astraea family hedgemaze high on the top of the Hill late at night to meet him beneath the moon and the stars.

*Be brave* were their watchwords, as much a part of their personal language as *right as rain* was part of the rebel vernacular.

The Wandering Wallace dipped his chin, his well-polished rhino horn glinting. "We meet again, Rowen," he said. "We live in a small, small world, do we not?"

"It seems you are a more integral piece of my world than I suspected," Rowen countered.

"It is a distinct possibility now I see your companions." He looked at the stormlights on posts surrounding the dais and main-taining the feel of daylight inside the manufactured storm cradling their ship. He addressed Evie. "Evening is falling. Shall we discuss business?"

The elevator made one more descent, the Topside deck cleared of human debris.

Ginger Jack was already seated at the table, tinkering with odds and ends of mechanisms he'd pillaged. He was already at work, determined to fix at least one of the damaged lightships.

The foxes zipped around his chair, whining.

Evie pulled a chair over for herself, turning it so she straddled its back, her arms crossed. "Might we include the Conductor in our discussion?" Spotting the circling foxes, she reached down and grabbed one, settling the snapping beast in her lap.

"Call her Jordan," a tall, dark-haired man said as he joined them. "Or better yet," his expression stayed strict as that on anyone Rowen had seen—except his mother; no one's expression was as sour as hers when Rowen disappointed her—"call her Lady Astraea."

Rowen rolled his lips together. As much as he did not like any other man suggesting how someone should refer to Jordan, at least this man referred to her with respect and encouraged others to do the same. That he could respect. That he could even like.

Evie smiled up at the tall brunette, stroking the annoyed fox so firmly its oversized ears flopped. Slowly its snarl faded. "And you are ... her agent?"

The man pushed dark curls back from his eyes. "No. Merely someone who believes in respect and equality. She is far more than a title or a rank."

"A dissenter," Ginger Jack said, not looking up. He pulled his hands back from the metal bits and watched them move without his help. Halfheartedly involved in conversation, he nodded to himself.

"You are not?" the other man asked.

Jack shrugged. "My actions speak more clearly than any label." He stood, gazing at heaps of parts still scattered across the deck. Stepping away, he chose one that appeared promising, and rifled through it until he'd found something interesting.

"Marion Kruse," the man introduced himself.

The name yanked Rowen's attention back from his friend's scavenging. "House Kruse?" Everyone in Philadelphia knew the tragic tale of House Kruse's fall. A Weather Witch dragged away from a birthday party and a poisoning that killed the remaining family—perpetrated by a household servant. The family name was rife with scandal. And Rowen had hunted with Lord Kruse and his eldest boy.

A boy evidently grown to manhood and now standing before him, dark hair falling into troubled gray eyes.

Marion gave him so sharp a look Rowen shut his mouth. Some topics were not his to address.

"Bring the Conductor—young Lady Astraea—over," the Wandering Wallace instructed Rowen.

"I'll fetch her," Marion offered.

The Wandering Wallace raised his hand. "No. Rowen."

Marion squinted at the blond next to him. "Rowen ... Burchette? It's been years ..."

Rowen blew out a sigh and stalked off to again try addressing Jordan and Caleb.

Behind him he heard more chairs get righted, wooden feet scraping across the battered deck planks. He left the noise and the intermingled scents and focused on the sound of his own feet clomping across the deck toward the girl who openly chose the company of a different man.

He paused a few feet from them, noting how comfortable Caleb was by her side. And how calm, safe, and secure she seemed to feel in his presence.

And how their hands slipped together, fingers entwining.

Rowen wondered briefly why he was surprised. He'd expected this. No, not *this* exactly—he'd expected she'd have given up on him, that she'd have been wounded by his lack of success in rescuing her. Perhaps that she'd thought he'd decided not to come and find her.

He hadn't expected that she would have found someone to

*replace* him. But Caleb and Jordan were so ensconced in conversation they did not hear him approach.

"Did the Maker do this to you?" Jordan asked, her fingers moving so lightly across Caleb's damaged cheek Rowen paused abruptly and looked away.

"No," he murmured. "It comes from a different torturer, a different time. Sometimes it seems a different lifetime."

"Many of my memories are like that, too. Distant. I want to run away, Caleb," she confessed desperately. "Run and never come back. Leave all this—all these problems to someone else. I want to go somewhere quiet. A place where there is only nature. Only nature and time."

Caleb glanced at the ship's ornate controls. "I fear there's no easy escape for any of us. Especially not *you*," he told Jordan. "You control a huge airship filled to the brim with dissenters and those thinking dissenters should be destroyed. They call you *Stormbringer*."

Jordan looked down.

"The name matters not," Caleb said. "Still you are one of the few truly capable of changing things for our people—you cannot abandon our kind now. Not when we are so close to having a chance for change."

"We aren't all of the same kind," Jordan protested. "Your kind, his kind," she jabbed a thumb over her shoulder toward Marion, "those kind are not *my* kind at all? I am an anomaly proving any one of us can be *your* kind if broken."

Rowen stepped more slowly, desperate not to draw attention to his proximity while they confided in each other, but even more desperate to know all that was being confided.

"You are not a Witch?"

"I should not have been able to be *Made* a Witch," she corrected. "I am the exception to a rule—an exception that proves the rule has been wrong all along. I am living proof that each and every one of us can be Made, each of us has storms brewing within. Making has nothing to do with heritage and everything to do with being broken. Every person alive makes as good a slave as a lord or lady—I am the living proof of *that*."

"Then you must stay the course, tell this truth, and bring equality. *You* are the key to changing the path of history with this revelation."

"What else might you tell me, Caleb?"

Caleb paused. "That whoever else knows the truth of this is in great danger. If it is desired that we are kept down—in our place —you are the key showing that no one's place is carved in stone. That is a very messy sort of thinking for those in government to allow the public. You bear a dangerous truth—the type that shifts paradigms."

"Yes," she whispered.

"That is the true definition of the Stormbringer, I think. You are in great danger, my dear," Caleb confirmed. "But now you are faced with an equally great choice: run or face down destiny?"

"What if running *is* my destiny?"

A board whined beneath Rowen's weight and Caleb faced him.

Glancing down, Rowen cleared his throat.

They released hands—no, Caleb released Jordan's hand. Jordan's fingers sought Caleb's once more, crawling up the tips of his to interlock again.

"Yes," Caleb coaxed, leaning slightly forward, a smile sliding up one side of his face.

Rowen focused on Jordan's face instead. On the scar that crawled along her neck and cheek, blossoming like some exotic and angry flower and yet unable to detract from her beauty. It simply gave her beauty another layer.

She glared at him before looking away.

"They request your presence," Rowen said, his breath tight in his chest.

She looked behind her, at the mechanisms controlling key aspects of the ship she Conducted.

She waited.

"Jordan," Rowen said.

She closed her eyes and stayed still.

"Jordan," Caleb whispered, and Jordan's eyes fluttered open and she nodded, her eyes never meeting Rowen's as Caleb led her to the table. Rowen trailed quietly behind until pride overtook him and he lengthened his stride, coming up beside Caleb.

The wind toyed with Jordan, playing around her dress's hem and spinning around her body to ruffle her short, dark hair. It rumbled across the deck like a playful puppy.

And then it snared the wanted poster from where Rowen had tucked it in his belt, tossing it to the deck where it rolled and fluttered before Caleb.

Caleb scooped it up, and Rowen swallowed hard, extending his hand for it and hoping it wasn't unrolled.

Without giving it a glance, Caleb smacked it into Rowen's upturned palm and continued on his way.

Rowen wrapped his fingers cruelly around the poster, rolling it tighter and no longer trusting it to his belt. But holding it started him thinking, as he worried the poster in his grip. If Jordan wanted escape—a way to be gone from the life she'd been forced into—perhaps Rowen could finance such a thing whether his parents had disowned him or not. The money from his wanted poster might not buy a huge house or the trappings she was born into—nor all she truly deserved ...

But perhaps she had lower standards now.

And if he gave the bulk of money to the revolution as he promised Evie, would the *Tempest*'s captain blame him if he kept something for his efforts—for the risk to life and limb he took in the process?

He didn't think she would begrudge him that. So, his eyes on Jordan as everyone arranged themselves around the table, his mind stumbled through a plan to somehow weave revolution into his happily ever after.

He knew they might yet have it all.

The falling rain silenced and soaked Philadelphia's Below, crawling into John's bones, carrying a chill. He clamped his teeth together to keep them from rattling and bent low, hissing to the girl still stooped and sopping wet. "Cynda!"

Her head came up and she scrabbled back farther from the water's edge.

He called her name again and she whipped around, her eyes slits as she peered toward the shadow holding him. "'Tis John," he said, stepping away from the building at his back so she could make out his form more easily. Light filtered out from a few nearby windows, yielding patches where vision was easier in the downpour.

Recognizing him, Cynda leaped to her feet and ran at him. John spread his arms for a hug, surprised when she shoved him back into shadow. Breath puffed out of him as he slammed into the wall. "Stay in the shadows," Cynda urged. "They left a gunman who makes rounds. It's not safe for you here, John."

"You will not make me leave you, child."

She shook her head and hugged herself, looking back up and down the strip of stones and wood that ran along the waterway. "The rain should start to lessen soon, don't you think?" she asked as she stepped away from him.

"Sure enough. Round 'bout another hour or so," he said to her back.

"That's when they'll come for her," she said. "The blood mixing in the water—it calls them. That's what they say ..."

"They'll not devour her," he fumed, fists hard at his sides, the complaints of an old man distant at the idea of such injustice.

"No, they won't," she agreed, spinning back to look at him, her eyes large and mournful. "But John, they aren't like we've been taught," she said, her voice cracking. "Not at all." Then she went back to her assigned position and knelt there, wrapping her arms around herself and rocking.

# Chapter Three

*Aboard the Airship Artemesia*

Bran's head snapped up when the Wandering Wallace announced, "There is a method to this madness." The Wandering Wallace took a seat at the table's head.

There were a dozen places Bran would rather be, and judging from the dull expressions on his companions' faces, he was not alone. They were all exhausted.

"We must make sure that we proceed swiftly but with caution. A nearly indestructible army works at my request, subduing any physical opposition. Its necessity will be short lived, and at the end of its usefulness many of its members will be retired."

"Will *be* retired," Jordan said softly in Caleb's direction.

Evie's gaze flicked to Jordan and then Jack before returning to the Wandering Wallace.

They knew something he was not privy to.

Jack continued playing with whatever the thing was he tinkered with—a collection of small bottles and hoses now. The tiny automaton he'd quickly crafted earlier waddled around the table, its form between that of a beetle and a tiny bear. Bran leaned over the table and partly around Marion to better watch Jack work while they all listened to the Wandering Wallace.

Jack's hands worked deftly, his fingers spinning a diminutive screwdriver as he pulled pieces out of a modest pile of odds and ends and, assembling the bits seemingly at random, turned the piece over. It was somewhat larger than his hand and an odd-looking conglomerate of the wreckage from the Wraiths' earlier attack.

Ignoring Jordan's commentary on his word choice, the Wandering Wallace said, "We'll be in Philadelphia in a few days if we encourage Lady Astraea to be swift."

"Please remember that *Lady Astraea,*" she stressed, continuing, "must keep *her* energy level high in order to make a quick retreat should your plan fail. Supposing I am the main route of escape."

The Wandering Wallace nodded slowly. "Yes. Yes, it is true that you are many things, including a means of escape."

"Then do not push me too hard nor too fast," Jordan suggested. "I carry the weight of two ships now."

Evie shifted position, kicking her booted heels onto the table's edge, drawling, "And you do it marvelously." She picked at the lace edging one of her voluminous sleeves. "I, for one, appreciate the lack of strain on my ship, and the fact I will have a fully stocked steam engine to fly us out of harm's way should we need it. The *Tempest* is far faster if we must needs beat a hasty retreat."

Jordan glared at her.

The Wandering Wallace smacked his palms flat on the table. "We will not need an escape plan as we will not fail. But we do need to reach our destination before the people of Salem spread word too far that we have missed our docking appointment and it is realized that an entire liner has gone missing."

Bran cleared his throat. "We should send Salem a message telling them that we are delayed. That should help."

"A good idea indeed," the Wandering Wallace agreed. "We shall do so tomorrow."

Jordan pressed her lips together. "This army of yours—they will not fail? You are certain their membership is vast enough ... And that they will come when you call?"

"Yes. Beyond any doubt."

Evie grumbled something under her breath before snarling, "Numbers. I would prefer higher numbers."

Jack said, "Agreed." Then, perhaps more for himself and Evie than the others, he added, "That's the best I can do until I solder some bits...." He held the contraption up for Evie's inspection and she grinned.

Bran recognized it by shape alone. "A gun."

Jack grinned, nodding. "Yes. Once I get this part ..." He pointed to a particular piece near the grip. " ... properly attached I'll have a long-range weapon like none other."

"Like none other," Rowen said, arching an eyebrow.

"Another weapon," Marion whispered. "Can we not do this peacefully? Can we not finesse this revolution without bloodshed?"

Jack, Evie, and the Wandering Wallace exchanged a look.

"I will also have at least one lightship repaired..." Jack tried.

Rowen glanced down at the table and Jordan pursed her lips. Miyakitsu quietly traced a finger along the inner edge of her kimono's collar.

Marion rapped his knuckles on the table, beating out a frustrated rhythm. "I want this to be a bloodless revolution. A coup d'état can be that, can it not?"

The Wandering Wallace turned to face him. "Yes, but only if the opposition allows that sort of overthrow. Frankly, such a thing will be up to them. If they allow a peaceful transition, I will certainly accept it."

"*You* will ... ?" Jordan twitched in her chair. The clouds darkened around them. "Please do remind me just how it was determined that you would be the one in charge?" she whispered.

The Wandering Wallace bridled at Jordan's insinuation. "Do you wish to take the reins then, young Lady Astraea?"

She shook her head, short dark hair rippling in the air's caress. "No, I want no such responsibility—I feel no such calling. But even I am wise enough to know there should be more than one man leading things."

"And there will be," the Wandering Wallace soothed. "There will be what we establish in Philadelphia and what still holds in other major cities as we sort things out. There will be a new, more inspired and forward-thinking Council."

"The last Council surely believed they, too, were forward thinking," she challenged. "Even if they held on to some of the past—even the worst bits—still I believe when those men entered the Council they hoped to make a better and brighter future."

"Perhaps for themselves," the Wandering Wallace murmured.

Jordan's fingers rolled into a fist. "My father was a part of that Council...."

"*Was,*" the Wandering Wallace emphasized.

Rowen's hand reached out for Jordan's, perhaps in an attempt to soothe—but she pulled her fist away, still seething.

Marion shifted in his seat. "Surely you do not think the current Council succeeded in crafting the brighter future you suggest they desired ..."

Jordan's head snapped up. "No. Not at all. Certainly not for our kind. But replacing a group with one man makes no sense—it returns us to a kingship—a sovereignty. We should not have slaves, but we should not have that either."

"I said I would include others...." The Wandering Wallace said, his tone going glum, like a boy pouting.

"You will," Jordan agreed. "We will see to that."

"And to a peaceable revolution," Marion added, giving the Wandering Wallace a firm look. "As peaceable as we can make it, yes?"

From within the depths of his rhino mask, the Wandering Wallace seemed to glance down at the table. "Yes, yes. Of course yes.

"If you have additional forces," the Wandering Wallace said, looking at Evie, Jack, Marion, and Rowen, "rally them. I do not care where they come from, nor their heritage—I only want assurance that they fight for us."

"I only want everyone to get settled in their cabins and get some rest," Jordan retorted. "Yes, we are on the brink of revolution, much must be done, but sleepless nights will come soon enough." She stood and looked at all of them—except for Rowen. "Go, eat, drink, sleep." She stared at them until they rose from their seats.

The Wandering Wallace, of course, had something to add. "I must deliver the headlines and sing," he said. "We must maintain and build trust."

Jordan shook her head, but, resigned, she pointed toward the small communications center with its flywheel and its horn intercom. He spoke into the horn, relating the headlines and news to the people stuck and static in locked cabins.

In all of her life, Jordan had never heard headlines such as the ones he delivered, things that sounded more fantastical than the reality she'd always been part of—things that seemed so foreign in form they might as well be dreams. Throughout Europe it sounded as if steam contraptions were on the move—and moving far more safely than the government of the United States wanted citizens to think was possible.

"And, in international news, The Baba Yaga has traveled into Moscow to discuss the terms of her surrender, leaving her steam-powered house to stand on its chicken-like legs outside of St. Basil's Cathedral."

The rest of their group made their way toward the elevator,

while Jordan adjusted the ship's controls and listened to the Wandering Wallace's song. Finally she, Miyakitsu, and the Wandering Wallace joined the last few of them riding the elevator into the *Artemesia*'s gut.

*Philadelphia's Below*

George slapped his hands together, looking up and down the street. All was quiet here at the edge of the Below. Wiping his brow with a rag before pressing the cloth back into his waistcoat's pocket, he headed home.

The falling rain, falling only Tuesdays and alternating Fridays, ran into his face again, undaunted.

There was nothing easy about his job. Not the searching out of the renegades and rebels who made steam contraptions, not the finding them at times no one else would be around, not the wanton destruction, not the fire-starting, not the need to cover his tracks.

He patted the belly he'd started to grow. All for a good cause. He assured the safety and sanctity of his son through his secret dealings with the Council. He assured his son would not be taken away, that what was left of his family would not fall due to Harboring a Witch.

Though, what could you fall from when you lived like church mice in an old woman's attic? There was no great honor left to his family name, no power he wielded in neither market nor government, nothing special about him unless one counted his son.

Todd was all he had—a clever child with a mind for artistry and design and a curiosity that George had never seen rivaled. Why, he'd be an inventor great as any, if George knew anything about anything. Which he was certain he did.

If only there were more inventors to model himself after ...

George knew of da Vinci and his flying devices, of Franklin and his—everything. Franklin tried it all, from printing to music-making with his glass armonica, to devising the postal service itself! Da Vinci's ideas were all used up, if you asked anyone in the businesses of building and design. And George had. The men he had spoken to assured him. Either da Vinci's ideas failed when tested or they had already been used to their full potential.

All good and godly things that could be invented *had* been invented—now was a time of revision, not creation.

And Franklin's remaining ideas were deemed worthless, Franklin earning himself quite a diabolical reputation—causing his inventions to be locked away in a cellar beneath his prized post office, if the rumors were to be believed. Locked away to be forgotten.

It was hard enough protecting a son who was a Witch, but a boy who might invent things akin to those that destroyed Franklin's reputation and eventually his life? To be guilty of diabolical dealings—how else did man manage such strange things as Franklin made except by dealing with devils or Wildkin? Had he not taken some Native as his lover at nearly the same time he'd been Ambassador to France? That was where the temptation and taint were found—the Wildkin or French.

Both had quite the reputation.

It was wiser—safer—to follow the crowd than test the government. Wiser to stay the path than stray and test your own abilities.

Far better he encourage his boy into something that brought no questions and no debate than something that raised eyebrows and made people look at him more closely. Because the more fiercely you examined someone, the more likely you were to find fault with them.

He opened the door, shouted greetings to the old woman sitting in the corner, humming as she rocked in her wooden chair, and heaved himself up the stairs to the attic.

At the top of the staircase he raised his hands over his head and pulled on a knotted rope hanging overhead. The ceiling opened, a ladder sliding out to nearly scrape the floor by his feet and, holding the sides as he went, he climbed his way home.

Rain slid down the eyebrow windows set at both ends of the attic and, by flickering candlelight, he saw his boy seated on the floor, playing.

He crept up behind him on tiptoe, heart swelling in his chest at being home, his son in view. No one but a parent understood such a sensation.

He clapped his hands down on the child's shoulders and the boy nearly jumped free of his skin, gasping, "Father!" His round cheeks flushed, he stood, turning to face his father and wrap his arms around him in a hug.

George squeezed him so hard he lifted him off the floor and Todd kicked out his feet, laughing. Set back down, Todd immediately began to lead his father away from where he'd been focused so intently on something.

"Whoa, whoa," George said. "First show me what you were playing with that had you so enthralled."

"It was nothing, Father," Todd insisted, slipping his hand into his father's and turning them toward the door in the attic's floor.

"No," George said. "It must be something grand." He pulled free of the child's grasp, picking him up and carrying him back to investigate.

Seeing the contraption there, George froze.

On the floor in fluttering light, stood a small and delicately wrought automaton in the shape of a cat. From its quivering wire whiskers to the tip of its long, jointed tail, it was all feline and fire. Beside it sat a small bag with tiny bits of crushed coal. A coal-powered steam cat.

George focused on breathing, trying to ignore the fact his son, a Weather Witch yet to be discovered, was playing with the very sort of thing George was hired to destroy.

A thing George had not given him.

He pushed breath in and out of his lungs, trying to fight a rising tide of panic. Just below his skin, a shudder raced, making the hair on his thick arms stand up.

Someone set up his son.

Someone had set *him* up.

And someone would be at their door by morning at the latest to make their discovery known.

In his arms Todd merely said, "Imagine if these were available for Christmas, Father. No child would ever regret being given coal by Old Saint Nick, would they?"

George stayed silent, stunned.

Perhaps no child would regret the gift of coal, but their parents most certainly would have regrets when they were discovered. And with men like George on the job they were sure to be found out.

Setting the boy down, George gave him his best smile and said, "I've got a surprise for you, boy." He ruffled Todd's hair until it stood straight up. "We're taking up residence elsewhere tonight."

"Moving?"

"Yes, my lad. Surprise!"

*Philadelphia*

The rain slowed—it did this, falling in patterns that, if one was observant, could be anticipated.

Huddled in shadow under a dripping roof's edge, John heard them before he saw them: a strange crying song rose out of the water and drifted across the edge of the land.

Cynda sat up straight, her eyes fixed on the water.

Footsteps sounded and John saw light glint off a gun barrel.

The song grew louder, slower, and sadder as the Merrow were singing a funeral dirge.

The water created a continuous blur—an ongoing sheet of moisture. John squinted against its onslaught, watching as something rose out of the water—something as liquid as the sea, as colorful as an oil slick and as beautiful as ...

He swallowed.

They *were* beautiful.

Shimmering and cloaked in rainbows, three sirens rose from the water, their faces transcending human—unearthly—angelic—an array of fleshy spines fanning out from the tops of their heads, crowning them. Their song shifted and changed as they neared the water's edge and the *words*—

—weaving, undulating words—

—the water streamed into his eyes and threatened to plug his ears and John thought for a moment he understood what they sang.

> Wide are the waves that keep me from you
> Far will my spirit now travel
> Without fear, without strain,
> Devoid of horror and pain
>
> Now will I move ever on, on, on ...

He shook his head, clearing the water from his ears, and their words returned to a weaving and weird otherworldly chorus.

Their heads part headdress and part nearly human hair, they swayed their way to land, long hands with webbed fingers reaching and pulling them up.

Onto land.

John jumped back, seeing how those waterbound angels flopped onto land, long coiling tails twisting behind them, mouths filled with rows of sharp teeth as they sang. Windows were shuttered and the light faded further in the already dim alley.

John remembered he was just an old man.

With bad knees.

Something slithered past his feet.

Cynda screamed.

The gun flashed, firing.

Another scream tore through the air and John counted three loud splashes.

A man snapped, "Do your duty!" and Cynda gave a startled scream. Then came the wet slap of footsteps and finally even they were swallowed by the rain.

Unnerved and exhausted, John slid down the wall, sitting in the cold and damp, joints aching.

*Aboard the Artemesia*

"I think I shall call that my nightly lullaby to the liner. What think you, my love," the Wandering Wallace asked Miyakitsu as she helped him tug off his boots of buffalo hide and contrasting stitching. The coin-silver buttons winked at him. They were the boots of a performer—not the boots of a revolution's leader.

Miyakitsu smiled at him, setting the boots down by the trunk that traveled everywhere with them.

He studied her, a man obsessed. Every line of her body and glimpse of her soul colored his world. But tonight there was something different about her.

She always moved with a fluid and animal grace—with good reason—but when she turned back to face him he wondered if her nose wasn't the slightest bit more pointed.

She reached out to take his rhinoceros head mask. Were her fingernails longer—a touch more like claws? He helped her tug the mask and accompanying hood free.

For a moment she stood there, cradling the head in her hands, staring at his face. Staring at his multitude of scars. He shouldn't have lived. He'd been told that many times. But he had been a child when he'd been set on fire along with his illegal contraption —along with his home and his family—he was too young to know he was supposed to die.

He had known pain.

But he discovered tenderness and healed under the determined hands of a young violinist in the Night Market. She took him in and nursed him, raised him as her own. In the Night

Market he might be an oddity, but there oddities thrived. He learned magick against her will. And one day, years later when he thought himself wise enough and man enough, he left her.

She probably blamed magick for his disappearance.

He shook his head. He loved her like a mother and he left her with not even a note to explain.

But no one ever explained his parents' leaving him either. They were murdered, and why? Because they bought him a toy that was steam-powered.

Miyakitsu's eyes roamed his scarred face a moment more and then she dropped the mask on the bed beside him and fell into his arms.

If his adoptive mother thought magick had stolen him, in a way, she would be correct.

Miyakitsu was magick personified. He held her close, wrapping her arms and legs around him and pushing the collar of her kimono open to bare one ivory shoulder. She snapped at him, clicking her teeth together with a giggle and knocked him back on the bed.

Magick had claimed him and he intended to stay hers for as long as he could, no matter her magick condemned her to not remember him come morning.

# Chapter Four

For evil news rides post, while good news baits.

—JOHN MILTON

*Aboard the Artemesia*

Morning found the *Artemesia*'s rebels tearing into a meal of scones, porridge, and dried fruit and waiting for the Wandering Wallace and his woman.

Rowen stopped eating when Jordan excused herself from the table, returning to the dais to Conduct the ship. The wanted posters had left his hands for longer than a few minutes only while he slept and now, under the table's edge, he unrolled them and thought.

If Jordan wanted to get away, to escape, he would do whatever was in his power to provide escape for her.

He promised resources to Evie to unite the rebels in their cause of freeing the slaves, but resources could come as readily in men as in money. Evie would not doubt his intentions if he pushed to go ahead of them on the way to Philadelphia.

Two birds, one stone. He rolled the posters up again and headed for his captain.

She and Jack had left the table to sit, heads nearly touching, on the very edge of Topside, arms slung over the banister, feet … Rowen slowed, realizing. His stomach lurched.

Seated at the very edge of the *Artemesia*'s deck as if they hadn't a care, were Jack and Evie, feet dangling off the ship, hanging loose in air that swept playfully around the big boat's body. Thousands of feet above the ground they acted like children sitting on a bridge above a shallow stream, letting their toes dip into the water as they chatted.

Rowen dragged himself forward. He was fine aboard an airship as long as he didn't think about what being aboard an airship truly *meant*—that they were traveling high above the ground at the whim of only one person—a person distinctly unimpressed with him.

Rowen stopped completely in his progress.

"Dear me," Evie said, turning to look his way, "it appears Rowen has again realized we are in midair."

"Damn," Jack added, turning so that one leg was fully aboard and most of the other was not.

Rowen swallowed hard as they eyed him, their smiles stretching from their lips to their sparkling eyes.

Kit and Kaboodle curled, one in each of their laps, napping. Rowen could only imagine Cookie, the *Tempest*'s cook, glowering and sweating as she turned the *Tempest*'s spit without either of her previously promised spit dogs.

"It must be something important racing round that brain of his to bring him so close to the edge. Perhaps we should be merciful and go to him?" Evie suggested.

"Be merciful?" Jack sniffed. "Well."

But Evie reached out and rubbed Jack's bristling chin with a sweep of her hand that made him follow her fingers for more. It was not the first time Rowen found himself wondering what happened between the two of them when they were alone. "Yes.

Be merciful," she whispered. "For a change. He is our friend, after all."

Jack eyed Rowen up and down. "Not just our ransom?"

"No," she assured. "And I get the sense he is readying to make himself useful to not only us, but also our cause." She pulled her feet out of the sky and, one arm wrapped neatly around one Fennec fox, popped to her feet and strode away from the edge.

Rowen took a long step back as Evie advanced. She had that effect. She was an odd combination: at one moment she could be playful as a kitten, and suddenly she switched and was fierce as a hellcat. Or so Rowen complained once. Jack had laughed and said, "That's what a woman is—soft as silk and hiding the strength and sting of steel." Rowen slid back another step.

"And what, dear boy, do you need us for?"

"If you recall our agreement—"

Her eyes scanning the deck and her words slow, soft, and wary, Evie said, "I most certainly do—you are to rally your friends, connections, and money to assist in our cause and in that way not be handed over to one of the fine folks willing to pay for your capture."

Jack slipped up beside Evie.

"I have a rather nontraditional method of retrieving the monies needed to better finance our cause."

Jack's eyes fell on the papers Rowen again gripped.

"I'm a fan of the nontraditional," Evie mused. "But is this a discussion best held Topside or belowdecks in a quiet cabin on the *Tempest*?"

"Ah," Rowen said, seeing the direction in which her gaze rested. Evie's eyes were fixed on Jordan. And most likely Caleb. "I fear we must start trusting each other sooner than later if this is to succeed."

"Sooner can still be tomorrow if later is the day after," Jack said. "If this is a conversation about either money or power, it is best spoken of in private."

"You fear there is no honor here?" Rowen asked.

Jack grinned. "Is there ever honor in a den of thieves?"

"Thieves?" Rowen asked.

"God, he's young," Evie chuckled, patting Rowen's cheek. "Yes, sweet boy—thieves. What more might we be when we seek to steal power from an established government? How better to describe those stealing their thunder?"

"Thieves," Rowen agreed.

"Let us discuss this elsewhere then," Evie said, motioning to the swaying rope and wood-plank bridge pinned to the Topside of both the airships. Evie led Rowen and Jack to the bridge, crossed to the *Tempest,* and went belowdeck where they discussed the importance of proper wording on wanted posters and Rowen's nontraditional way of obtaining money.

Then Jack and Rowen made their way to the ship's communication relays and contacted a few of Rowen's more interesting friends.

*Philadelphia*

George had made short work of packing their belongings—not hard to do when you owned nearly nothing. Telling Todd that their move was also to be a surprise to Mrs. Fammesh, they crept past her and emerged on the street just before dawn. "Stay close," George urged his son, "watch and follow me, and keep your head down. No matter what happens, keep your head down."

Todd obeyed, following silently and obediently.

Trusting that his father would guide him right and true.

And George did, guiding him past the alley where a young woman shrieked about Merrow murdering her friend and a crowd gathered to carry the corpse away, fists raised as they shouted for justice and for Merrow they might murder themselves.

George guided his son right and true. Past the brewing trouble and the burned-out shell of a house where George had done his most recent work. Up the Hill they went, past the sprawling Astraea estate where an exhausted African man with salt and pepper curls worked at a garden outside the main wall, already soaked, and to another house George had never stepped inside.

A household he hoped would understand better than most his troubles. And his intentions. Shouldering his bag, he took Todd by the hand and walked straight to the main door. He rapped on it with his knuckles.

The door swung wide, revealing a thin man in a smart suit looking down his nose at the two would-be visitors.

George doffed his cap, tucking it humbly under his arm. "I wish to see Kenneth Lorrington."

"And just who should I tell him has come calling?" the butler asked with a sniff.

"A man with secrets to tell."

The butler blinked and ushered them inside, closing the door behind them quickly.

*Aboard the Artemesia*

The Wandering Wallace finally joined his coconspirators Topside, today a peacock with less spring in his step than Rowen might have expected of a man in love. Miyakitsu lagged behind, her eyes wary, her posture strange. With obvious effort, he dragged everyone back to the dining table to continue plotting.

"There seems so much planning to a rebellion," Rowen sulked. "If this were a book, this would be the part I would skip."

"Very little comes from rebellions that are not well planned," the Wandering Wallace murmured, stretching across the table to study the map he'd spread before them.

"Still, I would skip this bit. Turn a page or two."

"Skip right to the fighting, would you?" the Wandering Wallace asked in a near monotone, his masked face close to the curling parchment. Peacock plumes swayed over their heads as he nodded.

Marion grabbed a teacup and tankard, placing each on a corner of the document to pin it down.

"Certainly," Rowen agreed. "Or the kissing." He stole a look at Jordan.

Blushing, Jordan rose from her place at the table, brushed down her broad skirts, and excused herself to return to the dais and her role as Conductor.

"Fighting or kissing," Wallace mused. "The books you read sound far more enjoyable than mine. But then, too, perhaps that is why I am leading a rebellion and why you, dear Rowen, are not."

Rowen snorted. "Just because I choose *not* to read certain things does not mean I cannot."

"Excellent," the Wandering Wallace said, pushing a stack of books across the table to Rowen. "Our rebels need leaders I trust. These books can enlighten even the dimmest."

Rowen blinked. "Even the *dimmest* you say?"

The Wandering Wallace nodded.

Rowen split his stack of books in half, sharing the workload with Jack. "There's hope for you yet," he said to the glowering ginger.

"I am still repairing a lightship," Jack muttered, and he rose, but the Wandering Wallace turned their attention to the Conductor's dais where Jordan worked and Meggie played.

"Look there. So beautiful, young and unaware of her own potential ... Why, every abolitionist and slave will rally to our cause when they realize the Stormbringer rides with us."

Rowen grunted and kicked his legs out under the table, folded his arms behind his head, and enjoyed his view.

Not far from his shoulder the Wandering Wallace said, "I have with me a precious cargo which requires I find a suitable Reader."

Rowen watched the dais as Jordan adjusted the ship's wheel and, turning, ran a tentative finger along the ship's main stormcell—a huge Herkimer diamond mounted on a post and ringed with jutting silver wires. She glanced at Rowen and color rose in her cheeks.

The sky around them darkened.

"You won't find many readers aboard the *Tempest*," Rowen joked from around a bite of scone.

Evie slapped him on the back and Jack laughed as Rowen choked.

Jordan froze, then adjusted other bits of the ship's mechanics quickly.

"Not that sort of reader at all, Rowen," the Wandering Wallace clarified. "A Reader like one might find dealing in soul stones. A Reader of use to a Reanimator."

Jordan rejoined them, her eyes skimming Rowen's face. He smiled and again she looked away.

Rowen grunted and picked up another scone. "And what sort of reader does a Reanimator require?" Rowen asked.

"A most accurate one," the Wandering Wallace said.

Jack stole the scone right out of Rowen's grasp, chuckling.

"You met a Reader in the Hill King's Cavern," Evie said.

Jordan wrinkled her nose and asked, "The Hill King's Cavern?"

Rowen perked up, food forgotten though a few crumbs escaped his mouth as he hurried to engage her in conversation. "Yes. In Bangor there is an amazing boulder cave beneath what Evie likes to imagine might be a library."

Jordan's gaze traveled to where Evie sat comfortably beside him. Comfortably between Rowen and Jack.

Jack was chewing his recently won scone but said, "The Hill King's Cavern is a meeting place—"

"—and partying place," Evie said, grinning at Rowen.

Jordan straightened in her chair, her eyebrows drawing together. Sensing her unease, Rowen pulled away from Evie's comfortable slouch and looked at Jordan as if he, too, was unnerved by Evie's attention. "There they trade, but there is music, and food—"

"—everything can be purchased for the right price," Evie said with a laugh.

"—and much needs to be avoided for one's safety," Rowen added, clearing his throat.

"And a Reader does what?" Jordan asked, refocusing the conversation.

"*Reads,*" Evie said, stretching the word out as she relaxed still further in her seat.

Jordan pursed her lips and then, sighing between them asked, "Reads *what*?"

Rowen leaned over the table to separate the glaring women. Jordan simply glanced at him and slid back from the table herself, her eyes narrow. "The stones?" Rowen asked the Wandering Wallace, hoping his intercession would squelch the rising tension.

"The crystals," the Wandering Wallace corrected. He pulled a small pouch from beneath the table and undid its drawstrings. Slowly he spilled out a few sparkling stormcells. Jordan's hand moved to a spot near her neckline where a crystal she'd found in her Tank at Holgate stayed. She relaxed, picking up one glittering stone. The Wandering Wallace continued, "Each crystal holds the spark of a person who has passed on."

"A bit of their energy?" she asked cautiously.

"A bit more than that ..." The Wandering Wallace paused, glancing at Rowen.

Jordan tapped the table between them. "Tell me what each holds. *Exactly,*" she said, her eyes narrowing further.

"An energy, like a spirit."

"A specific person's spirit is in each crystal?" Jordan leaned in. "You mean these crystals hold part of a person's soul?" She replaced the one she held and pulled her hand away, trembling.

"A bit more than that," the Wandering Wallace repeated.

"Their entire soul?" she asked softly.

His next words came slowly—carefully. "Yes. Each crystal holds a particular person's entire soul."

"They are trapped?" she asked, her pitch rising. "How can they ... if they're trapped ... how can they get to heaven ..." Rowen saw her pulse flutter at the base of her neck. "Or Hell?"

The Wandering Wallace leaned back. He drummed his fingertips across the tabletop, tapping out a rolling, rapid rhythm. "There are many things in life I do not know, many I cannot explain," he admitted.

"So," Jordan drew in a breath so deep it was audible, and said, "potentially you have a hundred or more people's souls trapped in a crystal purgatory? Souls you'll—what?—use for revolution?" She ran her fingers through her hair and shook her head.

"These are people misused by our system, people abused and killed because they were Witches. They will thank me for giving them the chance to change a broken system," he assured. "They deserved to live in a better world but were denied it."

"Have they slept since death? Is that what they do snared in a crystal palace? *God.*" She stood so fast her chair fell back, smacking against the floor. "What if they were so destroyed by what was done to them ... What if these spirits are damaged because of the way they died?" she asked. "What if they are more danger than asset?"

Everyone turned their focus to the revolution's self-appointed head.

Rowen rubbed his jaw. Evie's eyes were hooded and Jack's nearly glowed. Clearly Jordan was the first to raise such a legitimate concern.

"Don't you have a ship to steer?" the Wandering Wallace snapped.

"No one else has asked, have they? No one questions you. They're so caught up in the idea of abolition, of revolution, they aren't seeing the detriment." She waved one arm at them. "But you," she took a breath, "and I," she added, "know there are risks —great risks—as well as potential rewards in revolution."

"The rewards outweigh any risks."

"How can you be certain?" She stabbed a finger into the pile of gems, making a few jump and skitter on the table.

The ship dipped in flight and thunder boomed before Jordan regained control. Her nostrils flared, her eyes closed and Rowen's heart sped up. The ship steadied, the rumble of thunder receded, and Jordan opened her eyes to ask, "How do you know they will wake and remember who they were—that they will help us? How do you know they won't turn?"

"They will not turn."

"How do you *know*?"

"None of them have turned before." The Wandering Wallace examined the tips of his fingers nonchalantly.

Turning, Jordan looked at him from one eye. "Before?" She twitched. "You have tried this before? With other mechanical men —like those used by the Council in Philadelphia?"

He sighed. "Not exactly. But I have tested this method of using soul stones before."

"I am a fan of riddles, but only the ones he tells," Jordan said, hooking a thumb in Rowen's direction.

"You tell riddles?" Evie asked.

"More commonly dirty jokes," Rowen clarified.

Jordan rolled her eyes. "Explain how you tested this volatile method of powering an inanimate object, Wandering Wallace."

"Every time I Reanimate a person, I test the method," he specified, his eyes flicking from his fingers to her gaze. Somehow daring her. "Every time I bring someone back from the dead, I put my methods to the test."

"Now I see. You are a Reanimator."

Bran set his teacup down with a snap. "It is true then? You can reanimate the dead?"

"To a point."

"That sounds even less promising," Jack muttered, returning his attention to the mechanical thing he toyed with.

"Technically, yes, I Reanimate the dead. But there are limitations."

"Like?" Bran asked.

"If they've bled out too much it is nearly impossible. Or, if the physical damage is too great ... Being crushed to death. I cannot fix that. And I require a soul stone. Ideally the right soul stone: the person's own soul stone. Otherwise there must be a substitution made."

"A substitution?" Jordan hissed, her eyes wide. "You use another soul stone—another soul if you can't—what? Be inconvenienced by obtaining the correct one?"

"Do not," the Wandering Wallace warned.

"Do not *what*?"

"Do not press me on this, Jordan Astraea. Desperate times call for desperate measures and sometimes—to save a family, you sacrifice a soul. Sometimes someone does something so selfish and people panic to correct the situation—because so much has already been lost by so many." He paused and Rowen thought he saw a fire building in the depths of his eyes as he stood, pressing the beak of his mask to her nose and backing her up. "People might overlook a stone in their haste to save a life. The knowledge I have is not common. The upper ranks know nearly none of it and what the lower ranks know is mainly rumor and wrong. People do their best, but *time*—it runs out so very quickly, Jordan. And decisions have to be made. Suddenly."

Jordan's eyebrows tugged together and she stared at him. She shook her head. Eyelashes fluttering quickly, she stepped back a pace. "I do not want this going wrong on us," she whispered. "There is so much risk."

The Wandering Wallace laid a hand on her shoulder. "Far greater is the reward at journey's end than any risk we take along our way," he promised gently.

Down the table, Jack pulled out a tin of lucifers and struck one, sticking its burning head into the body of the automaton he'd been tinkering with. He withdrew the lucifer, waved it out, and nudged the tiny mech toward Evie. It jolted to life, staggering a few wheezing paces before, with a gasp of dark smoke, it toppled over. Righting it, he retrieved it and returned to tinkering.

"Rowen has some important contacts," Evie volunteered.

Rowen swallowed. "Yes. It is true."

"Have you been in contact with these contacts?" the Wandering Wallace asked.

"I have spoken to two," Rowen confirmed.

Jordan's eyebrows rose, and she leaned across the table, staring at him more directly than since he'd boarded the *Artemesia*. His throat grew tight. The Wandering Wallace asked, "And who are these contacts you have?"

"Kenneth Lorrington and Chadwick Skellish." Jordan gave a small nod, and Rowen continued, saying, "They have promised to gather more friends with military experience."

"More *sober* friends?" Jordan asked, her expression flat.

"Sober enough to do what must needs be done."

Jordan pulled her chair back up. She again sat beside Caleb and leaned back, pulling out of Rowen's view.

Rowen saw the tips of her slender fingers as she drummed softly on the tabletop. He stood. "That brings me to what my next task should be," he said. "I should go to Philadelphia in advance and organize my contacts."

Evie cleared her throat. "Into the viper's nest? And alone? I think not."

"The viper's nest?" Jordan asked.

"He hasn't told you?" Evie asked, doing her best to blink innocently. "He's a wanted man—and wanted for more than just simple companionship."

"Wanted?"

"Dear Rowen killed a man."

"What?" Jordan jumped back to her feet. "You did what?"

"I dueled over your honor. I won ..." The words came out weak, sheepishly.

She reached across Caleb and slapped Rowen. Hard.

"What the hell?" He held his cheek and stared at her, his jaw hanging loose. "What was that for?"

Jordan blinked several times and swallowed before addressing him. "That was for dueling."

"I was defending your honor!"

"Yes. And as noble a concept as that is ..." She rolled her eyes up and stared at the sky. Lightning sparkled above them. She drew a deep breath and eased it out slowly. "As noble a concept as that is," she repeated, "you could have been hurt. Or killed." She dropped her gaze hastily, her eyes shrouded beneath her lashes. "I will not stomach you doing any such fool thing again," she whispered. "I will not suffer losing you, Rowen Albertus Burchette." She raised her chin, but would not meet his eyes. "Not again."

"Ah, but dear, sweet lady," the Wandering Wallace cooed, watching them, "we will soon be marching to revolution. He must act as such dangerous moments dictate. Do not tie his hands so much he cannot defend himself."

She proclaimed, "I would never." She looked at Rowen and let out a weary sigh. "But take no unnecessary chances," she commanded. "Make no foolhardy choices." She hung her head. "Take no risks that outweigh the rewards," she said so softly he barely heard her.

Rowen stood there, mute. Stunned.

Jordan turned on her heel and walked away from the table, lengthening her stride in a way more warrior than woman. Rubbing his aching jaw, Rowen still enjoyed watching her walk away.

She threw her weight behind the lever on the Conductor's dais, hauling it back, snapping the *Artemesia*'s wings in close and reaching her hands out to pull at the distant clouds, drawing them tighter to maintain the ship's buoyancy.

# Chapter Five

Full lasting is the song, though he, the singer, passes.
—GEORGE MEREDITH

*Aboard the Artemesia*

At mid-morning the Wandering Wallace approached Jordan, saying, "Bring the ships down at noon. Not to land, of course, but to an altitude so the birds can land."

Jordan looked at him, raising one eyebrow.

"I may be creative, but even I cannot continue making up the headlines. That level of dishonesty requires government involvement."

Jordan's eyebrows jumped. "Making up ... ?"

He waved a hand at her in a trifling way. "Yes. I can be fairly certain most of the things I've said have happened, but I would prefer working from reality—even if it has been censored and twisted by the government."

Jordan gawked at him.

He cocked his head, the feathers on his peacock's mask rippling with color. "I cannot imagine you did not notice ... But then you did have many things on your mind, I suppose," he said, glancing at the way the surrounding clouds dimmed slightly. "Every noon liners of this class descend to a lower altitude to allow messenger birds to roost. We provide them feed and water and open the container tied to their foot to read the headlines. If we must, we add to the news before sending the birds on their way."

Jordan squinted at him. "At noon?"

"Yes. At noon. Unless there is real trouble and then they dispatch the owls or eagles when they must."

Shortly before noon, Jordan began the slow descent of both the *Artemesia* and *Tempest* as the rest of the group gathered at the dining table. She had set the ships to glide and barely taken her seat for the midday meal when it began.

Birds of all shapes, colors, and sizes popped through the cloud cover, skimming the deck's surface before setting down on a narrow railing by the airship's bow, each bird sidestepping to a particular spot.

Meggie clapped her hands at the aerial display. "Splendid!" she said as a hawk descended in a smart spiral, its wing tips nearly grazing the smaller birds who shifted, tittering nervously at its approach.

There were birds of all varieties, Jordan noticed, spotting pigeons, sparrows, blue jays, ravens, cardinals, bluebirds, and a selection of hawks settling on the narrow rail to preen and await their promised food.

The Wandering Wallace stood, shoving a bit of bread into the mouth of the peacock mask he wore. "Shall we see what news they bring?"

Meggie jumped up, an emphatic, "Yes!" bursting out of her mouth.

Jordan took a quick sip of water and set down her tankard, standing with the Wandering Wallace and Rowen.

Caleb set down his napkin and, rising, followed Jordan and

the rest of them. Together they crossed the deck to where the birds roosted.

Jeremiah, once only the ship's powder monkey, arrived on deck, led by a servant girl who had previously proven her allegiance to the Wandering Wallace. Quietly Jeremiah showed her how to feed each bird. He paused to address Jordan as he approached a blue jay. "You should have a special key on a ring," he said.

Jordan dug into the pleats of her dress and withdrew the key ring, saying, "I retrieved it," with a shrug, and flipping through the heavy iron keys, she paused on a very small and ornate one that looked more like a small charm for a bracelet than the key to a door.

"That's the one." Jeremiah slipped the key free of the ring and placed his left wrist in front of the blue jay, slowly pressing it into the bird's breast so it stepped up onto his arm with the soft jingle of a bell. Cocking its head it watched Jordan with beady eyes. Jeremiah untied a small metal canister lashed to the bird's leg with leather. On the bird's other leg was tied a bell.

Jeremiah untied the container and, inserting the key, opened it and slipped out a long, curled slip of paper. Setting the jay back on his perch, Jeremiah unrolled the paper and held it out.

The Wandering Wallace reached for it but Jeremiah passed it to Jordan. "It is your ship, therefore it is your mail."

Jordan turned her back on the Wandering Wallace, unwinding the paper between her fingers and thumbs and tugging it taut.

She read the small script carefully and when she was certain she could share its contents with a man as potentially powerful—or dangerous—as the Wandering Wallace, she read aloud, "Philadelphia Councilman Cowden Yokum has been found guilty of Harboring and imprisoned at Eastern Penitentiary."

"Interesting," the Wandering Wallace said, reaching up to stroke the blue jay's beak like any other man might stroke his beard. "He sounds most worthy of a visit."

Todd's feet kicked out and back where he sat on the plush divan in the parlor of the Lorrington household, staring up with wide eyes at the oddly high ceiling. George reached out and took his son's hand, passing him another biscuit.

Todd ate eagerly, crumbs spilling down his front, which George plucked off of him and placed in his own crumbled napkin.

Across the room from the awkward and shabby pair sat a long-legged man with narrow, bloodshot eyes. Whereas some might have been sipping tea this morning, Kenneth Lorrington raised a glass to his ever-present butler, saying, "Hair of the dog."

Whatever the dog's hair was, George thought, it smelled as foul as it smelled powerful.

Lorrington slugged it back, squeezed his eyes closed, and finally, opening them, managed something like a smile. "I have been told," he waved the empty glass in his butler's direction, "that you have things I would like to hear in light of the fall of the Astraea family and the *dastardly behavior*," at these words the smile became genuine, "of Rowen Burchette."

George opened his mouth to begin but Lorrington waved him quiet, adding, "I should make you aware, I have very recently spoken to Burchette. It is possible I already know what you do."

"Begging your pardon, sir, but you do not," George said. "And before I divulge these secrets I must have some assurance of my son's and my safety. We will need a place to stay."

Lorrington nodded gravely. "And what skills do you have besides telling secrets you were evidently meant to keep? Can you dust, mop, mend broken things?" he mused.

"Frankly, sir, I am in the business of breaking things more than fixing them."

Lorrington squinted at him. "Do you break things and then set fires, good man?"

George swallowed hard. "Yes, sir, I fear I do."

"Ah. I am familiar with your handiwork." He held his glass out for a refill, slugging the liquid back and then grimacing. "Coffee next," he specified to the butler as he shifted in his seat. The butler lowered his head. "Well, if I can say nothing else of you, you are quite thorough at what you do."

"But I am not so old that I cannot learn new ways."

Lorrington's fuzzy gaze landed on George's boy. "A good thing." He set down his glass and stuck out his hand, receiving a coffee cup. His gaze never left Todd. "Let me guess: he is a Witch."

George gasped but Lorrington chuckled. "Why else would anyone but rebels care what *you* do? Why else go to the lengths they have to control you? Why else would *you* run to a friend of Jordan Astraea's beau? Yes, you know things, but." He took a long sip of coffee, smiling over the cup's edge at his butler. "It is a good thing I keep the kitchen staff in beans, I see—such prompt service."

"Brews nearly all day long, sir," the butler mused. "Allows me to keep alert to your needs."

"Good, good." He looked at Todd again, though he addressed George. "You and the boy will be kept on as staff here. You will not question me or my family and you will keep your head down."

"And the fact he is coming into power ... ?"

"I will need more coffee before I can answer that. Now. Tell me a secret."

George glanced at the butler and scanned the room once before drawing a deep breath and leaning in to say, "Councilman Loftkin is tripling the number of patrols of men like me and beginning to plan troop movements."

"Do tell ..."

"He has maps and charts all over his desk. And tin soldiers populate them. He is planning something."

Lorrington kicked back in his embroidered chair. "Well luckily, so are we. It appears we will be mustering men, Scottin,"

Lorrington told the butler before he returned his attention to George. "Good man, do tell me more."

So, handing Todd another biscuit, George told Kenneth Lorrington everything he knew.


*Aboard the Artemesia*


Watching Jordan, Bran marveled at how accurate her touch had become and how quickly she had learned so much.

Meggie rose from where Miyakitsu and Maude now sat—talking?—Bran could never be sure as it seemed the beautiful young Oriental girl never said anything to anyone but the Wandering Wallace. At least he presumed she spoke to the Wandering Wallace —he could not imagine any relationship in which words never passed. His daughter moved across the dais to where Jordan, her face as dark as the clouds she called, Conducted the huge liner. Meggie set a tiny hand on Jordan's skirt and gave a tug.

Jordan looked down, her face brightening. The darkness of the clouds overhead softened, but their thickness and power never changed. Meggie petted Jordan's skirt a moment and then turned toward Bran and the diners. He'd seen that look before.

The look of a child with a sudden idea.

She skipped across the deck to him and tucked her hands behind her back, swaying up and back on her tiptoes. The move was one he should have grinned at—a move of pure joy a father should have reveled in—but instead he remembered the last time she'd skipped—the day of the ship's true overthrow.

The day she'd whistled with the Wandering Wallace and they'd all heard people screaming, thrown from balconies and windows for not going along with the ship's takeover.

A literal overthrow.

He had reasonable difficulty and a strange sense of foreboding sweep over him at the sight of her bobbing merrily before him.

As if she understood, she stopped mid-bob and pressed her

rosebud lips together a moment before speaking. "Miss Jordan keeps calling *angry* storms," she said in a voice distinctly tattletale.

Bran stooped over to look into her glowing eyes. He swept dainty curls back from her forehead and nodded. "I know, little dove. What do you expect me to do about it?"

"You know the most about Witches ... Can you not teach her a better way? A happier way?"

"Oh," he said in a whisper. "I do not think I dare try teach Miss Jordan anything ever again," he said. "She and I ... I would not blame her for not wanting to listen to me. I was horribly cruel to her." He swallowed hard, fighting back the memory of the tools, and the blood, and the pain he had inflicted to Make her a Witch. It amazed him she had not hurled him overboard, pushed by a gust of wind.

Even now her eyes were on him, watching him with cruel disinterest. When, briefly, her gaze fell to Meggie, the whole of her attitude changed and she was no longer hateful, but just a teenage girl.

A wounded teenage girl.

"Anil said Jordan should sing out her storms—call them with love and joy."

Rowen and Jack had frozen in the midst of their discourse. Rowen gave a snort. "Sing out her storms?" He shook his head. "I doubt you'll have much luck with that," he confided. "I frequently tried to get Jordan to sing—anything—she never would. Not a ballad, not a bawdy tune, nothing."

Meggie appraised Rowen. "Do *you* sing?"

"Not well, but with great gusto," he said.

"Perhaps that was why she did not sing," Meggie suggested.

Rowen snorted again.

"Papa, might someone attempt to fetch the violinist in hopes Miss Jordan might be inspired to sing?"

"Sing with a violin?" Jack scoffed. "A guitar is what you want for singing. Everyone enjoys singing with a guitar! Some even claim a man holding a guitar is more attractive to ladies." He looked at Evie. "Shall I play a ditty for you, darling?"

She laughed, but the smile hung on to the corners of her eyes long after the sound faded away. "You do have a guitar, don't you, Jack?"

"Of course I do. In the *Tempest* with the rest of my prizes. Traded to get a fine Martin, I did—none better."

"Shall we let the child see if her theory is correct or if Rowen knows our Conductor best?"

Jack slapped his hands together. "That's a fine plan. I shall fetch my guitar and we will have a right good sing-along at young Lady Astraea's feet."

Jack walked across the Topside deck toward where the *Tempest* was tethered, Jordan taking special care so the two great airships did not touch.

Bran imagined such work taxed her still-developing skills further, and gave him yet another way to judge her aptitude as her skill set grew at a startling speed.

Jack turned back to look at Rowen. "Come along, lad," he instructed with a tone so full of authority it seemed he was Rowen's senior by at least a decade, when in reality they might have a half-dozen years between them.

Rowen shrugged, pausing long enough to tousle Meggie's hair and shoot a gaze at Bran that was filled with daggers, then he followed the much shorter man.

It was Meggie, Bran realized, smiling down at her. They loved his daughter so they allowed *him* to live.

So far.

Because no one wanted to take away a child's parent if it seemed he at least did right by her.

Meggie trembled, tilting her head the other direction, her bright eyes taking on the strange and distant look he'd seen more often than he'd hoped. A look that showed Meggie was not quite herself, that the spirit of Sybil was nearing the surface of her consciousness once more. If Sybil was so near again—so often—

Bran knew as no one else did he was not doing right by his daughter at all.

They needed to land, give Sybil's skull the respectful burial it deserved before the frighteningly vocal ghost girl shared more than her pleasant memories with his darling daughter—before Sybil shared memories of torture at his very hands with the little girl he loved the most—his dear little dove.

*Philadelphia*

It was when Lady Cynthia Astraea woke that she seemed to reconnect with her true self, as if something lingered in her body —some bit of soul or spirit not ready to be whisked away to Heaven, Hell, or the crystal prison of a soul stone. It was as her ladyship napped that two of the Astraea household servants—two of the very few who remained after the family fell from social grace—John and Laura, decided to again rifle through her room in hopes of finding the missing soul stone.

John did most of the rifling, his large dark hands deceptively quiet as he rustled through her ladyship's recently growing collection of expensive gowns while Laura watched Lady Astraea sleep, all the way keeping her body between any view the lady, upon waking, might get of John.

He hissed in Laura's direction and she spun around to face him, seeing how he shrugged, his broad, creased face one large question. His ample lips moved, forming careful and silent words. "I cannot find it...."

Laura looked around the room, wracking her brain. Her eyes fell to the vanity. And the drawers there. She pointed.

Lady Astraea sighed and, heart pounding, Laura turned back to her, her mouth agape.

But, mercifully, the woman slept on.

Her shoulders slumping, she continued her watch, only briefly wincing when she recognized the soft sound of the vanity's drawer scraping open. Something behind her shifted, the drawer scraped closed, and suddenly John was at her shoulder.

He opened up his hand, and there, sparkling up from his pale palm was a glittering blue soul stone.

Laura's eyes popped wide and she fanned herself.

The smile lighting John's face was contagious.

She snatched the stone from him, put a finger to her lips, and, on tiptoes, she crept to Lady Astraea's bedside. Doing the lady's laundering had given Laura an uncommon advantage—she knew where a pocket had been secreted away near her lady's bust line. With trembling fingers she reached down and slipped the stone into the pocket. She raced backwards, bumping into John's chest, and felt his hands clamp down on her upper arms, a reassuring pressure.

The lady slept on, and with a thin sigh of relief, Laura and John both slipped from the room.

They paused a few yards from the door in the hallway, Laura grabbing John's arm. "A note was delivered for you, John. I have it."

"A note? From who? About what?"

She tucked the folded paper into his hand. "Open it and find out."

"Would that I could, but I fear I have little I can make out in written words."

"Oh. Shall I?"

He nodded and she took it back. "Oh, from Cynda. Have you seen her recently?"

He nodded grimly. "Indeed I have. Read on."

"John, it is with great fear I send this note. Having been in a new household these past few weeks, I have yet to forget the family of servants you spoke of me leaving and feel I must give you the truth of what you witnessed last night." Laura looked at him. "Last night?"

"Read on," John whispered.

"Merrow are not as we've been told. I have stood listening at enough doors of late to know that they are peaceful. They wish an end to war. Last night they did not come to steal and devour the body," Laura shuddered, "but to bury it at sea—a high honor."

John massaged his forehead. "Is there anything else?"

Laura's eyes skimmed the note. "She fears the truth will never come out. That those who know will die. But she is certain *you* are safe. She wanted you to know." Laura folded up the note. "We must burn this."

John nodded.

"What will you do now you know?"

He shook his head. "The same as any old man of my skin color with knowledge he shouldn't have should do. Keep my head down and pray for change."

Laura pursed her lips but nodded.

Aboard the Tempest

"If you're determined to go into Philadelphia and claim the reward on that wanted poster," Jack said, giving the paper Rowen held out a jab, "it makes sense to have a person with you acting as the collector of said funds. As if that person is your captor."

Jack bent over, reaching into the corner of his cabin on the *Tempest,* withdrawing what was obviously a guitar wrapped in a few pretty scarves the likes of which Rowen had seen hanging in the Hill King's Cavern in Bangor. Jack took a careful moment unwrapping the instrument, and turning it in his hands, he let the light from the cabin's stormlight lantern flash across its polished wooden surface. "Lovely, yes?" he said.

"Yes. May I?" Rowen extended his hand and Ginger Jack gently laid the guitar's neck in it.

Rowen grinned, strumming his fingers along the strings. He frowned at the sound of one and tightened a tuner, picking out that string and note again.

Jack laughed. "So you play?"

"A bit. Not very well and not very often, but I enjoy it when I can. This is lovely."

Jack retrieved the guitar. "Yes. So you'll let me play captor?"

"What?" Rowen rolled his eyes. "If you think you will make my task easier, then yes, come along. Besides, if I am to take a pod, I'd best have someone who can fly it."

Jack punched the air with the hand holding the guitar. "Excellent. We will sing for Jordan and Meggie and then, tomorrow morning so the light is best, you and I will start for Philadelphia."

Rowen pressed his lips together a moment, but he agreed. "Likely a nearly viable plan."

"Nearly viable! It's brilliant. We'll be the small ginger pirate leading the blond tree trunk to his appointment with destiny. As you so merrily pointed out, the wanted poster only requires your *delivery,* not that you remain. Then we'll meet up with your friends, organize them, and return to the ship." Jack stopped so suddenly Rowen bumped into him. "If ..."

"If what?"

"If we can land the pod on a mountain or a hill we should be able to bring it back to the ship. But she needs to catch air under her wings. She'll need lift."

Rowen smirked. "You want to land her on a hill ... ?" He felt his smirk grow into a full out grin and he rubbed his hands together. "I have just the Hill for you. With a wonderful potential landing strip. As long as you don't need it to be too long ..."

Jack considered and gave a sudden shrug. "I enjoy a challenge as much as any man."

"Good, good. Then our first challenge is finding a song or two for Jordan to sing. Start with that." He folded up the wanted poster and tucked it into his belt.

*Aboard the Artemesia*

Jack and Rowen crossed from the *Tempest* to the *Artemesia*, a bounce in their step, and Jordan spared them a glance before returning to her work. The task of having two ships in the fluffy arms of her self-made clouds was definitely more of a job than she had expected. She was doing her best to keep from telling Evie to take her ship and go.

Thankfully Caleb frequently made himself available to her, making sure she was drinking enough water to Draw Down so that, in turn, she might continue to Light Up the sky and maintain their course. Caleb made for a fine friend.

What did they have to be so happy about? They were headed into Philadelphia as quickly as she could get them there just so they might risk their lives in a cause she wasn't certain she supported fully. Yes, slaves should be freed. They had done nothing to deserve their fate and no one should be sentenced to toil as they did—and suffer as they did.

But the Weather Witches ... They were a dangerous breed. Releasing them on their own recognizance was a disastrous decision. She knew how quickly she pulled storms and lightning to herself when angry and if she—someone who should have been impossible to Make into a Witch—could do such things, what might happen if others who were more predisposed acted out in anger or fear or pain, too?

They would destroy the world.

She would sooner destroy her own kind than see that happen.

Rowen, Jack, Meggie (grinning), Maude, and Bran settled at her feet. Miyakitsu reclined nearby, lounging comfortably across the Wandering Wallace's lap while he stroked her hair. Marion sat alone at the table, glowering as only he seemed able to do. She looked at them each in turn. "It appears you are all gathered for a Sunday picnic. Should I have brought something?"

Evie crossed the distance and sat beside Jack.

Not Rowen.

Jack.

That was at least some small something.

Rowen pulled out the guitar.

Jordan stifled a groan. "If you begin singing something I don't like I'll crash us, I swear."

He grinned at her.

Her heart jumped a few beats before it settled into an appropriate rhythm again. She had encouraged him earlier by expressing the fact that she cared. She should not have done that, she realized, having seen the familiar gleam in his eyes. What could she offer him now she was a ruined woman and a Witch steering a motley crew toward insurrection?

There was no future with her. She looked down at the planks filling the space between her bare feet and the bend of his knees as he sat cross-legged and cradling the guitar.

Hopeful.

How could he still be so blastedly hopeful?

Caleb nudged her as if to say, Relax and enjoy.

But she could do neither.

"What would you like to sing, Jordan?" Rowen asked, strumming the guitar's strings. He made it look deceptively easy, playing a guitar. She knew the truth though. Playing an instrument—any instrument—was a tricky business. She had tried them all and failed dramatically at each.

"I would not like to sing anything, thank you, Rowen," Jordan responded, turning her back to them all to set gears spinning. She still wasn't certain what all the pieces and parts of the ship-based puzzle did, but she knew with enough force she could get it to obey.

She knew, with certainty, this ship was hers.

Except when the ship itself invaded her dreams and reminded her of the things—no, the person—she feared most. Even though he was dead. Gone.

"Jordan."

Meggie's voice jolted her back. "Please, Miss Jordan. Choose a song. It was so very generous for Jack and Rowen to offer to sing for us...."

Jordan stretched her hands on the ship's wheel, thinking. "As we are going into revolution, perhaps we had best sing something applicable." She leveled her gaze at Rowen. "Do you know 'Johnny I Hardly Knew Ye'?" She took some small satisfaction when his fingers slipped on the strings.

"Yes," he said, his tone dark. "But I thought we would sing a pleasant song ... you know, on account of little ears," he said, nodding toward Meggie. "Why not 'When Johnny Comes Marching Home Again'?"

"Some soldiers never come marching home again," Jordan said. "It is best she is prepared for what consequences our actions may bring. As the Wandering Wallace has pointed out, this overthrow is only as peaceable as our enemy allows it to be. And knowing the men of the Council, I doubt it will be peaceable at all unless we catch them totally unawares."

Rowen drew in a breath. There was a moment he fumbled to find the right chord to begin with, and she couldn't be sure if it was because he was out of practice or because of the song she'd chosen.

"I will apologize for not having the right voice for this song ... as much of it is sung by a beautiful young lady. Not unlike our dear Conductor," he added.

She closed her mouth and tightened her jaw, wishing she could harden her heart as easily.

Rowen closed his eyes and he began to sing:

> "While going the road to sweet Athy,
> Hurroo, hurrooo,
> While going the road to sweet Athy,
> Hurroo, hurroo,
> While going the road to sweet Athy,
> A stick in me hand and a tear in me eye,
> A doleful damsel I heard cry,"

Then, in the highest voice he could manage before sounding utterly ridiculous, he sang:

"Johnny I hardly knew ye.

With your guns and drums
And drums and guns
Hurroo, hurroo.
With your guns and drums
and drums and guns
Hurroo, hurroo.
With their guns and drums
and drums and guns,
The enemy nearly slew ye.
My darlin' dear, you look so queer,
Johnny I hardly knew ye.

Where are the eyes that looked so mild,
Hurroo, hurroo,
Where are the eyes that looked so mild,
Hurroo, hurroo,
Where are the eyes that looked so mild,
When my poor heart you first beguiled,
Why did you skedaddle from me and the child,
Johnny I hardly knew ye.

Where are your legs that used to run,
Hurroo, hurroo,
Where are your legs that used to run,
Hurroo, hurroo,
Where are your legs that used to run,
When you went to carry a gun,
Indeed your dancing days are done,
Oh, Johnny I hardly knew ye.

Ye haven't an arm, ye haven't a leg,
Hurroo, hurroo,
Ye haven't an arm, ye haven't a leg,

Hurroo, hurroo,
Ye haven't an arm, ye haven't a leg,
Ye're an armless, legless, chickenless egg,
Ye'll have to be put in a bowl to beg,
Oh Johnny I hardly knew ye."

He stopped then, muting the strings with the palm of his hand and setting a fierce and dreadful silence between them.

"It's not over," Jordan insisted.

Rowen looked at her blankly.

"The song is not over," she insisted. "It's not bad enough her Johnny has been reduced to an amputee who must beg his way through life, is it, Rowen," she asked, leaning so close he could see every detail of her scar and each spark dancing in her glittering eyes. "It's not enough that their war stole Johnny away from his love, but what next Rowen? Sing the final verse."

He swallowed hard, and slowly he began:

"They're rolling out the guns again,
Hurroo, hurroo,
They're rolling out the guns again,
Hurroo, hurroo,
They're rolling out the guns again,
But they never will take our sons again,
No they'll never take our sons again,
Johnny I'm swearing to ye."

Jordan snorted. "Because that is the truth of war and revolution," she said. "Revolution is bloody and nasty and violent and crippling and the moment you think it is done someone decides to roll out the guns again. I am sick to death of war and I have never been a participant in it! And when we are done with this coup—what of the Wildkin threat? What of *that* war? Do we simply turn our ships and our guns toward them next?" She struggled to catch her breath now and leaned over, panting, her heart racing, her vision tight.

The Wandering Wallace continued stroking Miyakitsu's long dark hair and said, very slowly, very calmly, "There will be no more Wildkin War. We shall make peace with them quickly, I believe. They will see reason."

"What?" Jordan pulled herself upward quickly and nearly swooned as her head spun. She clutched the ship's wheel and Rowen leaped to his feet to help hold her upright. She swayed against him, regretting immediately that she could not stay upright herself. Her vision swam and, licking her lips, she focused on the Wandering Wallace. "What do you mean they will see reason and make peace? We've been fighting them for generations...."

Evie groaned and stretched, raising her arms high above her before dropping them back down and draping one across Ginger Jack's shoulders. "They really keep your breed in the dark, don't they?"

"Now, now," the Wandering Wallace soothed, setting Miyakitsu to the side and standing. "Young Lady Astraea is not at fault for not knowing the truth of things," he said to Evie. "They keep young ladies of her rank well protected. Sheltered. They tell her what to believe and because she knows nothing different or, in this case, better, she accepts it. We must not blame her."

"He," Evie said, crooking a thumb in Rowen's direction, "thought the same thing. That we were at war and what?" She glanced up at him. "That we had good reason, aye?"

"Aye. Yes," Rowen stuttered. "It's what the military tells us. The war has raged for generations, ever since we accidentally killed one of their princes with a regular water-bound boat. They attacked, little Galeyn Turrell—not much older than you," he added, nudging Meggie with the toe of one boot—"was suddenly Made and flew the ship to safety on our coast. She was the first Weather Witch. That ship—everything started with it. And things haven't been right since."

He slipped an arm around Jordan's waist, but she pulled away.

"The war has raged on," she said. "They attack our people, we beat them back, they slaughter our horses for meat, we beat them back ... They keep coming no matter how we try to keep them at bay," she whispered. "I've seen them—I've seen what they do to both horse and man alike. If they have souls, there is no mercy in them." Shuddering, she wrapped her arms around herself to ward against memory. She had seen and survived an attack.

Once.

"There is more to the story," the Wandering Wallace said. "There is always more to the story. You just have to listen to where and when and *by whom*—yes, most importantly, I think, by whom—the story is told."

"How can we know? They are Wildkin. They don't even speak."

"Not true, not true. They speak, but not in a language we are familiar with. They speak not English, French, Latin, or German. That is true. But they most certainly communicate. All species do. All species *must*."

"Do you think all Wildkin speak the same language?"

The Wandering Wallace glanced at Miyakitsu. "I might hope that is the case, but I have my doubts. You have noticed they have only allied themselves with other waterborne species of Wildkin, yes? Pookas and Kelpies and the like?"

"Yes."

Now even Marion rose and crossed the distance to stand with them, listening intently.

"I believe their language is based somehow in the very water they reside in. Or, if not their language, their format for communication. I believe water is our key to understanding them. Water is the key to their power."

Jordan took a sip of the water that was always nearby on the ship—the water that allowed her to Draw Down. "Water seems to always be the key," she whispered.

"Which is why it is so very good that it is plentiful in this country," the Wandering Wallace said. "Cheers," he toasted her.

She drank and he turned to the discarded guitar. "Now that we are so full of somber thoughts, let's change things just a bit and make things better. Music is a wonderful tool for shifting a soul's perspective." He walked around the edge of their group, strumming and retuning as he went.

"Let's see, let's see ... Oh." He fixed his gaze on Evie. "I shall use your crew as inspiration, my dear. I took a brief walk aboard a ship like the *Tempest* once and my little journey has led me to believe that this song is quite suitable for your consideration when it comes to disciplining your crew."

He had only hit three notes before Jack, Evie, and Rowen all laughed, recognizing the tune.

> "What do you do with a drunken sailor
> What do you do with a drunken sailor
> What do you do with a drunken sailor
> Early in the morning?"

He leaned in toward Evie and she shouted:
*"Put a sparrow down his britches!"*
Leaning back, he picked up the suggestion and sang it, encouraging everyone to join in.

> "Put a sparrow down his britches
> Put a sparrow down his britches
> Put a sparrow down his britches
> Early in the morning.
>
> "Weigh hey and up she rises
> Weigh hey and up she rises
> Weigh hey and up she rises
> Early in the morning!

"What do you do with a drunken sailor
What do you do with a drunken sailor
What do you do with a drunken sailor
Early in the morning?"

The Wandering Wallace made his way around the group of them, dancing, singing, and gathering their creative suggestions for sobering up (or disciplining) sailors. By the end he had gotten nearly every person, from Caleb to Maude, to add their wild suggestion and nearly all of them were singing and tapping their feet or fingers in time.

Nearly all.

Jordan's feet tapped the rhythm—that she could not help. But singing? Her mouth was clamped as tight as the lobster-claw-inspired suggestion Maude made.

It was only as the final verse was spinning itself out and she felt certain he would not pressure her that she began to hum.

The clouds overhead began to change in both color and form. They lightened. Brightened. And the more she hummed, the more light was reflected off the clouds.

Yes, lightning still played there, but it seemed more like sparkles adorning the clouds—or dew drops pinned onto their soft fluffy forms.

She felt the faintest sensation of a smile tilting her lips and her jaw unclamped, her mouth softened. For a moment she was silent, but mouthing the words. Not singing, but she enjoyed the music and—as much as she hesitated to say it, the camaraderie of the people seated and standing nearby the Topside dais of the *Artemesia*.

Camaraderie she had never expected. And all because of Meggie's determined interference.

And Rowen's guitar playing.

# Chapter Six

Was it a vision or a waking dream?

Fled is that music:—Do I wake or sleep?

—HORACE MANN

*Aboard the Artemesia*

The Wandering Wallace clapped a hand across the strings and brought the music to its end, and Jordan's mouth clamped shut again. "I believe it is time for a bit of an education. Perhaps we can find a Reader and quickly, yes? There is much to be done before we send Rowen and Jack to Philadelphia and more before we set down ourselves." He handed the guitar back to Jack and motioned for everyone to stand. Jordan felt his gaze fall on her, and he asked, "Can you set the ship to glide?"

"So I might come with you?" she asked.

He nodded.

"Then yes, I can." She stepped to the controls, and squinted at the sky briefly. Motioning with her fingers, she cleared the clouds from a small patch of sky, taking her bearings. She nodded, adjusted the wheel by inches and leaned into the lever at its side.

Never far away, Caleb chuckled. "I think it's the grunt you give when you set the lever that makes the ship know you mean business."

Jordan's lips pursed.

Caleb's chuckle became briefly nervous. "It is simply not a very lady-like sound to come from such a lady as yourself," he amended.

There was a groan and the *Artemesia*'s massive wings adjusted, air catching them differently and helping to pop them into position.

"I do not often feel lady-like, so perhaps it is fitting I do not seem something I am not."

Caleb frowned and, looking away in sudden shame, Jordan rubbed her hands together, focused herself and announced, "We are ready. Lead on, oh great Wandering Wallace."

Rowen's eyes on her, she stiffened, her lips straightening out of their brief smile. He watched her as if he waited for something. Or someone.

Perhaps he was looking for a glimpse of the old Jordan.

The Jordan who quit existing—who died—sometime between the Tanks of Holgate and the takeover of the *Artemesia*.

Her spine stiff, she followed the Wandering Wallace and his entourage, allowing herself to be packed into the elevator with the rest of them.

They descended in the dim light provided by a single storm-cell lantern, pressed so tight together Jordan thought she felt everyone's heartbeat pressing against her. The different decks of the ship each registered with a *ding* as they passed by, and when the shared atmosphere grew most stifling with the scents of humanity and whatever floral perfume Miyakitsu was anointed with, the doors opened and they nearly fell out into the hallway, breathing deeply in relief.

"I suppose you've identified a Reader?" Jordan asked.

"Not completely," the Wandering Wallace admitted. "But ..."

He pulled the refilled pouch out of his vest and untied it, spilling a handful of stormcell crystals into his palm. "But *they* know. Soul stones know and shine more brightly when in the presence of a Reader."

"Why is that?" Meggie asked, standing on tiptoe to see the glimmering gems.

"Because every soul wants its story to be told," the Wandering Wallace whispered, leaning over to pinch Meggie's cheek. "Just as every heart beats with a desire to be understood and loved."

Meggie nodded sagely, watching as he straightened and held the sparkling handful of stones before him, staring at them intently through the eyes of the peacock mask.

"Watch," he whispered.

The crystals all glowed faintly, but a few nearest the Wandering Wallace's index finger glinted more strongly.

"Here we go: forward," he said, heading in the direction the glowing crystals seemed to be.

The rest of them followed him, all watching the stones to see which way they instructed the man holding them to go.

In a few yards, all the crystals in the right side of his open palm glowed brightly and they paused outside one of the many doors lining the long hallway. As the Wandering Wallace turned and approached the door, the glowing lights shifted, colors brightening at the front of his hand.

"This is it," he remarked, placing a hand on the door's knob. "The guards wander the entire ship in shifts, so who has a key?"

Jordan dug into the folds of her skirt and withdrew a ring of iron keys. "It must be one of these," she said, thrusting them at him. "I took the liberty of recovering them."

The Wandering Wallace nodded and flipped through the ring of skeleton keys with his left hand, searching for one that looked promising. He slipped one into the lock, tugged it free, and tried another. That one also failed, but with the third he announced, "The third try *is* the charm!" Tumblers clicked and rolled and the door unlocked, opening a crack. The Wandering Wallace looked at Caleb, Rowen, Jack, and Marion, "At the ready, boys. There might be some within that are not greatly pleased by being under house arrest."

The largest of them stepped forward, prepared to help restrain people if necessary, and the Wandering Wallace slipped into the room, the rest of them fanning out around him.

Inside, a single Wraith and Warden staggered back from where they had been standing in the room's center, moving so far away their backs brushed the room's walls. They stayed there, frozen and staring.

In a corner sat a few members of the Grounded population— people considered unable to summon the elements of weather. Only a few people knew the truth that Jordan did: that anyone could be forced into the strange mold magick made.

By a set of cots sat a young girl, a small dark-haired boy, and an older woman, her back stiff, an ornate hat with perfect feathers topping her silver curls as if she was merely waiting for a chauffeur, not a prison guard. She fixed her eyes on the intruders, glaring at them. She and the children were well dressed, and, considering that they had been contained in a room with both Wardens and Wraiths for a few days, well kept.

The older woman was obviously unimpressed by her surroundings and even less impressed by their sudden arrival. "What do you want now," she snapped, tipping her chin up in an attempt to peer down her nose at the people towering above her.

The Wandering Wallace ignored the question, opening his hand again to display the crystals. They glowed most brightly in the direction of the boy, girl, and old woman. He took a step forward. And another, watching as the glow trembled and adjusted.

The woman pulled the boy to her. "What are you doing?" she asked, her eyes so narrow in her wrinkled face they were barely visible.

"Good lady," the Wandering Wallace asked slowly, "might you be a Reader?"

"A reader?" she scoffed. "I am quite well educated, as is my grandson and his nanny."

Jordan's gaze flicked to the girl. She seemed young to be a nanny, but her large eyes told Jordan nothing.

"We are all readers," the woman said imperiously.

"Ahhh, but I mean another type of Reading," the Wandering Wallace corrected, taking another step forward. He stretched his hand out further, watching carefully. "Capital R," he specified.

Her brow wrinkled. "Capital R?"

The Wandering Wallace held his hand by the girl, then shifted his position to compensate for the glow, watching the way the boy squirmed away, pressing back into his grandmother's lap. Held before the boy's bright eyes the entire handful of crystals lit up like they had each swallowed a sun.

"And this, good gentles, is a Reader," the Wandering Wallace said. Jordan heard the grin in his voice. "One I'd wager does not even know his own abilities yet...."

The boy squinted at him. "My abilities ... ?"

"Good grandmother," the Wandering Wallace whispered, "we mean you no harm. As a matter of fact, if your grandson might briefly assist us, I can guarantee that your living quarters will be upgraded—made Weather Worker free," he specified.

The woman shook her head. "They have given us no reason to fear. But you—you have allowed this ship to be overtaken and you have let people be cast overboard like so much flotsam. Why should I trust your intentions and allow my grandson to fall into your grasp in exchange for a more private room ... ?"

The Wandering Wallace straightened, tipping his head as he pondered. "There are ways to make this happen," he said drawing each word out slowly. Jordan's heart thumped painfully in her chest, imagining.

She stepped forward, mouth open, hand out, but Bran slid in front of the Wandering Wallace and, facing the woman, knelt.

The Wraith and Warden hissed, their backs hunching and fingers flexing, curling at their sides.

In so charming a voice that Jordan shuddered, Bran generously offered, "Perhaps a private room with meals and tea the same as we are served Topside, your belongings returned, and the opportunity to depart at a port before we reach our desired destination of Philadelphia so that you will not be associated with our actions?"

The woman's eyes twinkled. "No threats, no going back on your word. You will provide what you promised and, most importantly, no harm will come to my grandson at any point in this ... activity?"

Bran nodded.

The Wandering Wallace set a hand on his shoulder and tugged Bran back, saying, "Yes, grandmother. All that and the safety of your entire party. It is all guaranteed. But only if you allow us to borrow your grandson for, at most, an hour."

Her pale lips pressed together in a thin line and she ran her rheumy eyes over them all. "Agreed—so long as I bear witness to this thing you ask him to do and am allowed to stop it at any point I feel he is in danger."

The Wandering Wallace sighed. "Yes, yes of course. We can do it all here. Now."

The boy wiggled, his mouth slipping around his face in doubt. "Gramma," he whispered, sliding his hands beneath one of her arms. "What do they want me to do?"

The Wandering Wallace was all showman again, and he bowed, reaching out a hand to the child. "Why, you, my boy, will tell us all amazing stories! Short and astonishing tales of people long gone—or perhaps more recently departed. You will help to assure that they have a little life well beyond their expectations."

The child allowed himself to be pulled out of his grandmother's lap and he stood face-to-face with the man in the mask. "How? How can anyone do such a thing?"

"Quite naturally, you will find," the Wandering Wallace said.

"Here. Sit yourself down. Be comfortable. This will not hurt at all," he promised.

The child obeyed.

"What is your name?" he asked.

"Lawrence," the boy said with a gravity beyond his years.

"Well, Lawrence, I am the Wandering Wallace but you may simply call me oh-most-wonderful-and-wise-Wandering-Wallace if you prefer."

Lawrence smiled and shook his head.

"Too much?" the Wandering Wallace asked.

"I can remember Wandering Wallace," Lawrence said.

The Wandering Wallace sat before him and motioned to the others in his group to follow suit and sit.

They settled around him, Jordan's eyes roaming the room and watching the Wraiths and Wardens at least as much as she watched Rowen, Bran, and the Wandering Wallace.

The Wandering Wallace spread the crystals out before Lawrence, the tiny gems sparkling in a wide array of soft colors, though many glinted clear as dew or white as pearl. The boy grinned.

"Have you ever played hide-and-seek?" the Wandering Wallace asked.

Lawrence looked at him and said with a haughty laugh, "I am seven. I am a master at hide-and-seek."

"Excellent!" the Wandering Wallace proclaimed. "What you will be doing is playing hide-and-seek with the stories inside each crystal. You will hold each one and find its story."

"How do I win?" Lawrence asked, his brow furrowing.

"You win by telling us the story within," the Wandering Wallace concluded.

The boy picked up a crystal, weighing it in his hand, the tip of his tongue sticking out as he concentrated on the tiny gem. A crease appeared between his eyebrows. He stared.

After three long minutes, he blinked and looked at the Wandering Wallace. "I think I am losing...."

The Wandering Wallace flexed his long, slender hands in his lap. "You cannot find the story?"

The boy shook his head slowly.

"Hmm."

Evie scooted forward. "Hello," she said, sticking her hand out for a hearty shake.

Hesitantly, the boy took her hand and let her shake his until his arm was loose and he was laughing at her antics.

She stretched forward, saying, "I think it has been a long time since the Wandering Wallace played hide-and-seek. He has forgotten a few of the important steps." She released his hand and said, "Hold the crystal, but close your eyes. And when we start to count to ten, you start to imagine finding the crystal's story—inside a beautiful sparkling crystal room. Can you do that for me?"

"Yes!" he said with a laugh. "I can do that!"

"I will need each of these stories found—every single one," the Wandering Wallace said, lowering his head to stare straight at her through the eye holes of his mask.

Evie nodded solemnly. "Now watch what good captain Elizabeth does," the Wandering Wallace instructed, grabbing Meggie by the waist and scooting her onto his lap.

Meggie giggled. "They are pretty," she whispered, watching the boy rifle through the stones with a single fingertip, rolling some gemstones over, and pushing a few aside. "But how will he know?" Meggie asked, leaning out to whisper into the Wandering Wallace's ear. "How can he tell?"

The boy looked at Meggie and blinked a few times.

The Wandering Wallace answered for him, "Each stone holds an energy that is specific. It is like investigating how a person signs his name on a letter. Each signature is different, and if you understand why in some people's signatures their letters loop and link differently than in others' you might understand a bit more of that person. This stone holds an energy signature. And he knows how to read it."

"Ready?" Evie asked. "I will count with you! Close your eyes and when we reach ten you'll be standing outside a line of crystal cottages. All you need to do is walk inside each crystal house at a time."

Lawrence obeyed and together they slowly counted to ten, Evie inserting calming instructions between each number. Jordan knew that more than simple counting was going on—this was what some called hypnosis.

At ten, Lawrence's face went slack, and when he began to speak it was with a slower cadence and a deeper voice. And with greater authority. "Alymyssa Georgine of Massachusetts. So sad— a young woman, her husband was lost in a Wildkin raid." His eyelids opened and Meggie gasped.

Only the whites of his eyes showed for a moment before the irises dropped back down and he peered out at the Wandering Wallace from dilated pupils. "She will serve you well," he whispered, the strange pace and timbre of his voice dissipating as his face regained its plump and childish appeal.

"*Serve* you?" Jordan hissed. She stood and slinked back from the group, watching the Wardens and Wraiths who clung to the walls with a cool detachment. "Serve you. Who are you to wake them from their slumber and enslave them for your own desires? Who are *you* to make slaves of abolitionists?"

The Wandering Wallace shook his head. "They will not be slaves, they will be empowered. And when we have succeeded they will be allowed to continue their rest or I will set them free. To do whatever it is that spirits do if not encapsulated in crystal."

"And how will you do that?" Jordan asked.

The boy continued to sort and sift the stones, muttering to himself in his strange, new voice as he worked.

The Wraiths shifted along the walls, watching as intently as the Wardens listened.

The Wandering Wallace lifted one shoulder in a shrug. "I will crack open each gem and release the power within. Let loose the soul. If that is what that soul desires."

"You promise you will give them all that choice?"

"Yes. I promise," he said with a heavy sigh. "I do not condone enslavement of any sort, Jordan. I am allowing them the opportunity to have a final say. I am giving them a chance they might have wanted but could not take when they were flesh and bone. Would you not want a chance like that if your life was cut short? A chance to say your piece—or act it out—before final freedom?"

She looked away, her gaze pinned to a small dent in the wall as she wrung her hands, distressed.

"Jordan, I am giving them a great opportunity and new bodies. Some will request freedom, some will know I've given it *to* them," the Wandering Wallace said.

"New bodies ... ?"

Rowen stood now, reaching for her.

She pulled away. "You are a Reanimator—that was why you thought you could help Anil's dead son."

"Yes."

"Are those the sorts of bodies you intend to use? The bodies of the dead?"

The Wandering Wallace kept his eyes on the boy, ignoring the drama on the rise behind him. But his shoulders slumped. "No, Jordan. I will not use the bodies of the recently dead for these stones," he said.

"Or the bodies of the long dead," she whispered, her voice thinning.

"No. Of course not. I have another set of bodies altogether. Mechanical bodies."

Meggie turned on his lap and grabbed the peacock's beak. "Mechanical bodies? Where?"

His body language changed immediately. "Shall I show you, little fawn?"

Meggie glanced to her father, "May I see them, Papa, may I?"

"If we all may," Bran said, his eyes narrowing the slightest bit.

"Of course," the Wandering Wallace said. "As soon as we finish here I will show you something amazing. Something that will change the destiny of this entire country—with a little help from my friends ..." he whispered, pressing the peacock's beak into Meggie's giggling face, feathers bobbing. He focused on the boy again. "Lawrence, can you play hide-and-seek a little more quickly, perhaps?"

Evie nodded and caught the boy's attention again. "Lawrence, this time you will seek a group of stories. Stories of Weather Witches or the families of Weather Witches—people who love the Witches. Are you ready?"

"How do you know so much about this?" Jordan asked her.

Rowen jumped in, allowing Evie to continue working with the boy, helping him fall back into his strange trance and separate the stones into the ones that would aid their cause and ones that would not. He whispered, "In Bangor we met another Reader. An old woman who seemed to know her from before. I can only guess she picked up a few tricks."

Jordan snorted. "I am certain she knows quite a few *tricks,*" she said with a derisive snort.

Rowen's eyes widened at her insinuation.

"I heard that," Evie snapped. She looked at the Wandering Wallace. "We will make short work of this now," she promised. "Perhaps you should send someone to help gather their belongings and find them a nice new cabin?"

The Wandering Wallace nodded. "Might you loan one of the gentlemen the keys?" he asked Jordan. There was a clink of metal in answer and Jordan handed the keys to Marion. Considering her options, she felt he was most appropriate.

She would limit Bran's control as much as possible for as long as possible, but she was beginning to believe she should consider taking the same attitude when it came to the Wandering Wallace.

Marion took the keys with all the seriousness she expected. "Your cabin's number?" he asked the grandmother. His voice was gruff but gentle. The fact he spoke so little only gave his every word more weight, more value.

The grandmother answered, and it was not long before

Marion was on his way to gather up their things and search out a new location. As promised.

The rest of the group lingered in the cabin while the boy Read the final gemstones and helped select the membership souls destined to serve in the Wandering Wallace's army.

# Chapter Seven

*Aboard the Tempest*

As the group of them walked across the swaying rope and wood gangplank joining the two airships high above the ground, the Wandering Wallace said, "The bodies you are about to see put to shame the automatons that the Philadelphia Council have as guards. Whereas they have heavy ceramic shells to protect their inner workings, we have steel."

But his words lost Jordan when she saw the woman moving back and forth near the *Tempest*'s ship's wheel—the woman lashed to her post ...

A hand dropped on her shoulder and she jumped. "Sorry," Rowen whispered. "I was merely going to say that *she* is the way the *Tempest* goes unnoticed as a steam vessel. Thanks to that puppet—"

"Puppet," Jordan sighed, squinting.

"—Tara," Evie inserted.

"—Tara," Rowen repeated. "Thanks to *her* there is no enslavement here and no reason for the government to suspect anything strange is up unless they board."

"And we pay our docking fees and all our taxes," Evie gloated, "and pass an inspection whenever required."

Both her eyebrows high on her forehead, Jordan conceded, "Impressive."

Caleb simply smiled a grin that he seemed to be becoming more and more comfortable wearing around the group of them.

The Wandering Wallace paused by a large tube extending about a foot above the deck of the Tempest and fitted with a large domed cap. "Shall we make our descent?"

Evie laughed and popped open the heavy cap to reveal a broad tunnel with a ladder running down its interior.

Jordan leaned toward it and corrected her previous thought.

... a ladder running down *part* of its interior.

Jordan felt eyes on her. Yes, Rowen's—they never left, gauging her reaction to nearly everything. But added to that relentless gaze was Evie's, challenge glinting in her eyes. She demonstrated as she explained. "We step in, onto the last rung, count to"—she looked at the gathered assembly and simply explained the rest—"ten, step off, and slide to the bottom."

Jordan nodded. "Easy enough," she said, though her stomach climbed a bit higher in her gut at the thought. If the descent was not far, it was no problem. But the way Evie grinned Jordan was relatively certain the descent was a good distance. "You first."

Evie grinned. "Last one closes the hatch."

"Agreed," Jordan said with a shrug she hoped looked casual.

With that, Evie winked at Jack and disappeared into the tube's dark mouth.

Jack went next and so on until only Rowen and Jordan remained Topside.

"I'll come last and make sure the hatch is secured," Jordan said, waving to the tube.

"And I'll be at the bottom waiting to catch you."

A smile twitched to life at the edges of her lips. "If my imagination is in any way accurate," she whispered, "I would launch into you and knock us both to the ground."

He pressed his lips together and nodded. "True enough," he agreed. "But I would make the attempt nonetheless."

She shook her head, trying to fight down the blush burning at her ears.

"Perhaps it is best if I go first and nobly step aside so my presence does not suddenly impede your progress." He looked so very grave a giggle betrayed her.

"That would be quite noble of you," she whispered.

He grinned. "I have missed that sound," he said, his voice going low and rumbling like the muffled thunder.

More than her ears heated at the sound, and she battled the feeling, fought her fear, hearing something more than simple fun in his tone. Her tone changed as well and, with clipped words she said, "I expect they are waiting for us."

He nodded and, stepping into the tube, gave her a solemn look. "I *will* see you laughing again," he promised. Then the darkness of the waiting tunnel swallowed him up.

Looking back at the puppet who appeared to Conduct the *Tempest*, Jordan muttered, "We might as well be one and the same, Tara," before she stepped onto the ladder and closed the hatch above her.

She jumped without hesitation.

Her hair blasted back from her face and her skirts blew up and she flew down the ship's dark throat. She smacked her skirts back down, pinning the fabric between her knees and her breath pounded out of her as she hit something soft.

Jordan opened her eyes to bright light and the sound of Evie's laughter. "Not even *she* screamed," Evie laughed, pointing at her.

Rowen crossed his arms over his chest while Jordan recovered her wits and sat up on the awkward stack of straw-tick mattresses.

"You screamed?" Jordan asked, a smile lighting her face again.

Rowen refused to answer, but stopped pouting long enough to reach a hand out and help her to her feet.

"Follow us," Evie instructed, leading them to a door in the room's floor.

"Another slide?" Meggie asked with an excited peep.

Evie laughed. "No, m'dear. Merely stairs this time."

Down they went, into the ship's hold.

The broad expanse was filled with wooden crates, most of them approximately the same size.

The Wandering Wallace stood at the foot of the stairs and swept his arms wide. "My army!"

"*Our* army," Jordan corrected.

The peacock nodded slowly and turned his attention to Evie and Jack who, Jordan noticed, seemed more and more frequently to act as one. The Wandering Wallace motioned them all to join him.

Jack reached into his collar and withdrew a key on a chain he wore.

Jordan's vision tilted and she balked, turning aside, remembering clearly the last time she had seen a man pull a key out of his shirt—

—when she was being kept by the captain.

Abused by the captain.

Her stomach quivered and she reached a hand out to steady herself. Thunder clapped close to the window and everyone jumped. Closing her eyes and catching her breath, she focused on steadying her breathing. She opened her eyes again to find everyone staring at her. Her mouth moved wordlessly, and she yanked her hand back, realizing the stability and strength she'd reached for—and found: Rowen's arm.

Nearly ever-present, Caleb leaned in and slipped an arm around her shoulders. Jordan slouched against him, her knees soft. Rowen took a half-step away, head hanging.

A pang of guilt rushed through her, but ...

... it wasn't like she could act differently. She couldn't help the way she felt.

Everyone moved away from Jordan and Caleb, drawing near the open box.

There were gasps and murmurs, and Jordan steeled herself, peeling away from Caleb, curiosity winning out over the nausea of her past.

Inside the box was, indeed, a mechanical man. Or woman, Jordan surmised, noticing there was nothing giving any clue to the contraption's gender. As a matter of fact, beyond that it had a discernible head, two legs, two arms, and a body segmented by a somewhat narrower waist, there was very little that marked it as human.

It was far simpler than the statues in any museum she had visited and nowhere near as ornate as the statuary found in some churches. In the center of its chest was a small hole, a socket the right size for a stormcell. It was this which held the group's attention.

The Wandering Wallace suddenly reached behind Meggie's ear, exclaiming, "Do look and see what I have found." He held a glinting green Herkimer diamond between his finger and thumb. "You had better begin scrubbing better behind those ears of yours or you'll sprout potatoes!"

Giggling, Meggie watched the Wandering Wallace carefully place the gem in the small hole.

The mech began to hum softly. With a gurgle and a whine it rearranged itself inside the box so it kneeled, facing them. Then it swung a leg up and over the box's edge and pulled itself out and stood. It promptly fell over, sprawling on the floor.

Jordan pursed her lips, then said, "So, rather than Philadelphia ... where shall we go?" She clapped her hands and blew out a breath. "I suppose it should be a place we can release our prisoners ..."

The Wandering Wallace thrust out a hand, silencing her.

She crossed her arms.

The mech scrabbled on the floor a moment, gears whirring as it struggled to get to its hands and knees.

The Wandering Wallace crouched before it and stretched his hand out, saying, "Welcome back to life, Lady Margo Penhurst."

The mech turned its face toward the Wandering Wallace. Its body shuddered, but it clutched his hand, and, after a long minute it repositioned its feet. It stood.

*She* stood, Jordan corrected herself, realizing something about the mech had changed since the stone had been inserted. Even its stance spoke of something different, something fresh, alive, and distinctly feminine.

"Where am I?" a voice echoed out as if someone called up from deep in a well. The sound was nearly as tinny—as metallic— as the contraption's body.

"You are on an airship. Alive in a new and more powerful body."

"Alive?" the automaton whispered, somehow sounding even more distant.

"Yes. Most certainly alive. And ready to take back some of the power that was stolen from you at your execution," he promised.

"Execution ..." she said. "I remember ..."

"Yes," the Wandering Wallace muttered. "Executions are memorable moments ... But let us dwell on the future rather than be mired in the past, shall we?"

The bald metal head cocked.

"We march on Philadelphia to correct the oversights of the current government and free the slaves. To free the slaves of all varieties."

"You would change the world so much?" the mech asked.

"Yes," the Wandering Wallace said. "Most definitely. Will you help us? Will you put your mark on history?"

"Yes," the mech replied. "I shall."

For the rest of that evening their crew worked to bring the

mechs to life and orient them to their new existence. Only once did they need to remove the soul stone and replace it with another.

Some souls could not be salvaged, some people were too dangerous to ever bring back.

*Aboard the Airship Artemesia*

On the *Artemesia*, the rebel leaders had reconvened at the Topside tables, Meggie, Maude, and Miyakitsu playing nearby the Conductor's dais, Somebunny propped up to watch. Taking off her hat, and shaking her head so her long red hair fell around her shoulders, Evie muttered, "At the best we have that army of automatons—"

"Automata," the Wandering Wallace corrected, picking at a cruller.

Evie blinked. "What?"

"Automata," the Wandering Wallace said. "Latin plural."

Evie rolled her eyes. "American singular," she said, pointing to herself. "I care little about the Latin plural," she confessed, "when we float at the brink of revolution."

"In stressful times it is important not to lose touch with appropriate decorum. One must not drop one's standards merely because war threatens," the Wandering Wallace quipped.

"Whatever," Evie conceded with a sigh. "Whatever they are. You have a small marching army of them, a handful of liberally aligned traders—"

"Let us call a spade a spade, shall we?" he said.

Evie sucked in a deep breath, straightening her shoulders and raising her chin. "How so?"

"Let us be rid of the misnomer 'liberally aligned trader' and speak the truth, shall we? Pirates. Your people are pirates. Not that there is anything wrong with that," he clarified, poking another piece of pastry into the space between the bird's dramatic beaks.

"You do not make conversation easy, do you, Wandering Wallace?"

"Conversation might not always be easy with me, but I am determined that it shall be clear and correct."

"Hmm," she said. She glanced to Marion for assistance, but he seemed more interested in watching the girls play by Jordan's feet. "Mind if I get to the point?"

"I rather encourage that," the Wandering Wallace said, cocking his head in a way so birdlike it unnerved her.

Her fingers tapped the table's surface. "We are undermanned and undergunned," she said. "You want revolution to come to the city that sets the precedent when it comes to Weather Working, but I do not think we have the numbers to do such a thing. This is a suicide mission."

"No. Most certainly not." He pulled cards from—from *somewhere*; as far as she was concerned he might as well have pulled them out of his ass—and fanned the cards out with a rasp. "We have something better than a standing army," he declared. He motioned with his glossy beak toward the dais where Jordan worked, tweaking the positions of mechanical things Evie understood the workings of well enough. "We have the Stormbringer."

Evie coughed. "Let us say we *do* have the Stormbringer."

The Wandering Wallace laughed. "You doubt the accuracy of my assessment?"

She lifted and dropped one shoulder, far too cynical to blindly accept some prophesied savior. "If King Arthur didn't return when the golems tore London apart stone by stone and brick by brick, and Christ didn't return when the Old World's churchyards vomited up their corpses and made war on the shrines, I feel relatively certain no barefoot teenaged girl in a worn blue and gold dress is set to bring an end to a war that's raged between humans and Wildkin for generations. I believe *you* believe we have the Stormbringer."

Marion's gaze flicked to her, and Bran shifted in his seat.

"And I am committed to the cause of abolition whether we have the Stormbringer or not—whether there *is* a Stormbringer or not. But I'd rather go into revolution armed to the teeth with men of matching intentions at my back and sides. At this moment, from what I know of Philadelphia, we are simply and brutally unmatched."

"Oh, ye of little faith! Regardless of the fact we have the Stormbringer, just *word* that we do—that the Stormbringer exists and is on this vessel—will be enough to gather every starry-eyed or desperate soul with a hunger for change. We will have our army— the entire Below will join us when they hear who rides with us. When they see the storms we've seen." The cards in his hands disappeared. "My magick will seem like paltry parlor tricks when the Below and servants on the Hill hear who we have."

"There is nothing more powerful and rallying," Marion whispered, "than a sign a promise has been fulfilled—that a prophecy has come to be. The Wandering Wallace is correct. People will flock to our cause—people who were not brave enough to stand alone will be empowered standing alongside the Stormbringer. Standing beneath the shelter of her power. The Council will quake at her name," Marion promised. "This coup may yet be bloodless."

The Wandering Wallace pushed back from the table, grating his chair's legs across the deck. "I certainly cannot guarantee *that—*"

"You may not guarantee it, but hope for it and perhaps it, too, will come."

Now the Wandering Wallace tapped *his* fingers on the table-top. "Your faith is remarkable, Marion. I shall set my course by its bright and leading light." He stood, stretching and peering at the people all around him.

With a jaunty step he made his way to where the girls played. "And what, dear dolls, are you all doing?"

Maude smiled up at him, and Meggie held up a black paper

figurine. The Wandering Wallace carefully took the figure in his hands, nodding his great beaked head and looking at Meggie with approval. "A shadow puppet. A carefully cut, well-jointed shadow puppet," he added. "Who is she?" he asked, noting the ruffled skirt and loose hair.

"Who do you think?" Meggie teased.

He held it up to the sky, framing it in a twisting mass of clouds. "I might deduce—from the dress"—he looked toward Jordan—"and the hair—" He winked. "Well, not the hair *exactly*."

"I like her hair more now than before," Meggie confessed, "but Mama is not as impressed."

The Wandering Wallace gave a sly wink. "So it is our Conductor, Jordan!"

"Yes! Oh!" She reached behind her and picked up the upper body of another figure. "Who is this?"

"Hmm. Strong brow, firm jawline, and broad chest ... Is it Rowen?"

Meggie clapped her hands together in answer.

"These are quite accurate."

"It is Mama's handiwork," Meggie beamed.

"Lovely. Lovely indeed!" he congratulated. "Maude, you have hidden talents."

"It is nothing, truly," Maude said. "Merely a traditional paper-craft. Though there is a fascinating story of the very first of the shadow puppets—a tale from the Far East."

Evie was prepared to drop her glare from where she hoped it burned into the Wandering Wallace when his demeanor suddenly changed, the raven's head raising, his gaze skimming over Maude and landing on Miyakitsu.

Odd.

Miyakitsu was twitching. Her head snapped from side to side, fingers flicking in her hair, her eyes darting. Something about her was distinctly disturbed.

The Wandering Wallace reached out, petting Meggie's head.

"They are lovely." The words were strained. "Perhaps your mama will tell the story of the first shadow puppets and you will put on a show for us?"

"Yes, certainly," Meggie said, bouncing beneath the palm of his hand.

"Good, good," the Wandering Wallace said, his voice falling into a whisper, his eyes still stuck on Miyakitsu.

"My love," he said, stepping around Meggie and Maude to be closer to Miyakitsu. "Dearest," he coaxed. He crouched there and Evie did the thing she ofttimes avoided doing—she used Witchery to pull his whispered words to her on a wisp of wind. "You do not seem quite well...." He reached down, grabbed Miyakitsu by her shoulders and pulled her up and to him, clutching her face to his chest.

The Wandering Wallace turned to address the group of them. "I am sorry, dear friends, but it seems I must take my lady to our rooms to rest. She is not quite herself," he said. Then, before they could ask him any questions or offer any help, he hurried Miyakitsu to the elevator and, sinking into the belly of the *Artemesia,* he sealed them away from view.

*Aboard the Artemesia*

The Wandering Wallace held Miyakitsu, not too tight and not too loose, feeling how her form slipped and changed within the circle of his embrace, her skin loose around her true self. She was slipping away, sliding, unbidden, into the fox. "My love," he whispered, "stay with me. Remember who you are—remember who *I* am," he begged.

The elevator bounced to a stop at their floor.

Too late.

Where once he held his beautiful wild woman, now the Wandering Wallace struggled with a frightened and snapping fox the color of midnight. He kept the kimono closed around her, wrapping her in fine silk as he rushed to their room, wrestled his way inside and dumped the crying beast on the bed.

He slammed the door shut, bolted it, and stared at Miyakitsu. "Please, my love. Not yet. Not so soon. I cannot do this ... I cannot do anything without *you*," he whispered, tugging off his mask and rubbing at his treacherously leaking eyes. "You are too young to give over to the magick," he whispered. "I was supposed to have more time. I was promised more time!" he shouted, hurling the mask to the floor.

The fox retreated on the bed, snarling.

"What do I do ... What do I ... ?" He paced before the distrusting fox, pulling at his short hair. "Set the stage, Wallace, set the stage. She might return any moment ..." He rushed to the trunk that was always among their belongings. With a few careful touches the lock released, buzzing and popping apart, pieces rotating out of position to allow the lid to open.

Inside, Mitakitsu's accidental doppelgänger, Tsu, slept, bound into the box and not to wake unless absolutely necessary. He had broken the promise to himself in the past—the promise to keep Tsu asleep while Miyakitsu was human and whole, but he had always managed to keep the girls from seeing each other. Tsu might see the fox, and Miyakitsu might see the closed trunk, but that was as close as they ever came to being face-to-face. And since Miyakitsu remembered nothing—*nothing*—after she slept or phased into her fox state—it didn't matter if Miyakitsu the fox saw Tsu the doppelgänger.

The Wandering Wallace raced around the room, setting the stage as he did every night, moments after Miyakitsu had fallen asleep and moments before he joined her in bed. Carefully, he placed the daguerreotypes and the masks, each in its particular place. He picked up the hand mirror and suspended it by Miyakitsu's side of the bed.

He looked at the fox. It still stood atop the bed, watching him with narrow and frightened eyes. It had not begun to sniff or circle, so it had certainly not begun to settle.

He had a decision to make and make quickly. If he left the fox in the room unchaperoned, it might do serious damage. If he went Topside without Miyakitsu and mentioned she was unwell, it would raise questions at least, and might invite unwelcome interest and visitors later. But if he stayed, some Good Samaritan might stop by and check on them. Most of them knew he traveled with a black fox, but if that black fox suddenly phased into a beautiful nude woman they supped with every night ...

He would be seen as a Wildkin collaborator. The trust he had built to help launch a revolution would be gone.

He returned to the open trunk, staring into it at Tsu. To anyone else she appeared to merely be sleeping. And she would remain that way until he dressed her up in the strands of soul stone crystals that kicked her body back into a semblance of life.

There were days he regretted his reaction to the panic that caused him to craft Tsu, but today was not one of them.

He scrubbed a hand roughly across his scarred brow and reached into the trunk, opening a smaller box within it. Inside was a set of compartments and inside each was a small stoppered bottle. There was one in the shape of a fish that held bitters, one in the shape of a cone that held liquefied ginger, and one like a pyramid that held molasses. A few bristled with strange protrusions.

He ticked them off, knowing each by touch: Absinthe, laudanum, heroin, opium, vodka, and ... His fingers paused on the last one.

*Chloroform.*

He'd never needed to use it. Not on Miyakitsu or Tsu, at least. He pulled out a handkerchief and withdrew the bottle, unstopping it and dumping some of it into the cloth in his hands—just enough to moisten it. He closed the bottle again, set it back in its compartment, and straightened, eyeing the fox.

It whined, a singsong sound, and flattened its body to the mattress, baring tiny, sharp teeth.

He pounced on it, covering the panicking beast's snout with

the dosed cloth and holding it—holding *her*—he tried to force himself to remember—her—until the scrabbling of her paws slowed, her eyes closed, and her fighting stopped.

He laid her limp body down on the bed, adjusting her position so she looked as if she had fallen asleep naturally, tucking her thick tail around her and propping her chin on her front paws.

He stepped back, staring at her, his heart racing. Sweat dotted his forehead even though the room was cool. He leaned over, kissed her forehead gently, and rocked back on his heels, thinking.

Like a man who had suddenly aged years in mere moments, he rose and stepped back over to the trunk. He looked from Tsu to the fox and back again. Then he crouched by the accidental doppelgänger and pulled out a strand of stormcell crystals. He swept her hair back from the nape of her narrow neck and attached the necklace. Then he moved on to the matching bracelets, the anklets, and earrings. He set each in its proper place and undid the belts holding her in the painted trunk.

There was one last thing to do, a strange thing straight out of myth and legend.

But magick was strange and so old it transcended memory and fell to instinct. So the Wandering Wallace, a man forced to make his way by selling illusion and sleight of hand in a land that outlawed any magick it couldn't control, let the tickle of power wiggle up from his heart to tingle on his lips, and, leaning into the trunk, he brushed his lips against his wife's mirror image.

And she woke.

The stormcell crystals around her throat glittered; a glow racing through them like lightning circled her neck. Her eyelids quivered and she blinked rapidly, eyelashes fluttering. She coughed—once, and softly, and then turned her face to where he always waited, watching.

This was magick. As magickal as a woman who was sometimes a fox, and as magickal as people who could pull clouds and wind and weather together to send ships and passengers flying. He reached into the box, holding a hand out to her. "Hello, my love," he whispered, "did you sleep well?"

She was always blessedly foggy in the first few minutes after waking, enough that, as long as he got her out of the trunk and lying or sitting on the bed, she had no recollection of regaining consciousness in a box where she was often stored like some forgotten doll. It was always a bit of a race then, to get her out of the trunk and to a spot she could truly wake and not be horrified at the reality of how he kept her.

"Here, sweetness," he whispered, helping her step free of the box. She stumbled, falling against him, her hair coming free of its loose knot and flowing around them both, the black of deep water. He breathed deep, pulling her strange scent down—a scent much different from the wild and sensual musk of Miyakitsu. Tsu's scent was cedar and spice, the scent of the trunk she slept in and its contents.

She seemed to have no scent of her own—no distinguishing musk, nothing that distinguished her as simply *Tsu*. Perhaps doppelgängers of briefly dead girls never truly separated themselves from the person they mirrored. He moved her across the floor to the bed, swept the fox gently aside, and laid Tsu down there, moving his hand slowly across her half-opened eyes and counting under his breath to ten before pulling his hand away again.

"Hello, my beauty," he said, bending down to kiss her lips in greeting.

She stretched, a long and languid move nearly precisely the same as Miyakitsu's. "Hello, my handsome love," she whispered. She yawned. "Why, when I wake, am I always so hungry?"

"Hungry?"

"Yes," she whispered. "Hungry. For the sight and touch of you." Stretching a hand up, she stroked his cheek.

His eyes drifted to the drugged and sleeping fox and he grabbed Tsu's hand. This was the trouble with magick—other than not knowing how magick truly happened, where it originated from—not knowing what rules were being reinforced and which were broken at any one moment.

Tsu was and was not, at any one moment and at none at all, his wife, his love, his hope, his fear, and his true love's simpler self. Tsu was as simple as shadow and as complicated as a cat. She was made from his wife, but had no idea there was any other woman in his life but her—and he was desperate to keep things that way.

When Miyakitsu had suddenly—he swallowed hard at the thought and pressed Tsu's hand tighter to his cheek, pinning it there—*died*, he tried to revive her, to save her.

But magick intervened.

Miyakitsu died that day on his Reanimating table, but he refused to give in so easily. He tried again. He used every stormcell in his collection then—used every bit of metal and wire, and he pulled the magick he'd learned from the Night Market people and those in the darkest of Philadelphia's alleys—places Marketers dared not go—and pulled every stitch of power Miyakitsu herself had taught him to manipulate and there, in his workshop, with only candlelight because he had no stormcells to spare, he leaned over Miyakitsu's chilling form and did everything to bring her back.

He had been a man possessed.

His heart hammered at the thought. That was what scared him most—how desperate he had been.

And the words he said—the promise he made in a moment of desperation. Words one part prayer, one part spell. And he had committed fully to something that drifted loose at the fringes of all magickal workings in the New World, something wild and ancient.

Something hungry.

He dropped to his knees at Tsu's bedside, still holding her hand to his cheek.

"What," she whispered, dark eyebrows sweeping together in worry. "What bothers you so, my love—what—" Her eyes searched his face. "What haunts you?"

He dared not tell her the truth, that a night three years ago haunted him. That *she* haunted him.

Because three years ago in the corner of his workshop something had flickered into existence, at first so faint he thought it was the lateness of the night and the emotional strain of losing his only love playing tricks on his vision.

But the stormcells glowed and pulsed, burning like each held the heart of a star in their faceted depths. A form in the room's corner slowly solidified, its edges firming to hold in whatever swirled within its boundaries—like a housemaid quickly stitching shut a bag she'd caught a snake in to keep it from biting.

The room and all its contents seemed black and white that night, all glare and shadow, nothing soft and in between, all color leached out by the stormcells and the thing that grew and stretched and found a familiar form in the dimmest corner of the Reanimator's workshop.

"Miyakitsu," he had whispered, his eyes burning, stretched so wide and unblinking. He had stumbled toward her, disbelieving at the same time hope grew hot in him.

He left rationality on his table with the corpse of his foreign bride and reached out to the form before him.

Long, loose black hair obscured her face.

He shivered now as he had shivered then, not at first sure what was behind the long locks. His hand shaking and his heart full of hope, he had reached out to the shadow, sweeping the hair back from her face to reveal Miyakitsu. Solid, safe, warm and soft beneath his trembling touch.

She was an impossibility.

A living, breathing impossibility.

She pushed past him, weaving toward the table, and he shouted as she stumbled, her hand reaching to steady herself—at least he thought so then—but she snared the tangle of stormcells and wires, pulling them down on her as she lost her balance.

There was a sickening sound as her head struck the edge of

the table. She collapsed, wrapped in a sparkling web that flared one last time.

And went out.

The only lights left in the cluttered space were the flickering flames of a half-dozen candle stubs.

He raced to where she laid, her eyes closed. He prayed one more time—to have her back and then lose her ...

He, a man who never cried, had sobbed then.

Until he'd heard her breathe.

"Oh, God," he whispered. "Thank you ... Thank you!" He pulled the webbing away from her.

He heard a cough and his name whispered. "Wallace?" came the frightened voice, and he snapped straight up.

"Miyakit—" he popped to his feet.

She was sitting up. "What—what happened?" she asked.

"Oh darling girl ..." he whispered. "I was so terrified ... So afraid I'd lost you ..."

It was then he knew he had a serious problem. He realized he needed to keep Miyakitsu and Tsu separated.

Forever.

It was then he knew he'd overstepped the boundaries of rationality and made some strange deal with—had it been God, or something else? Would God have given a man like the Wandering Wallace a second chance at love or would something else have shared what he'd think was an opportunity just to open the mouth to a trap?

He tried not to think too much about it. There was no going back.

He had two wives. The real one and her shadow.

He picked up a different mask, in a different mood. He settled the wolf's head on his shoulders.

He shook his head and said to Tsu now, "Do not worry, my love. Let us go Topside and feed you. And then you will begin to make masks for all our friends."

She smiled at him and stood up. Glancing over her shoulder,

she spied the fox. "Oh, sweeting," she cooed. She ran a hand across the plush black fur, watching it ripple beneath her fingers. "It has been a long day for her."

The Wandering Wallace's throat constricted.

"We must let her rest."

"Yes," he agreed. "It is true. Shall we go now, beautiful girl?"

She nodded, and he led her from the room, locking the door behind them.

# Chapter Eight

The smallest effort is not lost.

Each wavelet on the ocean toss'dAids in the ebb-tide or flow.

—CHARLES MACKAY

*Philadelphia*

Kenneth Lorrington, George quickly learned, was not known for throwing grand parties, or subtly working within high-ranking social circles.

But Kenneth was known for having friends of a distinctly divisive sort. Of several ranks, groups of them drifted into his household under the guise of making social calls. But instead of drinking, or gambling with cards or dice, these men gambled their lives, slinking into the household's library to discuss strategy and spar. They practiced sword fighting, boxing, and styles of fighting they claimed were learned as nearby as America's Fringe and as far away as the Far East.

Lorrington caught George watching them and motioned him forward. "Join us."

His chin tucked, remembering the warning to keep his head down, he obeyed.

Lorrington slapped him on the back and said, "Do you fight?"

"I used to."

"Good." Lorrington signaled another man over. "Skellish, give him a good one-two."

George's eyes widened. "I dare not hit a man of rank."

"You're in luck then," the one named Skellish said with a laugh, "I doubt you'll land a punch at all. But, please, for the sake of my practice time, do give it a solid try!"

Lorrington clapped, saying, "Quite right!"

So George obeyed. After he'd landed his third body blow to the ranking gentleman (and caught a few himself), Lorrington whistled and waved his arms for everyone to stop.

George dropped his hands, seeing how many men had gathered while he and Skellish were absorbed in sparring. The library was now crowded with men of varying ranks, and toward the group's center, Lorrington was steering an older man with spectacles and a large box.

"We have with us a very smart man. A few of you may have purchased watches and other fine baubles from him, but today he joins us to show us a far finer project of his."

The man drew up short, seeing George. "No. I cannot stay after all," he said, shaking his head.

Lorrington's tone was sharp. "I promise you that you are among friends. This man," he said, pointing to George, "is in my employ. Trust him as you would me."

"Kenneth," the watchmaker whispered, "you ask much of me."

"No more than your nephew Rowen might."

George moderated the surprise he feared would show in his expression.

The watchmaker sighed, and, his eyes never leaving George, he stepped to the library's center and began to unpack the box.

The library welcomed a few more guests, including Lord Morgan Astraea and Lord Gregor Burchette.

George's heart sped, aching in his chest. Had he still been in the Council's employ, he would have had quite the list of collaborators to hand over. He flexed his fists at his sides. Now, though, rather than enemies, he saw potential allies. It was a strange and heady sensation, being even a small part of such a group.

"Gentlemen," the watchmaker said, "I have a piece of technology to show you. A project in development that gives us more options and allows us to phase out Witchery."

He lifted a toy carriage out of the box and set it on the nearest table. "This will take but a moment to warm ..." he apologized, lighting a lucifer and sticking its burning head in a box toward the carriage's front wheels. After a moment he withdrew the match, shaking it out as the mechanism heated.

Steam poured out of a small chimney above the carriage's odd box, and the wheels, attached to rods that were attached to joints, and then to other odd bits, began to turn. The carriage began to travel forward.

The men clapped.

"So far," the watchmaker said, "we have been able to keep the model moving without incident for three hours. We have found that, by affixing a bellows, we can increase the carriage's speed to rival the trot of a horse."

The men murmured to each other, approval clear in their expressions.

Three hours at a trot was impressive.

Lorrington asked, "Who is the other part of the 'we?'"

"Old Sir," the watchmaker said. "A freed African with a mind for mechanics that is only rivaled by my own and a few others."

"That is precisely the spirit of this revolution," Lorrington congratulated. "That free men are freer thinkers. Good show!"

There was a round of hearty congratulations as the man snuffed the engine and repacked the box. He did not spare a glance for George, but hurried away.

"There are more like him," George told Lorrington as the crowd began to file out of the library, led by the watchmaker. "More inventive sorts in this city that might work well together."

Lorrington nodded. "I expect you know their names and locations?" he asked grimly.

"Names, yes. Locations?" George shook his head. "I left them with little reason to stay in the same spot."

"We will start with names and previous addresses, then," Lorrington said. "And we will seek to further revolution's grasp with fine inventions."

*Aboard the Artemesia*

It was as they again sat at the table, which was becoming far too familiar for Bran's tastes, that Evie growled out what he supposed they were all feeling: "Trusting a single soul in this endeavor is equally as nerve-wracking as knowing I should trust no one."

Bran tore his eyes from where Miyakitsu sat glittering with crystal jewelry, and focused on her man instead.

Peacock plumes twitched and the Wandering Wallace steepled his fingers together, resting the chin of his wolf mask on his thumbs, and peered at her. "You should be more than nervous," he warned. "You should be *terrified*. We risk everything by overthrowing a government. This is no small feat—no mutiny of a single ship in which we might simply hand the wheel back to her captain should we decide differently about our actions. This is life-changing. Or life-ending." He raised and dropped his shoulders. "We are rearranging all the pieces on life's chessboard so pawns may move unencumbered—so pawns might aspire to be kings and queens."

"We are *freeing slaves*," Evie responded, swinging her legs back to straddle her chair so she, too, leaned forward, her elbows propped on the table, her eyes grim. Or merely shrewd.

"If you believe that is the sum of it, perhaps that is best," the

Wandering Wallace said. "But, believe you me, freeing slaves is only part of a grander plan. It begins what's inevitable." Leaning back, he pulled one leg up to prop his foot on his chair's seat. He wrapped an arm around that leg, draping the other arm across the chair's back. "Can you imagine it, Elizabeth Victoria? A free world? A world without ranks. A world where *everyone* may vote. Where everyone learns to read and write. Where no one is judged by their appearance, or background, but by their achievements and heart. Where neighborhoods have faces of all colors, people of all faiths, and many languages are spoken—freely—in public, without fear of persecution. Can you imagine it?"

Evie snorted. "Quite an imagination you have."

"You are a pessimist," he accused.

"I am no pessimist, merely a weary realist. No matter what we do, no matter what we change, there will never be true equality. We are human. We live to subjugate others. We always complicate our existence, not simplify it. We are the only species behaving that way. We only feel safe with things—and people—we understand. And what we *think* we understand most—wrong though we are—are people most like ourselves. We are lazy. We do not wish to understand new things or new people. We prefer being comfortable with the evils we know rather than finding unfamiliar good."

"And you, Lady Jordan," the Wandering Wallace called to her across the deck, "what say you to Captain Elizabeth's theory? Are things so grim that true equality shall remain forever beyond our grasp? Say we free the Africans. Unionize the Irish. Free the Witches."

Her head snapped toward him at the last pair of words and she crossed to the table quickly, clouds darkening behind her. "You cannot truly *free* the Witches."

The Wandering Wallace's fingers tightened, whitening on the table's edge. "What?"

Close behind Jordan, Caleb hung his head.

Jordan locked her gaze with that of Bran.

His spine stiffened, a chill clawing beneath his shirt.

"Let *him* tell you why you dare not release us from our bonds," she challenged.

He looked away.

Marion shook his head, dark curls falling across his eyes. With a large hand he swept them aside, saying, "Why, Maker? Why might our Conductor, Lady Astraea, *Stormbringer,* believe we should not be set free?"

Jordan reached across the table, her fingers snaring Marion's wrist. She squeezed him so tight he tore his gaze from Bran to glare at her. "You need no answer except the one you feel inside."

Frost glinted where the edges of her fingers dug into his broad wrist—a cold so potent she hissed, pulling back, popping her stinging fingers into her mouth. From around them she whispered, "You know it—you feel it, too." Her eyelashes fluttered; moisture shone along the edges of her eyes. "More than any aboard these airships, our type—we Witches—cannot be trusted. We have been too ill-used to make kind decisions. We were brutalized to come into our powers and now we are brutal with others."

Her gaze volleyed between Bran and the Wandering Wallace. "You dare not truly free us. Use us to meet your ends, yes. But then destroy us."

Rowen jumped to his feet, color rising in his face.

Jordan reached out to him, and taking his hand, guided him back to his seat with a look and a touch. "It is the only way your type will go on."

"My type is *your* type," Rowen said.

Jordan drew back, watching him.

"I heard you tell Caleb the truth, that—"

"Hush!" she cried, her eyes wide. "You know not of what you speak!" Her hands shook and she dropped them to her sides and then plunged them into the generous pleats of her dress.

He stood again. "I *do.* I heard."

"I cannot win," she whispered hoarsely, turning away.

"I don't think there *is* winning in revolution," Rowen stated.

"I think everyone loses something during it. But you have to still fight." He rounded the table to stand before her. "Tell them," he urged. "Tell them the truth—there is freedom in knowledge: the freedom of choice."

"No!" she shouted. "No one else must know. I shouldn't have told anyone. It should've been only my burden and that of the Maker."

"*Be brave,*" Rowen whispered.

"I am. Braver than you know." She shook her head slowly. Sadly.

"This secret cannot be shared," Jordan insisted. "If others knew and used the knowledge ... It would bring chaos."

Bran glanced down, suddenly realizing he was no longer sure how many people knew the truth about becoming a Weather Witch—that anyone could be one if they were pushed far enough.... In his haste to leave Holgate (and the confusion surrounding his kidnapping) he had left some papers behind. And he had spoken to Maude and Marion ...

If they knew, and he knew, and Jordan, Caleb, and Rowen knew ... He glanced around the table. Only Captain Elizabeth Victoria, Ginger Jack, Meggie, the Wandering Wallace, and Miyakitsu didn't know. It seemed hardly a secret now....

"What is the harm?" Rowen pushed.

"Only think on it and you'll see."

Bran rolled it around in his own head. By telling the populace that anyone could be a Witch it did remove the stigma associated with magick. But ... He shuddered. What if people became determined to have more Weather Witches—perhaps for the military. There would be more Makers. There would be more cruelty even if it was accidental in the beginning. There would be Witches that triggered without guidance because, deep down, they knew it was possible ...

Jordan was right. There would be chaos. Marion had wreaked his own havoc as the meddlesome Frost King, but he'd never done anything hugely destructive. He'd never wiped out a population's crops, or destroyed a building with lightning, or sickened a population with an untimely chill.

But he could.

Almost any of them could.

"I shall prove it," Jordan said to Rowen, a determined crease between her brows. She spun to face Marion and Caleb. "When you are given a choice of action, do you not now turn to the darker of the paths presented? You, Caleb, who tried to gut the Maker? And you, Marion, who brought him and his family aboard this ship against their will?" They looked away from her but she was relentless as the dark that deepened in the sky around them. "Did you plan a relaxing vacation for them or fantasize where to dump his body?"

Both men scowled at the table, taking their scolding, storm clouds gathering in their eyes as lightning snapped distantly in the clouds Jordan called.

"This secret goes no further. And we Witches must be appropriately dealt with." Jordan locked gazes with the Wandering Wallace. "Use us however you must for the good of everyone else —that is why we were Made—" she added with a bitter laugh, "but you must destroy us as soon as you no longer need us—and before we realize you will pull the trigger." She groaned. "What I wouldn't give for a world without magick. Magick ruins everything." Regaining control of her shaking hands, she tucked them together before her. "You'll pardon me. I have a ship to sail. Philadelphia?" She looked at the Wandering Wallace for confirmation.

He whispered, "Yes," and they all watched her go.

Jordan stopped on the dais between the wheel and the sparkling stormglass, not far from where little Meggie returned to playing with her jacks and ball, the Fennec foxes dozing on Maude's wide lap.

He shook his head, the peacock's feathers fluttering. "What say you, Maker?" he finally asked. "Is there redemption for such souls or must we strip them from their bodies when the moment is right?"

Bran swallowed hard, his eyes squeezing together as he pushed out his most carefully chosen words. "Perhaps some are too far broken to be mended," he whispered, "but do not ask me who can be redeemed and who cannot be because I, more than any, hope redemption is available to all, no matter their sins. Men can change. Men can become better, stronger, wiser. But only if we try. So *you* will choose who to place in your sights when the time is right—not *me*."

Bran watched the Wandering Wallace pinch the bridge of his mask's snout in a vain attempt to reach his own flesh beneath the painted and fur-covered leather.

Miyakitsu pawed at his shoulder, cooing. He shook off her affections and rose to stalk in the space behind his chair, tucking his hands behind his back and shaking his head the whole time.

*Philadelphia*

The chambers of Philadelphia's Council were filled with men doing business and large government-provided porcelain and metal automatons wandering about as servants. Councilman Loftkin was focused on the reporter whom he'd called in. "Just write the bloody article," he demanded, rubbing a hand across his forehead.

The reporter, some new upstart from the newspaper who still had a fire in his eyes and an obvious inability to understand reality, leaned against Loftkin's desk. "Begging your pardon, Councilman," he said, not sounding like he begged at all, "we have an article about this poor girl murdered by Merrow and now *this*? I've caught no wind of this new news. Cynda Melkin's story was strange enough—what girls willingly wander the waterfront nowadays? And at night?" He clucked his tongue. "And now you claim there has been a fire related to someone's illegal experiments with steam, resulting in the death of the only child in a family's line? It sounds like quite the tale—but not one I've heard. Do you have a source? Witnesses?"

"Just because you have heard nothing," Loftkin strained past the words, "of this event does not lessen the reality or the heartbreaking tragedy of it all. And, in regards to Miss Melkin and her unfortunate friend: girls can be quite stupid."

"May I quote you?"

Loftkin fought down a growl.

"And *heartbreaking tragedy* ..." The reporter scrawled the words on his notepad and squinted at the Councilman. "You have a way with words? Perhaps you might consider penning a book compiling these tragedies?"

The Councilman snorted. "Politicians are expected to turn a phrase," he reminded. "A book. That is an interesting thought. Flattering even."

"The question would be, though, would your book be fiction or nonfiction?"

Loftkin sputtered. "What did you say happened to your predecessor? He never gave me a headache gathering news."

"It came to our attention that some of his sources were recycling news. And flat-out lying about certain aspects of what's occurring in this great country of ours."

"Really?" Councilman Loftkin stretched his mouth into an astonished gape.

"The man was living like a king—getting monies from somewhere. Imagine. A reporter living high on the hog. Not a clean writer's destiny, I daresay. Makes a man look suspicious, living beyond his means."

"Or stupid," Loftkin muttered. "Run the story or don't," he said, tucking his arms behind his head and leaning back in his chair. "The airships will run it and leave you and your newspaper wanting. Reporting is such a *very* competitive business."

Loftkin knew the reporter watched him—studied him—his eyes narrowed, pencil poised above his notepad.

"What a pity if news broadcasts between airships overtook

newspapers on the ground." Loftkin pulled forward out of the chair and, flexing his fingers, he folded his hands together on the desk. "News broadcast over the airways needs someone with a reassuring voice. I'm not certain there are many associated with newspapers having that quality ... Jobs might become scarce if you no longer compete."

The reporter tapped his pencil against the pad. "Let me get this straight ... The child's name was Terrence?"

The Councilman smiled. "Yes. With two r's."

"Very good," the reporter added, writing as quickly as he could.

*Aboard the Artemesia*

Most of their group had crossed to the *Tempest* to ready more automatons. Jordan stayed behind, insisting she needed to watch the ship closely a little while. No one questioned her—no one but Evie really understood what she did and it seemed, more and more, that Evie didn't care what she did as long as it got done.

It was never quiet on the ship—the storms that held them aloft whistled softly with distant-sounding winds and the occasional snap of lightning punctuating the steady purr of thunder. But the ship could still feel nearly peaceful if Jordan focused on Conducting and forgot everything else.

Their group reunited for dinner, though it seemed none of the ones who had gone to help with the automatons (other than Rowen) had any appetite.

Rowen always had an appetite.

Caleb moved food around on his plate and Bran simply stared at his, several shades paler than he normally was. Even the Wandering Wallace only ate a few bites.

"What is wrong?" Jordan finally asked. "Is the food not to your liking?"

Silent, they stared at the table.

"Something happened over there, didn't it?"

Rowen set down a chunk of bread and looked at her.

"Don't," Caleb said to Rowen.

"She asked."

"So you'll confirm her misconception?"

Rowen paused. "Just because one—"

Caleb slammed his scarred fist down. "He's pretty, Jordan," he said of Rowen, "pretty ignorant."

"Stop," she whispered.

Rowen stayed very still, watching her.

"Do not insult him, Caleb," she warned. "Tell me what happened. I'll choose what to think of it."

"Another automaton was switched out," Rowen said slowly.

"Switched out?"

The Wandering Wallace clarified. "A Witch was ill-prepared for rebirth."

Caleb covered his head in his hands. "He never stopped screaming ..."

"He couldn't be reasoned with. A storm erupted in the hold," Rowen added, "before we could pull the stone. Not horrible, but messy."

"It *sounds* horrible," Jordan said.

"Out of all of them, only two failed," the Wandering Wallace reminded.

The rest of the meal was eaten in silence. When people finally gave up on eating, they drifted away, taking the elevator to their rooms.

The Wandering Wallace curled by the horn and accompanying flywheel of the ship's intercom; Miyakitsu, decked out in so many stormcells it was hard not to notice, stroked a slow hand down his back soothingly. He twitched beneath her touch.

Caleb and Rowen stayed seated nearby; she felt them watching her work as much as they glared at each other.

The Wandering Wallace paused and took a sip of water before leaning away from the horn. He cleared his throat.

This was the most relaxing time of each night for Jordan—the time when the Wandering Wallace concluded the day's news and headlines and sang a soothing song to the passengers. His "lullaby to the liner." On nights the ship still felt haunted by its previous captain, the lullaby was what kept her sane.

She gripped the ship's wheel hard.

*Closer* to sane.

Caleb's hand snapped down on Jordan's and he sought her eyes. "Set the ship so you sleep tonight."

She conceded, adjusting a few dials and cogs before stepping away from the dais. Caleb was waiting for her.

Rowen just watched them.

"Are you escorting me?" she asked.

"Yes, darling," Caleb said with a smile so sweet Jordan's lips reflected its curve. In the dim light sifting through the cradle of clouds, she looked past his puckered cheek and only saw his undeniable beauty.

"Good night, everyone," Jordan said, but she meant it most for Rowen. She wasn't sure why she felt a need to say good-bye to him, but she did.

Caleb and she rode the elevator in silence. Caleb stepped out when she did, followed her to her door, and paused outside of it, every bit the gentleman.

Jordan did something she did not expect she would ever do— she invited him inside.

"Oh, darling," Caleb protested, looking at the cabin's Spartan decor. "You deserve so much more. If I were you, I would take the captain's apartments."

"No," she whispered, rubbing her forehead as she slipped out of her shoes. "Never." She nudged them underneath her bed and sat on its edge.

He cocked his head but nodded slowly. "Some other posh cabin then," he said. "But something grander than this."

Jordan shrugged.

"Go about your nighttime ritual," he encouraged.

She blinked a few times.

He laughed at her. "I see," he said. "You think my gentlemanly ways will vanish if you strip to a mere shift."

Jordan fought to keep her breathing steady and assessed his statement. She felt no threat from him. Not of any sort. "No," she said, sounding as puzzled as she felt.

"Good," he said, watching her closely. "Because I am one of the few who is absolutely no threat to you. You are beautiful, but not of my type."

She squinted at him, unsure. How could she be beautiful but not attractive? She thought back to their time in Holgate's grim Tanks.

"Quite seriously, you need some rest." He turned his back. "Please change. We can talk as you do and perhaps after, too. Perhaps it is time we exchange stories."

"Exchange stories?" she asked, fingers hesitating as she slowly undid her dress. Feeling air on her back, she paused, licking her lips, heart pounding. Her eyes closed and she fought to find logic. To find trust. Caleb never hurt her—he never acted like he might. But she had been hurt before.

Horribly.

Repeatedly.

Caleb's voice, calm and steady, brought her back. "I answer one of your questions with a story and you, in turn, answer one of mine."

Something deep inside her insisted she trust Caleb. She had to start with someone.

Stepping out of her dress, Jordan swept it aside with a tentative foot, snugged her shift modestly around her shoulders, and announced, "I am ready for bed."

Caleb turned, and looking at the crumpled dress on her floor, shook his head. "Dear girl, you are most certainly not ready. Pick up that thing you call a dress and at least hang it up. And run a brush through what's left of your hair. Just because you've been through a lot does not mean you should look like you have.

Tomorrow I will get a new outfit," he announced as she did as he had ordered.

She again sat on her bed. "May I ask you for a story first?"

"Strike for the heart."

She swallowed hard but nodded. "The scars—on your face," she specified, eyes dropping briefly to the others crisscrossing his fingers, "how did you get them?"

"Ah," he said. "I got them because someone disagreed passionately with my choice of lover."

She straightened at this, listening more closely.

"I was known for playing the pianoforte. I was considered quite the artist and held in some esteem. As you can imagine, artists tend to associate with other artists and so I met the most fabulous painter ..." His voice grew soft and wistful. "It was as he painted a private portrait of me that his father walked in."

Jordan wasn't immediately sure why she gasped—at the fact he loved someone of the same gender, that he had finally made it clear after alluding to that romantic love while in the Tanks, or the fact he had been caught? Perhaps it was a bit of all three.

"I was banished from his household—told to never show my face again." He sighed. "But love does not work that way. I had to see him. We were in love. I did not realize I had been seen until hours later as I strolled a quiet street. They grabbed me." He looked away, steeling himself. "They had knives. It seemed like dozens of them. One of them said, *He said never show your face there again—this is a face you'll think twice about showing.* And they carved into me."

Jordan's hands clamped over her mouth but a whimper leaked out between her fingers.

"When I did not die immediately, and did not die of infection soon after, his father did the last thing he could short of having me murdered. He accused me of Witchery. And I was taken to Holgate."

"You are not a Witch," Jordan whispered.

"No, just someone blinded by love."

"Oh, Caleb." Jordan stretched out a hand, but he waved away her concern.

"No, no, I will suffer none of your pity. I am alive and I have learned important lessons as a result of surviving. One: Money does not equate to class or education. Two: Those with the most power often have the least compassion; and three: Even in this most modern of ages there are barbarians."

Jordan's hand dropped and she hugged herself, staring at him.

"Now, dear child. It is your turn. Who did this," he moved his hand in a circle encompassing both her physical and spiritual self, "to you. You have been beaten far lower than Making could have taken you."

Filling her lungs and closing her eyes, she struggled to hold all the thoughts—all the pain—together long enough to explain what the *Artemesia*'s captain had done.

By the end of her stilted explanation, they were both seated together on her modest bed.

Crying.

*Aboard the Artemesia*

It was happening again. She was Topside, on the dais, the ship's wheel firmly in hand, a sense of control seeping in to fill her with warmth, when he appeared.

The captain. He strode straight to Jordan and grabbed her, pulling her from the ship's wheel and laughing as it spun loose, laughing until his mouth covered hers, swallowing her screams. Her arms were nothing but last night's noodles, soft, weak and worthless no matter how much she struggled ... He had a firm grip on her.

Body and soul.

The others stood watching her shame, standing still and solemn. Disapproving statues, their eyes were fixed on the captain kissing her, bending her body back, and sweeping her skirts away.

They watched. They knew.

They did nothing.

Why did she think *they* would stop him? *She* had not managed to.

Something inside her curled into a ball.

Withered and died.

The ship groaned beneath her feet, the deck splintering, boards popping loose. It opened, a cracked maw, sucking her down into the darkness, stealing her from his grip. The great and drifting ship fed her into its every fiber, running her like water until she flooded the ship's bow.

*She* was the figurehead with her arms flung wide and her head bent back. *She* was the woman with angel wings unfurled, not struck by the ship but guiding it forward with a joyful smile and a burst of song.

She and the ship were one, flying, merged beyond flesh, bone, and wooden beams, one living, breathing entity with only a solitary desire: to feel freedom fill her wings and speed her to bright new adventures and places unknown.

*Aboard the Artemesia*

Jordan jumped, her mattress creaking, waking to the image of a man by her bedside. He did not move. Did not jump or grab her, did not ... she forced the thought away and let the haze of sleep clear from her vision.

Caleb sat in the chair only a foot from her bed, his head nodding on his neck as he slept and fought sleep at the same time. Faithful as a hound, she thought. As unconditionally loving as the finest dog. And handsome to the point of being pretty—even though scars had rearranged the alignment of the features on his face years ago.

He was pretty inside and out.

She curled a fist beneath her cheekbone and watched him.

Pretty inside and out, and he understood where she'd been, how she'd changed. Why then did she not feel the things for him she logically should? Yes, he had mentioned a man when they had been in the Tanks together at Holgate with only most of one wall separating them. But the man could have been a brother or uncle or cousin. Or simply a faithful friend.

Defining a person's relationship status was a difficult thing when you barely knew the person himself. And how dare she define anyone's closest relationship when she couldn't even define her own?

He snorted in his sleep, his head lolling. He sniffled and snorted again, his eyes popping open, and he smiled drowsily at Jordan. "You're awake."

"And so are you," she said.

"I will leave you to your morning routine," he said, rising and stretching. "And I will return for you soon. Perhaps then you might indulge me."

She sat up in the bed, feeling the mattress shift beneath her. "How so?" she asked, wrinkling her nose.

But he was already by the door, and he merely turned to her and smiled, saying, "I guess you will need to wait and see, dear girl." The door closed.

Jordan rose slowly from her bed, her eyes fixed to the chair. It was the first time anyone had stayed in her room and not hurt her. She smacked her lips together. It was the first time she had trusted anyone enough to fall asleep near them.

Caleb was ... She rubbed her hand across her head, feeling the way the hair stood straight up or stuck out to the sides, creating what looked like a dark-brown painter's brush that resided on her head. Caleb thought she was beautiful. She knew she was not, and even his gentle attitude and the way he overlooked her obvious flaws—even that did not move her to finding him attractive.

Pretty, yes. Beautiful in an odd way. But ... Her stomach squeezed at the idea of finding him attractive.

She was not sure she even found Rowen attractive anymore.

The weight in her stomach warned her not to examine that line of thought too closely, and she obeyed, moving to the mirror to make her hair look less …

… offensive? She ran her fingers through it, managing to get most of it to point in a similar direction.

Well, it did not matter now what she thought of Rowen. Not after he had seen her looking the way she did. He was far too caught up in physical appearances to want to be seen with anyone who didn't look at least as handsome as he did.

Even with that awkward hairy growth on his face that some might define as a beard and mustache.

He was still Rowen.

# Chapter Nine

Love and hate are emotions that feed on themselves.



*Aboard the Artemesia*

Jordan turned away from the ship's wheel, surprised to see Rowen standing there, holding out a steaming cup of coffee. She blinked at him, not sure what to do or say.

He held it out, making it clear it was intended for her.

Hesitantly, she took it, holding both cup and saucer. "Thank you," she said, staring into the pale brown drink. He had added cream. She only had coffee with him one time, during an adventure into the Below. She had wrinkled her nose up at the black and bitter drink until he tempered it with cream ...

She took a long, slow sip.

... and sugar.

He remembered.

"Thank you," she said again, but more earnestly, closing her eyes and reveling in the rich scent that was all at once dark, sweet, and somehow spicy.

She felt the weight of his gaze like something solid and warm traveling across her face. Like sunshine had found her through the clouds.

It had been only a few days since they boarded the *Artemesia,* and though many things had changed, some things seemed as if they never would. His presence still knotted her stomach and made her eyes dart to every place but where he stood. His existence reminded her of how unworthy she was—reminded her at least as much as the regular nightmares that tormented her.

"You look tired," he whispered.

She shrugged.

Evie would have retorted with some joke. Meggie would have said something achingly adorable in explanation. Miyakitsu would have given a sweet and knowing smile. And Maude might have winked, depending on who stated such a thing.

But Jordan could only invest herself enough to shrug.

"This is too much for you, isn't it? Pulling two huge ships around the heavens ..." He looked around as if searching for Evie to make her take responsibility for the *Tempest.* Jordan nearly smiled, but instead she sipped a bit more, enjoying the warmth slipping down her throat.

Spotting Evie, Rowen moved to confront her, but Jordan reached for him.

Stopped him from leaving.

They both stood still, staring at her hand on his arm as if she had been possessed and lost control of her body. They had only touched a few times during his time aboard, and she remembered every contact viscerally. They embraced during their brief initial encounter, she slapped him when she learned he'd dueled, she reached out blindly and was held up by him on the Tempest, and she urged him to sit when she'd suggested the Witches not be freed.

But this was the only time she had stretched out a hand intentionally to hold him.

To *keep* him.

The coffee cup chattered on the saucer in her other hand and she stared at it, mystified. When had she put them back together?

She blinked rapidly, feeling the prickle of tears at the edges of her eyes. Her confusion mounting, she let her fingers slid from his arm—

—but he caught them and wrapped them in his hands. He stared at her more intently now, his eyes searching her face in a way that made her more self-conscious than she thought she could be.

The cup and saucer rattled so much she thought her hand might break off if she didn't regain control.

But Rowen was holding her other hand …

He stepped closer and everything happened at once: the cup fell, he released her to grab it, she reached for it at the same time, and their heads collided like two clumsy schoolchildren reaching for the same toy.

She groaned, pulling back and holding the side of her head, the saucer still in her right hand.

He straightened, holding the cup, his hand dripping with coffee and his cheek red from the impact. He was smiling in that bashful but roguish way of his that made her heart thunder.

She licked her lips and froze, stunned again when she realized she tasted him there, on her mouth. Her eyelashes fluttering, her mind replayed the comical not-quite-kiss, the less than romantic squashing together of the corners of their lips as their skulls plowed into each other. Her hand flew to her mouth and she blushed.

"Are you all right," he asked, grinning at her. "I never intended to clunk heads with you—and my skull is quite thick, as people gladly say."

"I'm … I'm fine," she said, stepping back. Perhaps he hadn't noticed their accidental kiss. Or perhaps he had but he knew that the better part of valor was not to mention it. Or perhaps he wasn't thinking about the press of her lips at all.

Perhaps she shouldn't think about it either. Her tongue

darted out and tested the spot her lips met his. She was mortified. What did she taste like anyway? Sweat and dirt and the potential of rain? She handed him her saucer—no, she pressed it into his stomach, so he grabbed it—and she turned away, focusing on the large stormcell mounted to the post and bristling with silver wires like a crown of thorns.

"You're a wreck," he whispered, stepping around so he was in her line of sight. "Are you not sleeping? Because if you're sleeping well than the only reason I can imagine you being so jumpy is because a handsome young man confronted you bearing gifts." He winked at her.

Jordan kept her expression as blank as she could and said, "I haven't slept well in weeks."

Rowen's face fell at the smack to his ego. "Ah. We must fix that. You must sleep enough, drink enough water—eat enough," he added, "to stay strong."

"—so I can keep both ships afloat."

"No," Rowen said, his tone sharp, "so you can keep *yourself* afloat. So to speak." He sighed. "Jordan. Do you not understand how very important you are?"

She allowed her gaze to flit to his eyes, his beautifully change-able eyes, today a shade between cornflower and gunmetal. Silver specks snapped like lightning bolts in their depths before she dared look away. That was the trouble with Rowen: he was captivating.

"I've heard the talk. I'm important to the Wandering Wallace's plan to take Philadelphia," she said grimly. "I might be the Stormbringer—I might not," she added hastily—"but to him I'm a valuable pawn on this chessboard only he clearly sees."

"I don't care about the Wandering Wallace," Rowen said. "I meant to *me*. You are important to *me*."

She looked away.

"Do you not see that?"

"Rowen." She groaned. "Rowen. Things have changed. Big,

sweeping things," she added. "Things that can never be undone. Although you are important to me," she admitted sadly, "I *cannot* be important to you. You cannot allow that. I am a Witch. You are the son of a high-ranking soldier. *You* might be redeemed, might return home. I might no longer have a home to return to. You cannot risk your future based on our past. What was it really?"

"It was *everything*," he murmured, brows drawn tight together. "There will never be so much of a change between us that I will not know you are the most important woman in—"

"Hush!" She stomped her foot. "Don't finish the sentence. Please. Don't. I can't be what you want me to be. Not today, not tomorrow. We do not share a future beyond this revolution. You cannot ruin your life over me. I'm not worth it!" She crossed her arms and added, "I doubt I ever was."

"—the world," he whispered. "You are the most important woman *in the world* to me. No matter what you do or say ... That will *not* change."

She faced him, hearing challenge ring in his words. "Don't be a fool," she hissed.

He said, "I leave for Philadelphia with Jack this morning." He scrubbed his brow with a fist. When his hand dropped she saw his eyes were dark and gray and cold as steel.

Her heart clenched. She had never seen his eyes turn that color before. She swallowed. Held her ground. She could not allow him to want her. Not at all. She was ruined but he might recover from everything. If he let her go. So she dredged the word up, hating herself as she pushed it from her lips, and said, "Go."

He blinked.

Suddenly Caleb was between them, one hand on Jordan's shoulder and one on Rowen's chest as he slid them apart. "Now, now, princess," he said, "mind your manners." He turned to face Rowen, slowly walking him backwards and saying under his breath. "She said it herself—she's not sleeping well. That takes a terrible toll on a person's personality."

"Are you apologizing for me?" Jordan called.

"No, no," Caleb said, pulling back as far as he could, "why apologize for perfection?" But Caleb slapped Rowen on the chest and turned him to face the dining table where Jack sat, working on another gun. Jordan swore he whispered something else to him before Rowen walked away, signaling to Jack they'd best be on their way.

Caleb faced her, smiling. "Well, you're not at your most charming this morning. Perhaps a nap is in order?"

"I thought you would understand," she whispered. "I cannot encourage Rowen's affection. I must push him away."

"Why on earth do you believe that?"

"Can't you see what I am? What I've become?"

Caleb's voice dropped. "Darling girl. What we see and what *you* see seem worlds apart. I see a beautiful woman only starting to understand her true power. A woman who is fighting to let that beauty inside come out—almost as much as she's fighting to keep it in."

"There's no inner beauty," she scoffed.

"Yes there is. I saw your foot tapping when Rowen sang. I heard you start to hum. There's beauty and love aplenty inside you yet."

"No."

"You're going to make this difficult, aren't you?"

"It won't be difficult if you just go along with me."

"Ha! The mantra of every spoiled child wanting a pony for Christmas."

"I can't let Rowen ruin his life over me. I won't. I won't let him be ruined because *I* am." She swiped at her face as tears raced down her cheeks, but Caleb stepped up to her, obscuring everyone's view of her, and whisked her tears away with a light touch. Jordan trembled, her eyes itching and her nose filling as she sniffled. "You *have* to understand ..." she whispered so softly the words might have been nothing but a wayward breeze whispering past, "I love him too much to let him be ruined by me."

"Ah."

Shaking, she looked up in time to watch Rowen and Jack cross from the *Artemesia* to the deck of the *Tempest.*

And disappear from sight.

"I love him, Caleb, but it can't matter now."

*Aboard the Tempest*

Caleb nearly vaulted across the bridge to catch Rowen's attention. "Might I have a word?"

Both Rowen and Jack turned. They looked at him, expressions flat.

"Only Rowen, please."

Jack snorted and walked a distance off.

Rowen faced Caleb, his eyes glowing and his face still flushed with rejection.

"Oh. You ..." Caleb's eyes went to Rowen's.

"I what?" Rowen asked.

Caleb's mouth moved, but no words came out.

"I. What?" Rowen repeated, shoving a full breath between the words.

Caleb stammered, "You don't understand."

Rowen peered down his nose at the other man, stepping forward to force Caleb back. "Enlighten me."

"She's different from how you remember her, yes?"

Rowen grunted. "I am also changed. And I know about the Making."

"Knowing and understanding are different things, friend."

A growl built in Rowen's throat and he slammed a fist into his open palm. "Get to the point. I know the Maker hurt her. I respect her wishes to not rid the world of him. I know Lightning Kissed her and marked her in a way never seen before. I know and in time *will* understand because I love Jordan. I know that, too. I *love* Jordan. I'm not sure I understand that either, but in time I will."

"There is more, Rowen," Caleb whispered. "You can understand the impact of torture because you have been a fighter: you know physical pain. And losing Jordan—you know emotional pain, too. But, she has suffered something you haven't."

Rowen's brow furrowed.

"Have you not wondered about the *Artemesia*'s lack of a captain?"

He squinted at Caleb, his gaze tracing each narrow scar lining the other man's face. "I presumed the Wandering Wallace had relieved the ship of its previous captain ..." He blinked. "The Wandering Wallace and Maker have been clear this ship is *Jordan's*, not the Wandering Wallace's. Why?"

"Because she deserves more than a ship, considering what that captain did to her," Caleb said, his voice going low and hoarse.

Rowen blinked hard once. Twice. His mouth and throat grew dry and he smacked his lips together. The promenade held a portrait of the captain. He had seen it—pictured the man alive. But what he pictured that man doing ...

... to Jordan.

The sound that rose from his throat was not one he'd ever made before and he turned, tearing away from Caleb.

"Rowen!" Caleb shrieked, racing after him, begging, "Don't tell her I—"

But Rowen spun around and Caleb slammed into him, breathless. "Don't tell her *what*? That you cared enough to tell me the truth?"

Caleb's head hung. "She will *hate* me."

Rowen's eyes went dark and he pounded across the bridge, Caleb close behind. If Jordan saw them, she gave no sign, said no word. In a grim silence they descended in the elevator and, when its door opened, Rowen stormed off down the hall without a word, Caleb running behind.

Rowen stopped in the promenade, facing the portrait of the *Artemesia*'s previous captain, facing the image of the man who had hurt Jordan worse than even the Maker or any direct blast of lightning could.

Ripping the portrait off the wall, he snapped its broad wood frame across his thigh, grinning as the canvas puckered and wrinkled, paint cracking and peeling, the captain's smile snapping into pieces that fell to the floor and were ground into the carpet under Rowen's heavy heel.

He shouldered past Caleb, making his way to the nearest balcony and shoving the door open. The wind whipped around him, ruffling his hair and blowing strands of it into his face. He sputtered, narrowing his eyes against the wind and the humidity hugging close. He dragged the canvas and its splintered frame to the railing and, looking into the swirling mass of clouds, hurled it overboard with a grunt.

For a moment it floated there, stretching out kite-like to glide, and Rowen's gut knotted.

Then lightning found it: a dozen slender bolts attacked like hunting dogs taking down quarry.

On fire, the captain's image curled, smoked, and burned its way through the clouds.

Behind him, he heard Caleb step back and out the door, leaving him alone on the balcony with only Jordan's conjured storm.

*Aboard the Tempest*

Nearly thirty minutes and one ship different, Jack stated, "That was ugly," as he led Rowen below deck and to the hall where the pods connected to the *Tempest*'s sleek body.

"That seems obvious. And it should be equally obvious I'd rather not talk about it."

"Of course not. The girl you love gutted you in public. No man wants to talk about *that*." He withdrew the key that hung around his neck and paused outside a particular door. "Which is *why* I think you *need* to talk about it. The things we don't want to talk about are generally the most important things to talk about."

"Let's go—put some distance between us and the *Artemesia*," he muttered. "I need to think."

Jack shrugged, twisting the key in the lock. He shoved open the door and waved Rowen inside. "This will be a tight fit."

One chair was set nearly dead center in the pod with only an arm's length around it on all sides. Directly before it was the main window—twenty individual window panes were cobbled together giving the appearance of peering out from behind the single eye of a gigantic insect. "Okay, big boy," Jack said. "Stand in the back and try not to move around. The shifting of your weight could impact the angle of our flight. Or crash us."

Carefully, Rowen picked his way to the back of the chair, placing his hands on either side of its headrest.

"Lovely," Jack said, reaching behind him to pull the curved door shut. He sat in the chair and pulled two belts across him, buckling them on either side of the seat. He wiggled in the chair before reaching out and flipping a set of switches.

"Hang on," Jack suggested, "I'm setting us loose and hitting the engine."

"Should I be strapped in?" Rowen asked, looking for his own set of belts and buckles.

Jack merely said, "Just stay calm and hang on."

Rowen knuckled into the chair and gritted his teeth.

Jack wrenched a lever back. A crack like thunder ripped through the pod, setting Rowen's teeth on edge.

And then they were falling.

Rowen screamed and held on as Jack laughed maniacally. His stomach wedged in his mouth, his hair flying up in a non-existent breeze as gravity tore them away from the *Tempest* and they tumbled toward the ground. Through the insect-eye window

Rowen saw the space the pod had snuggled into, the boards and painted sides of the *Tempest*. The pod fell through the clouds, puncturing them and whistling away from the world he'd come to know.

He was still screaming—the sound a thin wail—as the window showed blue sky and the last shreds of the clouds peeled away from them, leaving thin fingers of fluff pointing the way they'd come. Jack continued laughing and pulled back another lever and slammed down a series of buttons. There was a growl and a stutter.

"Shite," Jack said. He repeated the series of moves.

The growl resounded, the pod shivering as the engine roared to life. With a sudden *pop* the pod jerked upward as wings unfurled. Jack turned a small wheel.

The noise of the engine became a thin whine. It coughed. And went silent.

The pod was silent except for the string of curses Jack shouted.

And the roar of blood in Rowen's ears.

Jack pounded on the control panel.

There was a whine, but Rowen thought it was more likely from Jack than the engine.

"Damn it!" Jack shouted. He spun a wheel and there was a new noise—like a flag caught but flapping in the wind, buzzing. The wings had adjusted. Jack spun another wheel and they tilted as the rudder adjusted and the pod spun a half turn away from the *Tempest*. Jack leveled out the pod's snub nose, his hands flicking across the controls, pressing buttons, turning dials, and flipping switches.

Jack turned in his seat and appraised Rowen. "You're not going to vomit are you?"

Rowen shook his head.

"When you do, aim for the side, don't bring it over my head."

Swallowing hard, Rowen insisted, "I'm fine. Just ... startled."

"If that's what you do when you're startled, remind me to never throw you a surprise party."

Rowen grunted, unimpressed.

"This is the tricky bit," Jack said. "Now the engine's failed, we need to keep enough air under us to get us to glide all the way to Philadelphia. If we lose too much we plummet before we're ready."

Rowen squealed, "Before we're ready? It sounds like I should expect to plummet one way or the other."

Jack laughed, but the sound wasn't convincing. "We don't plummet quite as much as dive. Coast. Nose a path."

"Ah." Rowen's jaw clenched. He looked out the windows and along the nose of the pod, realizing how carefully reinforced it was. Bolts, rivets, and curving sheets of glossy steel led them on. "Nose a path," he repeated. "Vomit to the side, you said," he muttered, his stomach shifting in his gut.

Jack chuckled grimly. "Aye. To the side. Brace yourself, man, it's going to be quite a ride."

Aboard the Artemesia

Jordan sat at the very end of Topside's bowsprit, her bare feet kicked out over the ship's edge, toes dangling in midair, arms looped over the rail with her wrists crossed, her head tucked just beneath. It was oddly comfortable, this pose, these moments that seemed somehow out of both time and space. This passed as her leisure, rare moments she stared into the dark swirling void of her storm—the thin moments when she could push the *Artemesia* to glide and give herself space to wonder.

She sighed, glancing down at the wooden figurehead's carved curling hair, the upper sweep of her angelic wings and her bare and paint-freckled shoulder. It was an odd perspective a Conductor had.

They were not far from Philadelphia.

She chewed her lower lip, worrying it between her teeth until she thought it might pop. Releasing it, she blew between her lips. Only a Weather Witch understood her hesitancy about freeing her own kind.

Her kind brewed storms within themselves. They manifested lightning, gales, killing frosts, and tornadoes. To free people using such powers and give them equality—to let the secret out: that anyone had the same power inside them as she did—they were destruction waiting to happen. As much as she hated how far she'd fallen and the fact she'd taken her family with her ... Still. Perhaps the rank system had its place.

Perhaps everyone did.

Like the country's motto proclaimed: *A place for all.*

As a child, she thought it meant this was a land of opportunity—a place all immigrants were welcomed. But perhaps that wasn't what the founding fathers meant. Perhaps it was more of an "a place for all and everyone in their place" sort of thing.

Perhaps it didn't truly matter.

She swung her feet out and back, pumping her legs.

Not far from her, Maude sat petting Kit and Kaboodle while Meggie played with something the Wandering Wallace had given her. He occasionally brought her gifts he'd found while searching the rooms below for supplies that might benefit the rebel cause. He must do such things at night when they'd all retired to their cabins.

Perhaps, like she, he found sleep elusive.

Jordan puffed out a breath, her mind carrying the air away to drill a small hole in the clouds and afford her a distant view of the Grounded population's world—a world she missed greatly.

The map pinned partly under her hip shivered in the tickling breeze and she waved her left hand, clearing the clouds away like she'd seen her schoolteacher wipe the chalkboard clean. She traced a fingertip along the map's colorful features, reading labels softly as she went.

Below her, rolling hills spread between her feet, speckled with the bright but browning colors of autumn. She watched with wonder as they passed over the last bit of New York, keeping at a distance the city that bore the same name while they passed into the wilds of Pennsylvania.

The Susquehanna River rolled like a long and lazy snake through the world below them, a shimmer of silver winding from the middle of New York down through the rocky mountains and hills of Pennsylvania's northern border.

"Coal Country," she whispered, reading. "Wilkes-Barre, Mauchunk, Scranton ..." She squinted. Coal Country didn't seem to be much of a separate country to her at all, but coal was only used in a few things—a stove or furnace here and there, then to the west, the Colebrookdale forges made pig iron.

The Wandering Wallace had mentioned steam devices needed coal to heat water into steam, but in a world where such knowledge and devices were repressed and storm power fulfilled every need (and many whims) surely coal was only a minor fuel source. She frowned. How would things change if storm power ceased and steam took hold?

More coal would be needed, certainly. More men would enter the deep, dark heart of Pennsylvania to work the mines. More mines would be dug. More holes would dot the landscape and more steam and coal smoke would thicken the air.

But fewer Witches would be needed. Perhaps Making would truly cease and the secret she'd only let slip to a few—the secret she hoped pained the Maker most—would go unspoken and no one else would learn they all had the power inside them to change the weather.

And the world.

Meggie's voice startling her, she straightened, smacking her head on the rail above her. She rubbed the crown of her head, giving Meggie a smile.

"Yes, most wee one," she teased. "You called?"

"Would you teach me?"

"Teach you what?"

"How you do the things you do?"

Jordan felt she'd just sucked on a lemon. "No, pet," she whispered. "I would rather not. It requires a great deal of emotion—and can be troubling."

"I have a great deal of emotion inside me," Meggie volunteered.

Jordan tugged herself away from the ship's edge, swinging her feet back onto the deck and, with one hand on the railing, pulled herself back to her feet with a groan. "You have very *pretty* emotions inside you," Jordan said. "Things like joy and the seeds of laughter. Your emotions are wildflower pink, sunshine yellow, and summer sky blue."

Meggie wrinkled her nose, unsure.

Jordan pointed off the ship's bow. "See that," she asked, her finger crooked at the very darkest part of the clouds the ship nestled in.

"Yes," Meggie said.

"How would you describe those colors?"

Meggie's brow furrowed, and she concentrated on the roiling mess. "Gunmetal gray, starless night black, and the blue of a fresh bruise." She looked up at Jordan, hope twinkling in her eyes.

"Those are the colors of the emotions inside *me*," Jordan confided.

Meggie twisted back, staring hard into the darkness. "Oh," she said so softly the word was nearly stolen by a whispering wind.

"If I were you, I would keep *your* colors. Hold them tight and love them well. If I were *you* I would not wish to be like me. What I do takes a different sort of emotion."

Meggie's words were soft and slow but her eyes were bright as her spirit. "You are *not* me. And I remember what Anil said."

Jordan blinked. "And what was that?"

"That you needn't call a storm with hate. That any emotion —any strong connection with the weather will do. Calling a storm should make your soul sing—or you should sing when calling...." She paused and smiled.

"Ah. I see." Jordan's gaze drifted over Meggie's blond head, straying back to the clouds. "What if that is all the emotion I have?"

Meggie crossed her arms indignantly and stomped a foot. A wind whistled across the deck. "That is not all the emotion you have. Not at all. I've seen you play. I've heard you laugh," she accused. "There are lots of pretty feelings inside you. I know it. I've seen the way you look at Rowen—all the pretty things shine in you *then*." She popped a hand over her mouth, her eyes going wide.

The clouds went darker.

Meggie shrank back, her eyes pinned to the spot where Jordan's hand gripped the railing. Jordan followed her gaze, surprised to see her fingers had gone white. A faint trail of smoke drifted up from beneath her palm. Tiny sparks spattered in the space between her fingertips, crawling along the curved wooden rail.

With effort, Jordan peeled her fingers free of the singed wood and rubbed ash off her hand.

Shaken, she looked at Meggie. "I think perhaps you should not mention his name again." She rubbed her hands together, trying to wipe the remaining black away.

The ash smeared, spreading to her other hand.

"Because he left?" Meggie asked, her voice clear as a pipe.

The words reached her late. Her head lifted slowly and she heard the question again, this time echoing in her ears. Her chest tightened.

Meggie's hand slipped into hers but Jordan pulled back, the black staining her hand, but Meggie grabbed it, insistent. "He will be back. Both him and Jack," she promised.

"How do you know that?" Jordan asked, her eyes steady on Meggie's. "How do you know?"

Meggie blinked, her eyelashes fluttering rapidly. "Because they must," she declared. "Because home is where the heart is and both Rowen's and Jack's hearts are here." She shrugged as if it was the simplest thing to understand. "Our story will not end happily unless all our friends are home and safe. And this"—she dropped Jordan's hand and spread her arms to take in the *Artemesia*—"is home."



They had been gliding at a slow descent when Jack said, "Finally! One should be right *there*," pointing to a spiral of birds slowly climbing into the sky.

"One what? A bird?"

"No, the thing we gliders learned from birds."

"Something you learned by bird watching?"

Jack nodded. "There are plenty of things we can learn from birds. And other animals," he added. "Flight takes a great deal of energy if you don't do it right."

"And they ... ?"

"Do it right," Jack said. He angled the pod's nose toward the birds. "They are riding an eddy—a spot where air currents or different air temperatures meet and create an updraft. We're going to ride it like an elevator—take it to a higher elevation."

Rowen grunted.

They soared toward the promised updraft, descending by tiny increments all the way. Rowen pitched forward as the eddy caught them, tugging them higher in a slow spiral that Jack used and carefully controlled. Jack leaned back in the seat, setting his controls and watching as they drifted in a slow circle to the top of the eddy.

Rowen leaned over the chair, mindful of Jack's warning about a sudden and dramatic shift in his weight changing the pod's path, and peered out the window at the birds, watching them nearly as much as the world far below.

Jack whistled a tune that Rowen picked up and sang.

"Ah," Jack murmured. "We've reached the top."

He tweaked the controls, adjusting the wings and rudder, and they broke free of the curling wind, launching out at the higher altitude.

They glided uneventfully for another few hours, when Jack said, "If we keep going like this we'll make Philadelphia just after dark."

"The city lights up like a bank full of stars—should be easy to find our way."

"That brings me to an important question—just where are we landing?"

Rowen grinned. "There is a lovely estate with a long garden and a hedgerow maze at the very top of a hill I know right well," Rowen said. "We will be welcome there—or at least not unwelcome," he clarified.

"Ah. Your family's estate."

"No. Better. Jordan's."

The pod jolted suddenly to the side and Jack shouted, his hands darting for the controls.

"What the hell?" Rowen spread his feet wide and grabbed tight to the chair's back again. He followed Jack's example, squinting out the window. Something slipped past in the periphery of their view, large feathers stroking the top of the window.

"Brace yourself," Jack commanded.

"What's happening?"

"We're—" The words were smacked out of him when the pod was rocked again.

"We're under attack."

"By what?"

"Ala!"

"Ala?!"

Jack steadied his grip on the pod's controls, his eyes fixed. "Beast—demon, depends on who you ask or what you believe. From the Old Country. Wraiths have tried to wipe them out for decades."

"Why have I never heard of them?"

"Heard of the Lik or the Musussu?"

"No ..."

The ship bucked again and Jack fought to compensate. "Invasive species thought to be the stuff of legends—nightmares," Jack clarified, "but we're not that lucky. Lucky enough they aren't quite as horrible or huge as legend states, but, dammit!" He fell into a long line of curses before sputtering, "They exist!" He released the controls long enough to dig into the bag he carried. "Here," he blindly thrust a gun over his shoulder toward Rowen. "Lean out—"

"Lean out?!" Rowen shouted, gripping the homemade weapon. "Lean out of *where*?!"

"Pop the door, lean out, and shoot the damned thing," Jack said like it was the only sensible option.

"You're serious ..."

"Deadly," Jack clarified, gritting his teeth against the next jolt.

It came straight at them, talons bared and cruel beak open in a shriek that made Rowen's hair stand on end. Pulling up at the last minute, its feet smashed against the windows' edge.

The pod rocked onto its back.

Rowen tumbled into the back wall and they were falling, the pod's wings failing with a scream of fabric. "You have to go now," Jack shouted. "*Now*, Rowen. Cock the gun, pull the trigger, and blast that beast to nothing!"

Rowen pulled himself from the floor—no, from the back wall ... The entire world had shifted. He staggered to the door. Head spinning almost as fast as the pod, he braced one foot on the wall, one on the actual floor and shoved the door open. The wind tore past him, pulling moisture from his eyes and stopping up his ears with a blast that filled them with a rumble.

Squinting against the howling wind, he searched for his adversary. A shadow roosted atop of their pod, feathers whipping wildly to make it seem a black and hateful harbinger. Lightning flickered in the clouds and he glimpsed the curving beak, battered and cracked, something metal glinting at its corner.

He pulled the gun's hammer back, took aim, and fired. There was an awful noise as the bullet struck, throwing the Ala backwards and peeling its talons free of the ship with a squeal that set Rowen's teeth on edge.

It plunged like a rock and Rowen fell back inside the pod, pulling the door shut behind him.

"Nice job, tree trunk," Jack said. "Now act like ballast."

"Huh?"

"Stand in front of me with that hulking mass of yours and just be."

"Just be?"

"Yes," Jack said, teeth gritted. "Stand. *Be.*"

Rowen lurched forward, not able to keep his feet on one surface. He straddled the floor and the wall, one foot on the base of Jack's chair.

"Lean toward the window," Jack demanded, leaning as far forward as his chair would allow.

The pod shifted with Rowen's weight, slowly pulling out of its backwards dive and straightening.

The wings caught with a bang as air filled the fabric and they were gliding again. Rowen dropped to his knees, his world righted.

"Well," Jack said, relief clear in his voice, "I'd like to say that's the worst of it, but ..."

Rowen followed his gaze out the window. They skimmed the treetops—branches brushing the belly of the pod. They weren't climbing. They were still descending.

"Pull up?" Rowen asked.

Jack laughed, but the sound was hollow and tight as a freshly finished drum. "I'm bringing us down."

In the distance the trees thinned and parted, fields spreading out below them, dotted with grazing sheep.

A large pasture sprawled beneath them. And at its far edge? More trees. Pine trees soared up, daggers spearing the sky.

"This is us," Jack said, pulling the wings in.

They moved like a pebble skipped across a pond—a very large pebble across a very solid pond. Words fell out of Rowen's brain and he flew up, his feet clipping Jack's head as the pod dug a furrow in the soft earth, screaming its way to a stop, sheep scattering.

Rowen's head cracked into the back wall. He collapsed on the floor. His world went black.

*Aboard the Artemesia*

After the new headlines were read, and the Wandering Wallace had sung another song, Jordan wrapped a shawl around her shoulders, gathered a dozen pierced paper stormlanterns she had been given, and left her room to do what she had recently become accustomed to doing—wandering the halls of the *Artemesia* at night, after the ship's course and controls were set. Wandering in the silence and solitude and trying to make peace with the things that haunted her, trying to erase the captain's touch, trying to truly make the *Artemesia* her own.

Past the shuttered storefronts in the promenade she went, knowing they'd been shuttered against her crew as much as against disagreeable shopkeeps now spending their time in newly assigned rooms instead of behind counters at mercantiles, confectionaries, bookstores, bakeries, and apothecaries. It was better not to allow the temptation of open shops and better to give merchants assurance that their stock, at least, was safe.

She continued past the store window where ribbons, hair combs, and mirrors were displayed, and beyond the tailor's place where a dress form stood abandoned in the dark display window, strips of half-stitched cloth hanging from shiny steel pins. As the captain's Conductor she had never been allowed to visit the stores and the shops or explore the place where the daily puppet shows had been performed for children. She had not been allowed to stop in the ship's chapel to bend her knees in prayer or take communion.

They had kept her apart from everything good or gentle. They left her unloved. Unblessed.

In each shadowy corner she set a stormlantern to dispel the darkness, adding to the glow of each crystal with a single touch of her finger and a thought.

She paused outside a door with a cross on it and set her hand on its cool metal handle. She tried the door. It opened on silent hinges. The hall deserted, she slipped inside. Pausing in the chapel's nave, she closed her eyes and summoned the stormlights lining the sanctuary's walls.

A glow rose in the room, growing brighter and brighter until it seemed daylight climbed across the walls. On the still-dressed altar a silver cross and matching candlesticks shone as if freshly polished. The room echoed with her every hesitant step.

Empty.

She shuddered.

Was a chapel ever truly empty? She hugged herself, her eyes roaming up the walls and across the vaulted ceiling. This was the one room on this deck that soared so high. The beams from the regular ceiling had been interrupted to provide more room for God. Or, at least, voices raised in praise of God.

She itched, standing in a holy place. At home they attended church every Sunday as was proper for a young lady of her standing. At home she studied the word of God, learned the popular hymns, and memorized the appropriate scriptures, though her mother commented once that she lingered too long on the Psalms.

And what had it mattered? Had God been here, listening to prayers when the captain pinned her beneath him two floors below? Had God's ears been too full of songs to hear her muffled screams? Or had God never been here at all?

Or had God never been?

Lightning found her when God had not.

She shifted her weight from one foot to the other, feeling the crush of the rug beneath her bare feet and, making her decision, she wiped her eyes and, finding her way to the nearest pew, sat and rested her head on the back of the pew before her.

Quietly, she prayed.

Because sometimes there was simply nothing else to be done but take it all to the Lord in prayer.

# Chapter Ten

He'd make a lovely corpse.

—CHARLES DICKENS

*Aboard the Pod*

His ears ringing with the sound of someone's voice and sheep snuffling and bleating around their pod, Rowen woke.

He recognized Jack's voice.

And Jack's cursing.

Rowen rallied. He was bleeding. Not much and not from a vital spot, but it was a red that matched nothing he was wearing and he hurt. It only took him a moment to join Jack in some cursing of his own. His was somewhat more creatively phrased.

"Help me get unbuckled," Jack said with a groan. "I'm bleeding."

Rowen dragged himself to his feet and lurched toward Jack. "You aren't the only one," he muttered. He reached for one set of buckles while Jack fumbled with the other.

"You're not the one who got kicked in the head by a mule ..."

Rowen grunted. "At least you didn't say *ass*," he said, freeing him. Extending a hand, he pulled Jack out of the seat, amazed the pod's interior had so little damage. Even the glass panes making up the window only bore a few stars and one small, jagged crack.

"Hear that?" Jack asked.

Rowen froze. There were more voices coming from outside the pod.

A colorful coat waved as someone walked near the window's edge.

"Who is it?"

Jack's voice lowered. "Don't know. But that was clothing and the Wildkin aren't fans of western dress. Or fans of much dress at all if you read accounts from the Fringe."

Rowen bent over and retrieved the gun. "Are they friendly?"

"Friendly is questionable—optimistic—but *human* seems a safe wager. Open the door. Slowly," he specified.

Rowen did as he was told, the door's hinges groaning, strained from the crash.

Rowen got the first glimpse of the men standing outside. Short and dark with pale blue eyes, they wore boldly patterned clothing in bright colors. "Liberally aligned traders," Rowen whispered to Jack a moment before he bent over.

And vomited.

The men jumped, suddenly animated. They had not expected *that*.

"*That* was a delayed reaction ..." Rowen groaned.

"Better outside the pod than in," Jack said, smacking Rowen's back. He pressed between Rowen and the doorframe, appraising the men outside. "These are no liberally aligned traders," he concluded. "These men are something far bolder. These men are Travelers."

They spoke to each other in a fluid language tempting Rowen's educated ear with hints of Greek, English, and ... Hebrew? And something else. Out of all of it, the only thing Rowen could be clear on was that their guns were leveled at him and Jack. "Any idea what they're saying?"

"I think I hear Gaelic ... Maybe. Smile. And, for God's sake, lower the gun," Jack commanded, reaching around Rowen to place a hand over the weapon and press it down.

The Travelers' guns lowered, too, but their eyes remained threatening.

One of their number stepped forward, thrusting his chin toward their ship. "You scared our sheep. Sheep are unhappy. Not good for milking today. Unhappy milk sheep mean unhappy milkmaids. Unhappy milkmaids mean—"

"—unhappy men," Rowen said, unfurling a grin. "We apologize," he said. He swept an arm out, giving a generous bow. "It was not our intention to fall from the sky here—or anywhere."

"What caused your fall?"

"Ala attack."

The Travelers looked at each other, a few words passing between them. "The Ala has harried our herds and crushed our few crops by bringing hail," the man commiserated. "Voracious. Demonic. Children go missing."

"There is a reason men are paid to hunt these things," Jack muttered.

"I am sorry for your troubles. But—" Rowen's expression brightened, and he said, "One less of their number will nip your heels. It lies dead not far from here."

More words were exchanged between the group of strangers. Their self-appointed representative asked, "What did it look like?"

"Tall as I am with dark feathers, black and bleak with a smattering of gold in its long sword-like tail."

"Its beak?"

"It was split—cracked at the edges—"

The man stepped forward, the single pace eager. "At the corner of its mouth ... ?"

Rowen closed his eyes, remembering. He caught himself, swaying. "Something glittered there ..." he said. He still bled.

The man spun to face his peers, exclaiming something that made them all chatter happily.

"You killed their queen!" the man explained. Staring at the ship, he rubbed at his chin and then looked at the nearby gathering of brightly colored wagons. "How far did you wish to get in your ship?"

"To Philadelphia. As fast as we can. Our goal is a just one," Rowen assured.

The man shook his head and stepped over to the ship's wings, easing one skeletal frame open. The fabric was tattered, torn in a few places.

Rowen's heart sank.

"Your wings need patching and there may be more that has been damaged. I doubt you are flight-worthy. Philadelphia ..." He looked in the direction their pod's nose still pointed. "We can take you by wagon, but it will take days ..."

Rowen winced. "We must get there sooner. Much depends on what we are doing."

The man nodded. "Explain your task and perhaps we might be inspired to speed your journey," he offered warily.

Rowen and Jack exchanged a hesitant glance and shrugged at each other. Their ship was down, they were lost and friendless. What more harm could be done? "We are headed to Philadelphia to express our displeasure in the inequality of men. We mean to encourage abolition. Freedom for all to seek the pursuit of happiness promised by our forefathers."

"Abolitionists," the man said with a grave nod.

The men behind him muttered among themselves, needing no translation.

Rowen and Jack stood still, unsure and uneasy.

A smile spread across the man's face. "Come with us. We have an option that may suit your needs. And women who can patch those wings if you give us a night to do such work. We are a people who can mend anything," he promised.

Jack grinned. "That sounds promising."

The man again turned to his peers and said a few words, pointing toward the wagons and then the pod. They debated something a moment, and then an older man who spoke loudly puffed out his chest and strode away from the knot of them and toward a wagon. In a few minutes, he and his horses and wagon backed around in front of the pod. The other men surrounded the small ship, each of them placing his hands somewhere on its side. Their translator motioned for Rowen and Jack to join them, too.

They stepped in, and the man said a few words and clearly began to count. On what they took to be "three" all the men grunted and together they hefted the ship up, heaving it into the wagon's back. They slid it in, slinging ropes over its body and beneath the wagon and lashing it to any available fittings. The pod was secured in a matter of minutes.

The men moved to their separate wagons and Rowen and Jack sat on the bench with the translator. He snapped the reins across the backs of the horses and, together, they trotted along, Rowen and Jack nervously eyeing their environment and smelling the air for the scent of nearby water. The gun rested in Rowen's lap, his hand remaining on its handle.

The translator noticed and gave a little cough. "You expect Wildkin?"

Rowen shrugged, but his back was stiff and straight and he knew that his body language told more than any words.

The wagon bearing their pod turned on the winding path, disappearing into the trees.

The translator laughed. "There are no Wildkin threats here except those from the air. We have streams and lakes, that is certain, but the Merrow have never tried to come this far inland and their allies prefer the waters further down the mountain." Now he shrugged. "Certainly keep your weapon at the ready—I would never tell a man not to do something that makes him feel safe, but it is unnecessary. By the way, my name," the Traveler said, "is Tommy Toogood."

"A pleasure, Tommy. I am Rowen and this is Jack." But he kept his eyes sharp all along the path as they became hemmed in by trees, the world around them growing dim. They were in unfamiliar territory with horses aplenty to tempt hungry Wildkin.

*The Wilds of Pennsylvania*

The scents and the sounds reached them before the sight of the Travelers' camp unfolded in their view. It was sprawling and strangely liquid; small campfires marked the forest and spread between tents, wagons, and tree trunks. From every tree hung dozens of flickering pierced paper lanterns. Horses were tied to tree trunks and munching on handfuls of hay and small piles of grain, their tails flicking against flies or mosquitoes.

Rowen's stomach growled at the smell of meat roasting over a fire. He ran the tip of his tongue along his lips appreciatively.

Tommy pulled their wagon to a stop and hopped down from his seat, Jack and Rowen leaping down to help him release and secure the horses.

The sound of a violin singing through the tree branches caught Rowen's ear, somehow familiar. He paused by the wagon, scanning the area and wondering.

A small dog raced between the campfires begging for scraps from each small gathering's cook. It teased them with entertainment, hopping on its hind legs and dancing in tight circles. Rowen froze, recognizing the dog. He knew that the violinist was the same he'd listened to in Bangor. He squinted. In the distance he saw her—long and lithe, her bow sliding across the violin's strings in a supple way that seemed magickal—otherworldly.

Magnetic, people drifted toward her, carried by the tune, and the crowd around her campfire grew. Dozens settled, lounging at her feet.

Rowen and Jack watched her, struck dumb by the sad song she spun out with only her bow and violin, her body swaying under the weight of the notes.

"She is lovely, is she not?" Tommy asked. "She wandered into our camp again a day or so ago. She is always welcome. Older than she looks, they say. She travels the New World—searching, always searching. Always somewhat sad and soulful."

"Searching for what?" Rowen whispered, his eyes never straying from the mesmerizing violinist.

Tommy shrugged. "Some say she searches for the son magick stole away many years ago. But she never speaks of such things. At least not to me."

"A son magick stole away? Sounds like another Witch the Tester snared," Jack grumbled. "Sad stories those. And far too many of them. No doubt there are many mothers missing their children—many families will never be reunited."

"What if the boy's become a Wraith," Rowen murmured. "Kissed by Lightning and deaf as a doorstop. He'd never even hear her song ..."

"That's depressing," Jack muttered. "Would a Wraith even remember a time before Lightning toasted him from brains to biscuits? Not being able to hear his mother play seems less pitiful than not even remembering her."

"Now *that's* depressing," Rowen conceded.

They fell silent again, simply listening to the music weaving through the woods.

Rowen's stomach growled again.

Jack chuckled. "That was a beautiful mood you ruined," he said, smacking Rowen's shoulder. He leaned around Rowen and addressed their guide. "We'd best get my friend some food before he starts to gnaw on things at random. Would you ..."

"Be so kind as to feed you? Of course." Tommy led them to a modest campfire where a small boy turned meat on a spit. "Lamb," Tommy said. "Fresh and tender."

The boy lifted the lid of a nearby pot. Inside was bread so fresh and warm it steamed. Rowen's mouth grew thick with moisture. The boy closed the lid again and lifted the lid on another, last pot.

"Mutton," Tommy said. "We have both mint sauce and mint

jelly," he added, crouching by the fire. He motioned for them to do the same.

Jack crouched and Rowen sat in the moist loam by the fire, transfixed equally by both meat and music.

The boy pulled out the loaf of bread, split it handily with a knife bigger than any Rowen might have imagined him carrying, and slapped long strips of dripping slow-cooked mutton on pieces for each of them before putting another slice of bread on top. He handed it over, Rowen waiting neither for jelly nor sauce but attacking the sandwich.

"What did that ever do to you?" Jack chuckled.

Rowen grunted. And kept eating.

"Amazing how quickly you recover. We crash landed, you spewed your guts, we took a bumpy ride through a forest where fading light was flashing, and yet here you are downing your dinner as if you needed to kill it again."

Rowen wiped at his mouth with a fist. "Emptied guts require refilling." He returned to devouring his food. His eyes drifted from the crackling, popping fire to the still-performing violinist. She changed songs and a new tune drifted in their direction. Rowen could not help but sway in time to the music while he munched.

Tommy Toogood talked as he pulled apart a leg of lamb, separating the slightly charred meat from the bone, "We will put you in a wagon to sleep tonight, giving you our finest hospitality. In the morning, as part of our camp begins again on its way south, you will take to the air."

"How exactly?" Jack asked. "Our pod—"

"Your glider's wings are being mended by capable hands," Tommy assured, "but we will take you up in the air our way."

"*Your* way?"

Tommy tossed the bone into the fire and brushed his hands over his trousers, brushing ash from them. "If you are ready, I will show you." He rose.

Jack followed, looking to Rowen. He twitched, pressed his

lips together and began to rise but hesitated, looking back at the pots and the campfire.

And the young cook.

The boy grinned at him, opened the two pots and put another sandwich together.

"Thank you," Rowen said, his pained expression gone as he stuffed the sandwich into his mouth.

Jack rolled his eyes. Tommy grinned and led them through the woods, around campfires where Travelers reclined in colorful clothing, and past the area their pod still rested in the back of a wagon. Lantern light fluttered in shadowy tree limbs. The pod's wings had been stripped, making it look like a giant wood and metal hickory nut with bare branches poking out of either side. Huddled around the nearest fire sat a group of young women sewing with needles the length of fingers, the slim metal darting in and out of the thick fabric of the pod's wings.

While they worked, they sang. Rowen picked up the tune easily, humming as the men skirted the group. The girls noticed and turned, looking at Rowen and smiling around the song. One motioned to him, inviting him to join them. For a moment Rowen hesitated, the easy openness in her expression, the generous lips curving in a smile, and the thickly fringed laughing eyes forming an expression he'd seen in many women.

Many times.

But he shook his head, clearing it, and realized the thing that attracted him to her was the thing he missed most about Jordan—the laughter. The smiles. Those were the same things he was determined to bring back to her. So he left the singing girls behind because he loved a girl who still felt she had no voice with which to sing.

He trotted after Jack and Tommy. The trees thinned, finally parting, and they came to the foot of a hill. Spread across its base were huge swaths of fabric attached to ropes and baskets large enough to hold several people.

"Hot air balloons," Jack exclaimed. "A mob of them."

"We've given up on government-sanctioned transportation. But we are not ready to align with other established trading orga- nizations, so we have found our own way. It is not easy and it requires us uncovering some information the government kept quiet, but ..."

In the distance someone straightened, seeing them, and moved away from where he had been bent over examining the fixtures on one of the large baskets. He moved toward them instead.

Quickly.

"We should return to camp," Tommy whispered. "Now," he suggested, turning back.

There was a shout and Rowen and Jack straightened, hearing a woman's voice come from the seemingly male silhouette. The tall top hat, waistcoat, and trousers could not completely disguise the curves of their owner once she was directly before them.

Yelling at them.

Not exactly yelling at *them* but yelling at Tommy.

"You bring strangers here—"

Tommy protested. "*Friends*. They killed the Ala queen."

"That makes them friends? Makes them trustworthy?" Her voice rose and she tugged off her top hat, long hair tumbling free. She waved the hat at Tommy in exasperation. "So the enemy of my enemy must be my friend?" She threw the hat on the ground between them.

Tommy calmly leaned over and picked it up. Gently brushing it off, he straightened its brim as she stormed on about secrets no longer being secrets and not being able to trust her own people to keep their technology quiet. Tommy kept quiet and let her finish fuming.

Finally she stood still, silent before them. She snatched the hat from Tommy's hands and awkwardly stuffed her hair back under- neath it. Thick strands of it stuck out but she straightened her back, pulled back her shoulders, and regained some small part of her masculine posture. With an exhale that sent hair hanging near her eyes fluttering, she stomped away.

Rowen coughed. "What was that about?"

Tommy shrugged. "Salanna is a fine spy. A beautiful young woman, still she disguises herself and masters her voice to seem a man."

"She seems quite an attractive woman—why play at being a man?"

"Men are able to get into places a woman may not," he said. "Salanna ventures into places we have no man to go and gathers information. We have tried sending men but they are too often discovered. She did what they could not. Do not ask me how— some things I do not know or understand." He groaned. "We should obtain her support before we transport you to Philadelphia. She will want assurance you are trustworthy."

"How do you suggest we do that?" Rowen asked. "She seems distinctly unimpressed with both of us."

"Talk with Salanna. Show her you are good men. Filled with abolitionist ideals. That might be enough to let her see why we should transport you."

"Actually, I don't think your balloons will be fast enough to get us to Philadelphia," Jack said. "They depend on the winds and tend to be slower ... We need the pod to take us in. It cuts through the air like a hot knife through butter—it outruns most other airships."

"Then take it," Tommy said. "The wings will be mended by morning."

"It's not quite so easy," Jack said. "We need to be at a very high altitude to catch the wind and hold it long enough to complete the last leg of our journey."

"But you are in the foothills now. The altitude is higher than Philadelphia, true, but only by a small amount."

Jack shook his head. "Shite. There has to be some other way."

"The *Artemesia* can't dock without us there in advance," Rowen murmured. "We set the plan into motion."

"A plan?" Tommy asked. "This is more intriguing than meeting with the Council to express abolitionist views."

Jack shook his head. "The council needs a more serious shakeup."

"That I do not disagree with," Tommy said.

"We are setting a plan into motion to provide that. But it must happen in a certain order."

"Is this a coup?"

"Would you support it if it was?"

Tommy's lips grew thin. Rowen shifted from foot to foot.

Jack pressed the point. "Will you support us?"

"Not only would I support it, but I'd wager Salanna would, too. But if balloons are not fast enough ... our wagons won't be either."

Jack nodded grimly. "Correct. We need to get the glider to a good altitude."

Tommy rubbed his chin, looking back at the huge balloon skins lying limp against the grass. "The pod is not very heavy," he said, more to himself than them. "We have a significant length of heavy rope ..."

Rowen's eyes narrowed.

"And a few men who know how to tie strong knots that release when given just the right pull." He looked at them both again and grinned. "Come now. We'd best set this plan into motion quickly so we are ready to greet adventure in the morning!"

*Aboard the Artemesia*

Out of prayers and long out of stormlanterns, Jordan found her way back to her room and locked the door. Caleb had provided her with a new nightgown, which lay draped across the foot of her bed. She slipped into the heavy linen shift, appreciating its weight and coverage. Longer than her dress and more modest, she considered wearing it as well tomorrow to better cover the bits the captain had been so determined to expose.

She woke after a few hours, panting, her heart thrumming. The misty remnants of a dream lingered, filling her room. She opened her hand and the stormlights blared to life, so bright they nearly peeled paint from the walls as she tried to clear her memory of the stain hovering so near.

The stain of the captain.

She shuddered and pulled her knees to her chin, wrapping her arms tight around them. Squeezing her eyes shut, she reached a hand out to the bank of windows lining her room's wall and pulled her fingers in. Lightning split the sky and thunder boomed, rattling glass. With a muffled sob, Jordan sank back under her quilt and covered her head with her pillow.

Tomorrow would be a new day, she promised herself. And with the new day she would no longer be anyone's victim—especially not the victim of a dead man.

Day could not come soon enough.

*Aboard the Pod*

The pod's wings repaired, the skins were slipped onto the skeletal fixtures and secured under the glow of torchlight. Tommy led Rowen and Jack to a large wagon sporting tall wheels, colorfully painted walls, and a curving roofline. He held a punched tin lantern up, candlelight giving a soft and wavering glow. "This is where you will sleep tonight," he explained, leaping up three attached stairs and tugging open the door. He hopped down, handed them the lantern, and ushered them inside with a flourish.

"I leave you now," Tommy said, dipping his head and doffing his cap.

"Thank you," Rowen said.

Inside space was tight, only an aisle flanked by two narrow beds ending at a wall lined with shelves dotted with oddities.

There sat stumps of candles that had melted together in rivulets of colored wax; a variety of different sizes of marble mortars and pestles glimmered, and there were dried flowers, and glass jars filled with herbs, spices, and liquids Rowen couldn't determine the origins of. Some jars looked like fish, and some bristled with little glass thorns or tiny bumps that reminded him of toad's warts.

"Those are the dangerous sorts," Jack muttered, motioning to the bumpy bottles. "I'd wager we're in an apothecary's cart. They bottle the dangerous things in glass with remarkable textures so, even in the dark, they grab the correct drug—or don't grab the wrong one."

Rowen nodded, taking a seat on a bed. He pulled his boots off and swung his feet up. "Tomorrow we make the rest of the journey to Philadelphia," he said, folding his arms and putting them behind his head.

"Then things get exciting," Jack promised, kicking his own boots off.

"Yes," Rowen agreed, opening the tin lantern's door and blowing out the candle.

*Aboard the Artemesia*

Meggie woke in the middle of the night, wet with tears and the water of untamed Witchery. Maude had rolled out of their shared cot to comfort Meggie first, even as Bran was rousing. Maude was always quick with fresh bedding and gentle words—always the first to soothe the wounds of—Bran yawned and rubbed at his eyes—any wounded.

He still didn't understand how he'd won Maude. He sat up and swung his legs over the bed's edge.

He smiled, hearing Maude softly sing, *"Rise Gentle Moon."* Nearby Marion shifted in his bed, the ropes supporting his mattress groaning under the young man's weight. And length,

Bran thought, noticing the way Marion's feet hung off the bed's end.

What might Marion have been if he'd remained unMade? Would he have cared about abolition or revolution if slavery had never touched him directly? Would any of them have cared, or did it take the lurid touch of a thing to make a person care enough to change it? Combat it?

Conquer it?

What was any man's tipping point?

Were not more physicians and nurses people who once suffered the cruel touch of death or disease? Were not the hardest workers and most clever entrepreneurs the ones who grew up in poverty's grasp? And the finest artists and authors—were they not the ones who had only imagination to entertain them as they developed?

Or perhaps they were merely the most frequently drunk ...

But the strongest proponents of steam power—why did they support what they did? Had all of them known a Weather Witch?

Why was the Wandering Wallace so passionate about this movement? There must be a story behind such dedication.

Bran sank back into the mattress, hearing the muffled noise of Maude saying a fresh "Good night and sleep tight, my dear little mite."

Maude crawled back onto the cot, her toes running the length of his leg before she nestled in beside him, resting her head on his shoulder. "Her dreams are becoming darker."

He rolled toward her in the dark, his heart thumping solidly inside his ribcage. "How so?" he whispered, lips brushing her forehead. "What has she dreamed?"

"She dreams of water mostly, but sometimes someone chases her."

"A typical dream," Bran murmured, relief sighing out of him as he sank deeper into the thin mattress, ready to give himself over to sleep once more.

Maude buried her face in the crook of his neck. "Tonight she ran from someone trying to tell her a scary story."

Bran stiffened. "Oh?"

"The girl's name is Sybil."

"A common name," he said.

Halfheartedly.

"You know the Sybil chasing her," Maude insisted. "We need to get to ground, Bran. We need to do what is proper by that dead child. She lost her life too soon, far too soon. We must appease her spirit."

He groaned softly. "I know all that and accept the blame. But we aren't on the ground and I cannot get us there faster. I cannot appease Sybil yet. I promise I will, just not yet."

Maude shifted beside him, her breath hot on his cheek. "But we need Sybil out of Meggie's head before ..." The sentence fell away, leaving the unspoken truth hanging in the night air to haunt them both.

Before she saw what her father had done ...

... to the Witches ...

... and to a little girl ...

... just like *her*.

# Chapter Eleven

This world is not so bad a world
As some would like to make it;
Though whether good, or whether bad,
Depends on how we take it.
—MICHAEL WENTWORTH BECK

*The Wilds of Pennsylvania*

The *Tempest*'s pod was packed tight in the camp's largest wagon, its wings repaired and made ready for flight. A secondary set of belts and buckles had been installed for Rowen because, as Tommy Toogood pointed out, "This is a far-from-standard launch."

Because, beyond the belts, buckles, and fixed wings, there were balloons.

And specially devised rigging.

"When you promised things would get exciting, I didn't expect *this*," Rowen said, eyeing the heavy ropes and metal fixtures that ringed the pod like tentacles.

"It will be much different than any launch I've done before," Jack admitted. "But what's the worst that could happen?"

"We could die."

Jack coughed. "True ... But the odds ... You are a hero in the making. Heroes never die until their story's reached its end."

"What if mine has and we don't know it yet?"

Jack scoffed, "We've got a few chapters in us yet!"

"As long as they aren't all dénouement."

"True, true. Falling action is not what I'd wish right now ..."

The wagons arrived at the foothills where the large silk balloons lay spread flat in the blossoming dawn. The balloons had been rearranged, the baskets forming a large circle. The wagon holding the pod pulled into the circle and a group of men surrounded it, hefting the pod and setting it down in the center of the balloons.

The wagon pulled away and the men stretched the ropes, tying each to a metal link on a different basket.

A half-dozen ropes were knotted to a half-dozen balloons, every action overseen by Tommy and the woman, again dressed as a man, Salanna.

"It is time," she announced. "Light the balloons."

The men started small fires nestled in fancy metal cradles chained to the base of each balloon. They worked bellows by each, rhythmically pumping to fill each balloon while other men kept hold of more ropes—two per basket—acting as living anchors.

"Careful now," Salanna warned over the rhythmic blasts of the bellows. "They must fill at the same rate so we rise together."

The carefully stitched balloons rose into the air, flaming cradles and bellows hanging beneath them in a spiderweb of rigging, and more men clung to the ropes, the baskets beginning to rise off the ground, skimming the grass. Men hooked a foot into a well-placed hole in each basket and swung their legs over, finding their proper place so the bellows and fires might be well-tended.

Salanna looked at Jack and Rowen. "Time to buckle up, boys," she said.

Together they entered the pod, Jack again taking the seat as

Rowen stepped to the back wall. The made quick work of their assorted belts and buckles, strapping themselves in.

"You ready?" Jack asked.

"Hell no," Rowen answered. "If by *ready* do you mean will I vomit or scream? Scream? Undoubtedly. But we will remain vomit-free."

"That is good news. Perhaps miraculous."

The balloons slowly rose, their baskets tottering on the ground like children balancing on tiptoes. The baskets rose higher, the ropes connecting them to the pod slowly straightening, and the baskets drifting out of the pod's view. Men counted in unison and anchor ropes flopped to the ground, loose, with a *slap*. Rowen braced himself, saying, "Not miraculous. I ate nothing this morning."

"That explains your piss-poor attitude. A sacrifice made in the name of revolution," Jack said with a snort.

The ropes went taut and Rowen couldn't be certain if the groan and growl he heard were the straining ropes, the places they joined the pod, or his stomach determined to make him a liar.

"Hold on!"

Inside the pod their world shifted, the entire ship rocking forward onto its nose. Jack and Rowen hung facedown, staring at the grass and held in place only by their snug belts and heavy buckles. The pod scraped a few feet along the foot of the hill, sounding like it found every rock to rub against, and then it swayed free of the ground.

Rowen swallowed the lump rising in his throat as his stomach matched the movements of the heaven-bound pod.

The world grew smaller below them, drifting away as they left wagons and carts and the remnants of smoldering campfires behind—or *below*, Rowen thought.

The hills and the trees became tiny toys—models made to surround an ornate dollhouse. They climbed into a clear sky, outstripping the rising sun, which spread like a painter had overturned his colors across mountains and valleys alike.

And still they rose higher and the world below grew smaller.

"Not long now," Jack said, his voice deeper from the weight of his body pressing his ribs into the leather belts. "Brace yourself."

"I have been ..."

They hung silently then, the world below sliding to the side but the sizes of things remaining the same.

"Any minute," Jack whispered throatily.

Shouts came from above. The din of voices cleared and a rhythmic count began at their backs.

"They'll cut the ropes any moment ..." Jack stretched his arms out, his hands above the pod's controls, fingers poised and twitching.

Rowen wondered if it was wiser to keep his eyes open or squeeze them shut.

But it was too late.

They were already falling.

And Rowen was screaming as the world rushed toward them.

Jack growled out his determination, slamming the lever down and popping the wings wide open. Rowen's back slammed into the wall as the pod was hurled upward again. Their altitude leveled out, and Jack adjusted their path, pointing their nose toward Philadelphia with the knowledge new allies followed them below, transported by colorful wagons.


*Aboard the Artemesia*


It was while the Wandering Wallace stayed belowdecks—the time he spent in his cabin seemed longer and longer each day—that Jordan took her chance. She had stared at the charts and maps so long she nearly had them memorized. So it only took a brief sweeping aside of a small section of clouds to sight the sun and adjust their course.

To nudge them just a bit away from Philadelphia.

She needed time to think.

She needed distance between herself and the idea of revolution. Between herself and the idea of Rowen. To consider setting Meggie and her family down for safety's sake. She reached into her sleeve and felt the brass heart he'd given her, nested and hidden in its folds.

She needed time to make sure the Wandering Wallace would be true to his word.

She was struggling with trust—with most men. She shouldn't be surprised, shouldn't blame herself, but frustration stung her nose and threatened to make her eyes stream nonetheless.

Revolution and freeing the Witches meant more than simple freedom. It meant an overthrow of all rank and order. It was potentially a disaster. A bloody disaster if the gleeful way the Wandering Wallace secured the *Artemesia* was any mark of his true methodology.

Her jaw clenched and she remembered the screams of people being thrown off of balconies.

The sun fell on her face, warm and reassuring.

Her stomach shimmied in her gut at the thought of leaving Rowen, but knowing she must take her chance while she had it and keep the Wandering Wallace from leaving her kind to their own devices, she sealed the clouds and held the slightly adjusted course steady.

*Aboard the Artemesia*

Meggie stood before the longer of the Topside dining tables, smoothing out a bedsheet slung across it and spilling to the floor to create a makeshift stage for a puppet show. The Wandering Wallace, now wearing the wildly ribboned and thickly maned mask of a lion's head, had donated the frame from his knife-throwing background to their cause, and it now hung with another plain sheet. Behind the sheet and the draped table an array of strong white stormcells glowed, casting a powerful light against the fabric.

Meggie turned, noted everyone's attention was focused on her, and puffing out her chest, began. "Once, long, long ago in the far, Far East—"

"So far east it is west to some," Maude's voice rang out from behind the cloth, the words followed by her easy laugh.

Meggie pursed her lips a moment and then continued. "—there was a handsome king—" A sleek silhouette rose from behind the covered table, dressed in a sweeping coat and pants that ballooned out just above the ankles. "—and his beautiful queen." A second figure joined the first and Meggie slipped behind the table. The puppets bowed to each other and began to dance together. In a more fiercely focused voice, Meggie continued, the slightest bit hesitant, her attention split. "She was his light and his love, and he, as rich as he was—"

"—which was very, *very* rich indeed—" Maude quipped.

"—he was far richer having her in his life."

The puppets parted and the queen, silhouetted in her broad ball gown, blew her king a kiss. But she stooped, and she shook.

"But a cold wind blew across the sea—"

Bent, the queen was wracked with coughing and the king rushed to her side. More figures appeared on the scene, and the silhouette of a bed rose from somewhere behind the table.

Meggie said, "And the queen fell ill," as the queen collapsed into her bed. "But no matter how many doctors came when the king called," the new puppets gathered around the queen's bed, poking and prodding the queen while the king paced across the stage, "there was no saving her."

The queen's arms rose, waving like a flag of surrender before falling flush to her body. The doctors drew back, hands flying to their mouths. Across the stage the king straightened as if he somehow knew.

Beside Jordan, the Wandering Wallace shifted in his seat. He reached out to Miyakitsu, taking her hand so fast and hard she gasped before slouching, relaxed, against his shoulder once more.

Jordan's attention returned to the puppet show.

The queen's hands were folded on her chest and the bed holding her was lifted onto the doctors' shoulders. In procession they walked her body past the inconsolable king and sank beneath the table.

The king fell to the ground, distraught and destroyed.

Meggie was silent for a long moment.

"The king was devastated. He was alive, but he no longer *lived*," Meggie said as the king twisted in agony on the stage and finally stood, raising his hands to the heavens, pleading. "His kingdom suffered. His people suffered. His advisors knew something had to be done. Somehow he needed to come back to life."

A new puppet emerged—a short man in a dramatic cape. He raised his hands, moving them slightly up and down, and the shadow of Meggie's hand appeared, a small ball pinched between her finger and thumb. She moved it back and forth between the puppet's hands as if he juggled.

The king sat up.

The short man did a back flip and when he popped back to his feet, Maude whistled and Meggie threw confetti into the seated crowd. "A magician was called to court," she explained, "and although he performed many amazing tricks and the king regained some sense of himself, still, he was not nearly as he was before."

The king sank below the table.

"His kingdom needed more from him," Meggie continued, "so his advisers took the magician aside." The doctors returned, cornering the little magician. "They made it clear he had to make the king as good as he was before."

The magician shrank away from the threatening postures of the doctors. The doctors stomped away, leaving the magician to pace and rub at his head in worry. Then, suddenly, he raised a hand to the heavens and gave a little hop.

Meggie cleared her throat and said, "After much thought—"

"—and even more worry—" Maude chimed in.

"—the magician had an idea!"

The magician bent over and appeared to be hammering at something. From behind the table came a frame with a thin napkin pinned to it. The magician next wrestled with a real pair of scissors (Meggie leaning out of the backstage area and saying, "We ran out of time!") before disappearing again and tossing snips of black paper into the air. The scissors disappeared with a flash and the magician wrestled a real stormlantern onto the table. The magician stepped to center stage and raised both his arms in triumph.

"The king was brought in for a special show that the magician hoped would catch his attention."

The king appeared and sat stiffly on a throne to watch, surrounded by fierce-looking advisers. The magician stood in front of a curtained display of his own—a miniature mimicry of what the crowd sat watching. The magician waved his arms and disappeared. Another stormlantern flared on, making a spotlight behind the miniature display. And from behind the second, and much smaller, illuminated screen another puppet rose.

The queen had returned.

The king jumped to his feet.

In a squeaky voice, Meggie said, "Greetings, my king! Your love has brought me back once more—"

The king rushed toward his queen, but she waved her arms to keep him back.

"You and I might be separated by death but we are held together by something far stronger–love. You must stay on one side of the curtain and I must stay on the other. But," she said when the king began to pace before her, "we can still have this moment and you might have this message to keep you warm now my body lies cold in the ground."

The king nodded slowly and, stepping back, sat cross-legged before his queen.

The Wandering Wallace adjusted his position and laid his masked head on Miyakitsu's shoulder, watching the story unfold.

"You are not the same man I first married," the queen said.

"How can I be that man when part of my heart is forever gone?"

"You think you have lost part of your heart? That you have lost your love?"

He nodded.

"You are so wrong, my love! I am not gone from this world at all—merely changed. You can find me in the seeping and strong colors of dawn. I am the notes that make the nightingale's song sweet. I am the sustaining power of the ripened rice and the light in the eyes of our people. But when the joy and prosperity fades from our countrymen, *I* fade as well. Our people need their king. *I* need *my* king," she whispered. "Your love of our kingdom and the prosperity of our people honors me."

The king nodded. "That is what I want—to honor you. For all to know that you will always be my love."

"Then give the devotion you once gave me to our people. Do good by them in *my* name. In this way your love will return to me and you will see me again in their smiles and in their laughter."

"As you wish," he said.

The queen shifted, her dark form wavering behind the illuminated curtain. "My time in this form is over. Find me in others and my love will never leave you." And then the figurine shook, sinking behind stage.

The king leapt to his feet. "Our people shall prosper under my renewed attention and in my queen's name!"

"And, so they did," Meggie announced, crawling out from behind the table to stand. She brushed off her skirts. "Inspired, the king set about to improve his people's lot in life and he never lacked for love again."

The king disappeared, the glow of the stormlanterns faded, and Maude rose from behind the table, dusted herself off, and joined Meggie.

Meggie piped up in a practiced tone: "As the king was inspired that day, so we hope our play has inspired you! No love ever leaves us if we act with love in our hearts."

The two took each other's hands and bowed low to the cheering crowd, their fingertips brushing the deck.

It was as Bran helped Maude disassemble their makeshift stage that the Wandering Wallace approached. Bran busied himself with the magician's props, hearing the Wandering Wallace ask Maude, "If I might make a request … Might you craft a few paper puppets for me?"

Bran spared the masked man a glance. There was something changed in the Wandering Wallace's posture—something meek, something humble.

Not far from them, Marion and Caleb picked up swords to practice fighting, their every move overseen by Evie and Jack.

Revolution was on its way, and the Wandering Wallace wanted Maude to make puppets.

Maude nodded slowly. "Puppets of … ?"

"Of myself, Miyakitsu, and my fox."

"Yes, of course," Maude murmured.

"Excellent well," the Wandering Wallace said. He pulled himself up straighter and, as he left Maude and Bran to talk, it seemed his step was lighter.

Maude pressed close to Bran, her breath teasing across his lips. All thought of revolution and puppets and the sins of his past fled. "Should I not be set other tasks? Miyakitsu makes our masks, Evie trains fighters …"

Meggie pounced on her, wrapping her arms around Maude's hips. "That was wonderful! I kept the lights good and steady, yes?" she whispered.

"You most certainly did," Maude agreed. "You are learning so much!"

Bran smiled. "See?" he asked Maude. "You *do* have an important job in the making of this revolution," Bran whispered, looking meaningfully at little Meggie, squeezed merrily between them. "No doubt."

*Philadelphia*

Their landing near the hedgemaze on the Astraeas' property had been less than flawless but far from horrendous. Rowen even managed to keep his stomach from turning inside out, which Jack gave as proof of a gentle landing. They had stepped out of the pod and, grunting, groaning, and straining, dragged the small ship out of direct sight of the sprawling Astraea mansion.

They took their chance, slipping out of the hedgemaze and creeping unnoticed through one of the estate's gates.

"I dislike this entire situation," Jack confided, his hand resting on his gun. "This area is too genteel. Too clean, too neat. Everything and everyone in its place," he muttered, eyes roaming.

"It's where I grew up," Rowen countered, his hand finding his sword. "This is home to me."

"I distrust everything about your home."

Rowen nodded. "We agree on that. Have a care," he warned Jack, thrusting his arm out to move Jack back into the shadows. Men in watchmen's uniforms strolled past, chatting as they occasionally snapped the butts of their staffs down on the cobbles, enjoying the ring of metal on stone. "They usually stay at their posts," Rowen said, peering through narrowed eyes.

"They have reason to be out and about," Jack muttered. "Word has surely reached them about the Wraiths and Wardens vacating Holgate."

"Mmhmm."

Several dozen feet away, the watchmen shouted and ran after a ragged-looking boy. Catching him quickly, they held him up by his collar and yelled at him. Rowen picked out a few words, one of which was "curfew" and the other two were not to be repeated in polite company. He looked up at the street lamps. They had started to glow. Dusk was crawling across the Hill.

Jack pulled his pocket watch from his waistcoat, popping it open to check the time. "We'd best get moving or our contact might decide better than to wait on us."

"Your contact can wait," Rowen assured, watching as the watchmen dropped the boy and shoved him in the direction of the Hill's slope. The watchmen might not afford lodgings on the Hill but they were eager to move along any ranked below them. If they couldn't stay longer than a patrol, no ragamuffin would either.

Another minute passed as the watchmen returned to their seemingly normal circuit, continuing.

"Wait," Rowen urged.

They waited in the thickening shadows, watching the men's backs grow smaller. When Rowen was certain they were out of earshot, he grabbed Jack's arm and hurried down the street the opposite way from the watchmen. "Where are we meeting this contact?" Rowen asked.

"The big oak in the old park. Does that mean anything to you? Any guess as to who this person is?"

Rowen shook his head. He'd considered who might be willing (and able) to pay a bigger reward than the government, and why they might want him badly enough to do it, but the list in his head was short.

His mother? Yes, but she'd never be caught in the old park. Not when the new park was far more fashionable. And she certainly would not be in such a location after a curfew. The family of Lord Edwards? He knew little about them. It was possible one of them had motivation and money to lure Rowen into their grasp for the purpose of exacting revenge. Not honorable, but possible.

Beyond those options, Rowen could fathom no one else with such ready cash and keen interest.

If things went well it wouldn't matter. They would show up, take the money, disarm the person and be on their way.

They had a plan.

A negligible plan, but it was something. "Take my sword."

"What?" Jack's eyes roamed up and down the streets and the occasional alleys shooting off at crisp angles.

"Take my sword," Rowen repeated. "If I am to appear your prisoner, should you not have disarmed me?"

Jack blinked up at him, lips thin.

"I would hope *I* would disarm a prisoner of *mine*," Rowen muttered. "Especially a prisoner who is so much *bigger* than I am."

"*Fatter.*"

"*Heavier.*" Rowen straightened, sucking his stomach in. "Muscle is heavy."

"So are the rocks in your head," Jack muttered. "Fine. Give me your sword."

Rowen shoved it into his hands.

"Is there anything else a proper captor would do to better give the impression of having dealt in ransoms?"

Rowen snorted. "I find it very strange that, having obviously dealt in kidnapping—"

"—shanghaiing—" Jack corrected.

"—that you are not be better versed in such things."

"Generally we *impress* a captive, they like us, and there's not a need to deal in ransoms or rewards for their return," Jack explained. "You are an odd exception to many of the things we once supposed were rules."

Rowen nodded. "As is Jordan," he whispered. "What a pair we make."

"You don't seem to be making much of a pair at all."

Rowen shot him a look that could've been lethal, but placed a single finger to his lips and said, "Shhh. There. That's our destination," pointing to a copse of broad-trunked trees surrounded by a handful of stone and wooden benches.

They could see a shadow move by the far bench—a shadow partly obscured by a tree's trunk.

Jack stepped out and around him, slipping a sash around his wrists.

"That's a bit weak, don't you think?"

"No, *a bit weak* is what you'll be if I stab you in the leg with your own sword," Jack corrected, snugging the sash tight.

Rowen rolled his eyes.

"Remember, you are my prisoner. Behave accordingly."

Rowen lowered his head and muttered under his breath, but Jack led him, carrying Rowen's sword at his suggestion.

They approached the trees and benches, muscles taut and coiled like springs—expecting ambush. They stopped before a seated figure engulfed in a voluminous cloak.

A Kinsale cloak.

A woman.

*Aboard the Artemesia*

A knock on her cabin door revealed Caleb outside. She let him in, relieved to be in a room where she controlled who entered and exited.

"Bring it in," he instructed in a most authoritative voice.

Jordan stepped back, watching as a guard entered, a folded screen tucked beneath his arm. He moved to the edge of the room, and adjusted his grip, set the screen—still folded—before him.

A man entered backwards, carrying the first part of a large copper tub, and he and a partner set it down in the room's middle. The first man opened the screen and then they all removed their hats and bowed in her direction. They turned and left.

Caleb entered, closing the door behind him once more. He gave Jordan a glance and then moved the chair to the far side of the screen so that now the chair and the tub were separated visually. He peeked back around at her. "It took some doing, you know. To bring a tub down here. That elevator isn't exactly spacious. But, as you have made it abundantly clear you will not move to the captain's quarters—"

She winced. "Of course I cannot," she whispered. Aghast, she stared at the gleaming tub.

The door opened again and a group of maids carrying buckets of steaming hot water entered and began to fill the tub.

"Is that his ... ?"

"No. You deserve to have his, but his is firmly attached to a wall and the floor with a system of pipes and a drain to provide running water. There was no easy way to remove it."

"Good," she said, letting out a sigh. "I want nothing that reminds me of him," she whispered, stepping forward to rest a hand on the tub's tall edge.

Lightning flared outside her windows, its reflection tripping across the rippling surface of the water as its volume grew. A girl paused and threw a handful of herbs and flowers into the bath water and Jordan couldn't help but smile. She remembered baths like this. The servants, the scent of herbs steeping in warm water.

The peace it all brought.

"Thank you," she said. She meant it. Suddenly it was not simply a reflexive response she had been trained into, but she meant it.

Truly and deeply.

Caleb smiled. "This is only the beginning, dear child," he assured.

"You really need to stop calling me that," she said. "We are surely of an age."

After sufficient time soaking to leave her hands as wrinkled as walnuts and her mind clear, she stepped out of the tub, her body alive, fresh, and gleaming with water. She snatched a towel from a waiting servant's hands and wrapped herself in it, using a second to rub most of the wet out of her hair.

"Are you decent, dear one," Caleb asked.

"I most certainly am not," Jordan snapped, pulling the towel more tightly about herself.

"Oh, dear," he muttered, coming around the screen to look at her directly.

She gave a little shriek and turned her back to him. "Go away, Caleb. Go away now—it is not seemly for you to see me like this ..."

"Well, that is most unfortunate. Because I am not the only one who will be seeing you like that, my lady."

She gasped and spun to face him. "What do you mean by that?"

"I mean that if you do not slip into your shift shortly, the people who are bringing you new dresses to choose from will be quite surprised." His gaze traveled the length of her and he winked. "But not disappointed. No," he added as she snatched the waiting shift and disappeared around the screen to change, "certainly not disappointed."

# Chapter Twelve

*Philadelphia*

Her face hidden in the shadow of her voluminous hood, the mysterious woman rose to address them.

Jack spoke, his hands shifting on the scabbard he held. He squinted at the woman. "I've brought you Rowen Burchette, as requested, at the appointed place and time."

She nodded, pointing toward a waiting carriage.

Rowen tilted his head, examining the figure before them and the horses in their traces. Mentally he berated himself for not spending more time in the stables that housed Philadelphia's steeds and were under his father's control.

For not spending *more* time? For not spending *any* time. If he had, he might have recognized the woman based on her horses alone. His father would have. Gregor Burchette was like that.

Jack asked, "You want us to go to the carriage?"

The hooded woman nodded.

"Then why not say *that* was where to meet in the first place?" he grumbled, steering Rowen. "Typical woman," Jack muttered loud enough she might hear, "says to meet her one place than decides on another. Bad as moving furniture. An indecisive lot you are, you ask me."

The horses stamped at their approach. Their driver, bent and narrow with a high top hat's brim resting low on his brow, hissed them into silence.

The lady stopped by the carriage's door.

Jack and Rowen watched her with equal measures of trepidation.

They stood like that a long moment, waiting.

With an exasperated sigh, she knocked on the carriage's side. On her gloved hand a ruby ring flashed.

The driver turned in his seat and, leaning awkwardly backwards, peered down at the hooded figure. Reaching across, he yanked the door open.

She gestured toward the open door.

"No," Jack said. "No, nay, never. No one's getting into any vehicle be it cart, carriage, wagon, or unicycle until I get my money. I delivered him. I want compensation for my pain and suffering. Because this one? His presence brings pain and suffering."

"That's because I have superior reach in a brawl," Rowen said with a smirk.

Jack snorted. "Yeah? I'll whoop yer ass right here and have you crying like a babe without his bottle. Right before milady, if you don't have a care."

The cloaked figure waved her hands anxiously. Again she pointed to the carriage's open door.

"I want my money," Jack returned.

She stomped her foot.

"Gentlemen," the driver said with a sigh, "I believe the lady suggests the money is not on her person at the moment. As a precaution against vandals."

Jack rubbed his chin, fingers rasping across his bristly beard.

Rowen cleared his throat.

Jack acted as if he hadn't heard.

Rowen cleared his throat again. Both the driver and the lady looked at him. Jack, however, ignored him.

"If the money's not on you, it does seem we should go to wherever my money's at ..." He reached behind Rowen and, grabbing him by the waistband, shoved him forward.

Rowen paused at the carriage's single step, thinking he recognized the carriage—that he had vomited out of its window one night after a bad go of drinking. If it was the same carriage, the woman in question was certainly someone he should recognize. He opened his mouth to say her name at the same moment Ginger Jack hit his rump with his own scabbard, sending him right at the opening and leaving him no choice but to step up. "Bastard," he growled, now inside the carriage.

Jack grinned up at him, motioning for the woman to join them. "I assure you—they were married."

They settled in to the carriage; the driver closed the door, snapped the reins, and sent the horses into a trot.

Jack leaned back against the plush seat's back, one finger tracing the quilted stitching. "Comfortable."

The sharp noise of the horse's hooves echoed, as did the hissing of wheels spinning through water. That's right, Rowen mused. It was Tuesday. One of the scheduled days rain fell in Philadelphia.

"Loud," Jack added.

Rowen shifted on the seat. It did not matter how well appointed—that was gilt, was it not?—or comfortable the carriage was. What mattered was completing their mission. "Take down the hood, Catrina," he snapped. "I know. I do not understand, but I know."

With a disapproving sniffle, Catrina Hollindale, ranked Fourth of the Nine, reached up and lowered her hood, trying her most winning smile on Rowen Burchette, wanted man.

He shook his head. "Two questions," Rowen said. "First, why? And second, do you have the money? Because, if not, I expect things will go very badly. And they will go very badly very fast."

Jack nodded.

"Why?" She looked surprised by such a question. "Because the government was unwilling to see reason. Had they succeeded, Rowen, dear," she said, though he flinched at the endearment, "you would have been taken in and summarily made an example of. Or used as a pawn to keep your father and the military he controls more beneath their thumb." She shook her head. "They would have seen you captured, tried, and hanged on trumped-up charges. To save you I had to have some dolt—"

"Dolt?" Jack protested.

"—find, capture, and bring you to me. For safekeeping."

"Safekeeping," Rowen repeated.

"Dolt?" Jack snapped again, bristling.

Catrina only had eyes for Rowen. "Yes. You will stay with me until I can get to your family and tell them all that has transpired. Then we will move in appropriate steps to have you exonerated and reinstated as Sixth of the Nine. You will return to your family, begin courting, and be at the right place and time (and the right mind) to serve your enlistment."

Rowen blinked. "And I suppose we will marry and have a dozen babies."

She sat back in her seat. "A dozen might be a bit much, but I will not stop you from trying to reach such a goal."

He slammed his head back against the carriage wall in frustration. "I will do no such thing."

"But, without sufficient trying there can be no such number of offspring. Surely some carousing friend has explained how such things happen...."

"I know how such things happen."

She pulled the fan off her hip, waving it between them. "Then what—?"

"—do I mean?"

She nodded.

"I mean that this myopic vision of yours will never work, Catrina."

"Myopic? Why not?"

The carriage had rolled to a stop and Jack let out a long, low whistle, peering out the window.

"I have the means and motivation to make it happen. I have some pull on the Council. I can—I will—" she corrected "—make this work."

"You can't, Catrina," Rowen repeated, almost sadly.

"Why ever not?"

He fixed his eyes on hers and said slowly, carefully, "Because I do not love you."

She flicked the fan closed.

The carriage door swung open, and it seemed she could not get away from him quickly enough, tripping on the carriage's step and nearly falling onto the sidewalk.

Jack jumped out, looking up and down, admiring their change of venue.

Rowen joined them, a quick glance registering what he had expected was their destination—the Hollindale estate.

"No," Catrina murmured. "No. I do not believe it," she said, her voice shrill. She walked in a tight circle, snapping her fan open and then closed.

"My lady," the driver said, "you had best get inside and out of sight of the watch. They will return shortly."

"Yes, yes, of course," she agreed with a sharp nod. "Go, put up the carriage and horses. I will pay you a bonus tomorrow."

The driver nodded, and, with a crack of the reins, set the horses into motion.

Catrina addressed Jack, who had the good sense to take the sash binding Rowen's hands as if they were truly captor and captive. "You want your money, yes?"

"Yes," he said without hesitation.

"Bring him inside. I will give it all to you. You did as I bade and should be rewarded for such action."

They followed her up the steps to the large manor with its carefully pointed brick walls and elegant trim. Inside the foyer, she stopped.

"You do not love me? Perhaps that is true now. But you loved me once," she insisted, searching his face for some confirmation.

"No."

"Yes you did," she said, more to herself than to anyone else. "You have just forgotten. You will learn to love me again."

"The money?" Jack reminded.

"Yes, yes. Untie him."

"I did not ever love you. And I will not. You cannot *make* someone love you," Rowen said, gentling his tone.

"You did, you will again—I mean, why would you not love me? I did everything I could to get you to notice me." Catrina stomped her foot so her heel on the tile echoed. "There was not a day that went by that I did not dress to my utmost, that I was not coiffed and styled to seek your appreciation. Your approval. I gave you my complete and undivided attention, I afforded you every kindness even though you were two ranks below me. It was like a knife in my heart when you started spending more time with Jordan than me. Even though my parents scoffed about my affections for you, even though they said you were a waste of my time and good graces, still, I silenced their protests. I silenced their doubts about you. Forever," she added, a mad light flaring in the depths of her eyes.

She caught her breath and continued. "Did you truly not heed me? I knew you first, I introduced you to each other! When I realized you were falling for Jordan ... I knew what I had to do." She was breathing rapidly, her hand on her stomach, her chest heaving in her tight dress. "You were destined to be mine. You just needed a distraction removed."

Rowen stiffened, his eyes narrowing.

"So I had Jordan's dress ingeniously designed, made, and I contacted the Councilman."

"You did what?" Rowen was still as a viper poised to strike, but Catrina was so wrapped up in her own admittance she no longer had sense enough to stop herself from rattling on.

"I commissioned the dress—such an expensive thing with its intricate little cage of wire netting—but necessary to get the sparks to run as they did. It was a piece of genius. All I had to do was convince them that she was the Witch—all it took was some planning and a touch at the right moment ..."

Rowen's jaw dropped. "Shite, Catrina," Rowen whispered.

"Please! I am a lady!" she admonished. "So they took her away." She made a shooing motion with her hand. "Off to whatever palace they keep them in as they educate them for their lifetime of travel and adventure ... I arranged for her to go to a different place, live a different life, and assured that you and I would eventually come together." She reached out to lay her hand on his arm, but Jack slid between them.

Jack sought Rowen's eyes. "She didn't know what she was doing."

"Just who are you," she asked Jack, "captor or confidante?" She wrinkled her nose up at him. "And you are wrong," she told him. "I knew precisely what I was doing," she said with a snort of dismissal. "I knew that by sending her off on a lifetime of travel I was keeping you for myself. That was all I ever wanted."

"Rowen," Jack warned, "she didn't know what the conditions were like. She couldn't."

"What?" She rounded on Jack, blinking. Her hand reached out to touch Rowen's arm and he shook her off, rage making him tremble. "I did it all to win you, dear Rowen. How could I have guessed that you and that servant of yours—Jonathan— Where is he, by the way?"

Rowen's nostrils widened and he sucked in a deep breath, everything about his form tight, wound like a spring.

She again waved her dainty hand. "How could I have known

you and Jonathan would traipse into the wilds to find her? You'd never done anything that bold before. And certainly not something that went so strongly against your mother's wishes …"

"Stop."

"But you went plowing ahead like a bull!"

He dropped his tone and volume, every bit of breath warning her. "Stop now. Before I stop you …"

Jack cleared his throat. "My money."

Catrina hurried to a nearby chest and wrenched it open. She pulled out two sacks of coins with a grunt and, hefting them beyond the trunk's edge, shoved them into Jack's waiting hands. He took a half step backwards under the sudden weight, releasing Rowen.

Rowen thrashed at the knotted sash, worrying it loose.

She stepped into him then, her bodice brushing his chest.

He stepped back, glaring.

"I was so worried I had to set up a wanted poster with a reward that was more valuable than any others. I couldn't bear you being dragged before the Council, knowing I set this entire thing into motion! It just didn't seem right!"

"My being hunted after the duel didn't seem right to you, but what you did to Jordan and her family, *did*?"

"I never had qualms with her family, that's my one regret," she admitted. "But I would have done anything to have you returned. And here you are! Safe and sound! Thanks to—"

"Jack," he replied, working his way more firmly between them.

"Jack. Well. Isn't that just a wonderfully common name?" She patted the sacks. "This is what you're due. Thanks ever so much for bringing Rowen to me and," she leaned in, placing one finger against her lips, "we must never speak of this again. It is important no one know he's in my keeping."

Jack merely blinked at her.

"Now, Rowen, we must get you out of those—clothes—and into things of a more distinguished sort."

"Catrina. That is not my priority."

She wrinkled her nose and pulled loose her fan. Flicking it open, she waved it between them, nearly smacking Jack in the nose. "And a bath. I daresay you could stand a bath."

"Catrina," he said, heaving her name out in exasperation.

"Yes, dear boy? I apologize for rushing you along, but there is much on our agenda you do not yet know about."

A door opened and they spun to face the intruder.

Disheveled-looking as always, Catrina's uncle paused in the doorway. He straightened. "Oh, isn't this interesting ..." He strode forward—no, staggered more than strode—and stopped beside them to stare at each in turn through bleary and bloodshot eyes. He rubbed his chin. "Fascinating." He waved at his niece, grinning at Jack and Rowen with the look of one who knew too much and said too little. "Go on, dear girl. Don't let me stop you." He peered at her again through half closed eyelids. "Your agenda ... ?"

Aboard the Artemesia

Jordan had barely dropped the towel and slipped into a simple linen shift when she heard the door open and close and more footsteps roam the floor space of her room. She peeked around the screen and heard Meggie laugh.

The child slapped her hands together and said, "Oh, Miss Jordan, this is so exciting!"

Jordan shot a look at Caleb.

He raised one shoulder in a shrug. "I have an amazing sense of style, but I thought Meggie would also rise to the challenge of giving you a fine new look."

Meggie just grinned up at Jordan, her heart-shaped face glowing.

Maude glanced from Jordan to Caleb, regaining Meggie's

hand. "I was told you and Caleb would watch my dear little sprite, but you do not appear ready …"

Caleb waved a hand at her and detached Meggie's hand from hers to take it in his own. "I assure you she will be well taken care of. You may go about your day and we will bring her Topside when Jordan is more suitably attired. Good enough?"

Maude smiled, leaned over and gave Meggie's forehead a kiss, and then left the room.

"Jordan, come join us," Caleb said, patting her bed. He moved to a waiting chair, his eyes following her as she came out from behind the screen to sit on the edge of the bed.

Meggie jumped up on her lap and clasped her hands together, waiting for the show to begin.

There was someone at the door nearly immediately. "Oh!" Meggie slid back down and raced over to open the door wide.

A maid walked in, holding high a broad gold gown with wide skirts and a deeply pointed wasp's waist. Jordan didn't need to try it on or even have the girl turn it around to display its back, but said with a snort, "No."

Caleb's eyebrows rose.

"Ah, yes. You never saw me in my gold ball gown that I wore the whole time I was housed in Holgate. The gold ball gown lined with a net of metal thread that caught lightning and led people to believe I was a Witch. And that my family was guilty of Harboring."

Caleb swallowed hard and clapped his hands together, signaling a change of view and the girl spun on her heel and exited before a new girl stepped into the room, this one holding up a bright purple dress trimmed out in both gold and silver. Its sleeves puffed at the top before narrowing near the elbows and flaring again, growing heavy with lace at the wrists. The skirt was narrower than the first and Jordan rested an arm around Meggie's shoulders, leaning lightly across her.

"What do you think?" she asked the child.

"Show us the back!" Meggie declared.

The girl smiled and turned the gown around.

"Your derrière will look gigantic!" Meggie whispered.

"From out of the mouths of babes," Caleb said with a chuckle, reaching out to tousle Meggie's pale blond curls.

Jordan snorted, noting the ample bustle. "My rump would look quite huge," she agreed.

"Ah, but my darling girls," Caleb announced, "such things are quite in style in Europe."

Jordan wrinkled her nose. "You would have me wear something that is stylish abroad and has not yet caught one's fancy here?" she asked.

"Oh, just try the blasted thing on," Caleb muttered, leaning so far back in the chair that its front legs came off the floor.

"Shall I?" Jordan mused, going nose to nose with Meggie.

Both their noses wrinkled, their tips touching, and they squinted at each other with sparkling eyes that made them look mean if one didn't know how they joked or watched the way their lips twisted into crazy grins.

"Yes," Meggie insisted with a sharp nod.

"Then I shall!" Jordan said, leaping to her feet. She snatched the gown away from the maid with a softly spoken, "Thank you," and disappeared behind the screen.

She wrestled with the fixtures on the back of it, and then stepped into the voluminous gown and tugged it up around her shoulders. It did not come up as far as she had hoped.

Her neck and most of her shoulders were bare to the air, and she shivered, knowing how much of her flesh could be seen. And how much of her scar.

"Come out, come out, come out," Meggie insisted at the top of her voice.

Jordan heard her bed squeak rhythmically and peeked around the screen.

Meggie was bouncing as hard as she could and giggling each time her rump reconnected with the mattress.

"What if I don't like it?" Jordan asked.

"Are you getting cold feet, beautiful girl?" Caleb called.

"No," Jordan muttered, "cold shoulders, technically." She disappeared back around the screen and thought she could hear Caleb's eyes roll.

"Be brave, child," he insisted. "You are among friends here. Well, among friends and one anonymous servant girl," he added, obviously remembering the maid still stood there, obedient.

Jordan rested her hand on her bust, feeling the way her chest rose and lowered as she breathed. And noting that her chest was rising and falling rapidly. She closed her eyes and gulped down air, sucking in breath after breath as she tried to steady herself. Caleb wouldn't understand—couldn't understand. She barely understood! There were just times—moments, triggers that caused her vision to constrict into a dark tunnel, moments her pulse rose in volume in her ears to the point she could hear nothing else around her—not even the thunder booming when she lost focus for a few minutes and let it slip loose. They were times her stomach tried to turn itself inside out and her throat tried to close, shutting down the panicking bellows of her lungs.

She drew down a bigger breath yet, and it turned into a yawn.

Caleb chuckled. "We are the ones growing bored out here, Jordan," he teased, "you have no reason to yawn."

She bent over at the waist and rested her hands on her knees. She could do this, she repeated over and over again in her mind. She was among friends. Caleb would never hurt her—they had shared too much already. And Meggie adored her—there could be no doubting that.

So she stayed leaned over, her eyes closed, her focus tight as she tried to regain control over her breathing and her racing heart.

"Jordan?" Meggie's voice so close startled her so much she straightened right back up and she grabbed the screen to steady herself, dizziness making her sway.

"Are you all right?" she asked, her eyes wide and soft.

Jordan nodded stiffly, equally to convince Meggie as it was to convince herself. "Go," she whispered. "Go sit down. I will step out momentarily," she promised.

Meggie chewed on her lower lip a moment, but she nodded and disappeared from sight again.

The bed began squeaking again, but now it was slower, softer, a more tentative echo of her previous behavior.

Jordan steeled herself, brushed her hand lightly along her shoulders and, setting them back and raising her chin as she'd been taught, she carefully stepped out to be viewed.

Caleb examined every inch of the outfit. Or perhaps he was reading her body language, she thought, seeing a cast of disapproval color his face like a faint shadow. There was a line on his forehead she hadn't noticed before. A worry line. It was prominent now. "You don't like it?" he asked gently.

"No."

"It's pretty, Miss Jordan," Meggie insisted, her tone reflecting puzzlement. "You're pretty in it," she specified.

"Thank you, Meggie," she whispered, though she didn't feel thankful at being seen when she felt so horribly uncomfortable. But that was no reason to be rude. Especially not to Meggie.

"What do you not like about it, sweetheart?" Caleb asked.

Jordan froze. She had not expected to be asked something so specific. If she was going to be honest, what she didn't like about it was the way it made her feel exposed. But that was irrational. She was fully dressed and many women wore things with an even more open décolletage. Her neckline was modest when compared to some.

She cleared her throat and wiggled her jaw in thought. "It is pretty," she remarked slowly. "Of that there can be no doubt, but it does not feel right to me."

"Ah," Caleb said. He rubbed his chin, speculating. "If it does not feel right than it cannot be right, dearest one," he agreed. "Go on, take it off and we will see another."

Shamed by the fear that kept her from enjoying something so

lovely, Jordan dragged herself back to the other side of the screen and stepped out of it.

Standing there in her shift alone, she was suddenly keenly aware of how little fabric separated her from the rest of the world. "Caleb," she squeaked. "I am not sure I can ..."

His voice was low, soft, and soothing. So patient she wanted to cry at his generosity.

"I shall have Meggie bring you the next one, love," he conceded, "and you may stay back there between modeling for us. And you will only model what you like," he guaranteed.

She breathed out the words, "Thank you," and this time she meant it.

True to his word, Caleb sent Meggie around the screen with the next dress. Well, as much of the next dress as she could carry. It was a struggle for one so small to carry so many yards of fabric, but she gave it a most valiant attempt, only tripping over it twice.

It was powder blue. Soft and light and free of cares and worries. It was a dress made for brighter days. A dress Jordan hoped someday she would wear merrily. So Jordan leaned over, kissed Meggie's forehead, and sent her back without even trying it on. The next three dresses yielded similar results and Meggie began to huff and puff.

Jordan couldn't be sure it was from exhaustion or frustration.

And then Meggie appeared with a dress that made Jordan's heart stop.

It was steel blue—the color of glossy gun barrels and threatening skies—the color of trepidation and promises yet to be kept. She loved it immediately because she knew it like it was her own scarred skin. She leaned over and Meggie closed her eyes, waiting for another kiss—another rejection—and she sank her fingers into the glossy satin fabric and pulled it out of Meggie's hands.

"Go," Jordan whispered. "Let me try this one."

"Really?" Her eyes lit up and she grinned. "Yes!" she exclaimed as she disappeared back to Caleb. The bed squeaked faster now, and Meggie again was giggling in anticipation.

Jordan worked her way into the dress timidly, unwilling to accept it—to love it and need it too fast. There were bound to be flaws with it, she imagined as she slid into it, her eyes scouring it for any imperfection. Finding no problem with it was nearly as frustrating as knowing there was no rational problem and yet being unable to enjoy it. She settled the neckline on her body and noted with satisfaction that it was the most modest of all so far. She turned, examining as much of the skirting that lay in heavy pleats behind her as she could. The bustle was large but not overdone. The sleeves were beautiful but not dripping with lace or ribbons that might be tiresome when working on Topside. And the fabric was the right weight for a Conductor.

Dammit.

With a sigh she stepped out from behind the screen and presented herself to them.

Caleb stood. And clapped. "Lovely. Simply lovely," he repeated, shaking his head admiringly. "You, my dear, look stunningly powerful in that dress."

She felt heat rise in her cheeks and she brushed her hands across the skirt, feeling the way the rough skin of her hands tugged slightly at the fine fabric. "I will ruin it," she said sadly, but Caleb just laughed.

"Do your worst, child!" he challenged. "Any dress would be lucky to be worn to shreds by a woman of your power and talents."

She couldn't help it. She smiled.

"I think we are done here," Caleb said to the girl standing by, arms still open to receive the dress, having seen so many rejections. She blinked and, shrugging, gathered up the discarded gowns and left the room.

"Well," Caleb said with a grin, "I think we have time to play a game and then it's off to dinner!"

"A game, a game!" Meggie shouted. "What shall we play, Caleb?"

"Hmm," Caleb rubbed at his chin in thought. "We could play hoops, or the Game of Graces or jacks ..."

Meggie scrunched up her face at the offerings, and drawing herself up to her full (yet inconsequential) height, she asked in a very serious voice, "When was the last time you played hide-and-seek?"

Jordan blinked and Caleb laughed.

"The last time I played hide-and-seek," Jordan admitted, "I was your age or a year older."

Meggie let out a long, low whistle. "That long ago?" she asked, her eyes wide and unblinking.

"It's not so awfully long ago," Jordan sputtered, crossing her arms. "And I was quite good at it, I will have you know."

"Mmhmm, yes, yes of course you were," Caleb said, though his tone was clearly mocking. "For we all gladly stop doing something we are aces at."

"I outgrew it," Jordan clarified.

"You don't outgrow having fun," Meggie said, shocked and disapproving of such a radical idea.

Jordan smiled at her wistfully. "That is a good way to live your life," she said. "By never stopping doing what's fun."

"That is a good way to live a life," Caleb agreed. "I wish everyone were allowed to live in such a fashion—having fun and no worries."

"Then we are agreed. We must play," Meggie commanded.

"We must?" Jordan quirked an eyebrow at her. "And just who do you think should be 'it'?"

Caleb's mouth unrolled into a savage grin as he swept Meggie back into his arms. "Well, I believe the one who is the hunter should be the most professional of the lot of us, since I can say with fair certainty we will be most excellent hiders." He gave a generous wink to Meggie and she mimicked the move.

"I agree," she said. "Miss Jordan, it is your ship. It seems only fair you be the one to root us out, as we are merely passengers."

"Your logic is impeccable," Caleb whispered.

"And how high am I to count?"

Meggie's mouth swished from one side of her face to the other and she looked at Caleb for counsel. "Fifty?" she whispered.

"Oh, dear little fawn, I fear I am far too old to find a good hiding spot by the time she reaches fifty. I say go higher." He motioned with his thumb for her to raise the number.

"Seventy-five?" she asked.

"Higher still," he urged.

"One hundred?"

He looked to Jordan and said, very slowly, "Why yes, I do believe that one hundred will do quite nicely."

Jordan placed her hands on her hips and said, "Fine. One hundred it is. I shall turn around, cover my eyes, and count, and you shall hide—on this floor of the ship only," she clarified. "If I have to hunt the whole ship through we shall never make it to supper!"

Meggie nodded in very serious and sage agreement while fighting down a smile.

Jordan turned around, covered her eyes with her hands, and began to count. Very loudly. She heard the door open and close and she continued counting, occasionally exchanging a nonsense word for a number just to make things on her end more interesting.

"One hundred!" she shouted, spinning around. With a quick peek under the bed she determined her room was empty of geese (though it would have been brilliant in her opinion to hide in the same room as the hunter and go uncaught). She threw open her door and poked her head out, scanning the hallway.

She had told the truth. When she was round about Meggie's age she had been very good at playing hide-and-seek. But things had changed—her sisters had been promised, one was soon wed, and they were both gone far too fast. So it was not a lack of interest that had stopped her from playing, but rather a lack of participants. Her parents had never been the playful sort—there was decorum to remember—and so, at five or six, Jordan had simply stopped playing and started conforming.

She turned left down the hall, thinking the way seemed somehow brighter and that a child would be drawn to light, especially if she knew soon she'd be hiding in the dark. She popped open door after door, peering inside and rifling her way through the rooms until she came to one that held prisoners.

Stache stood outside, leaning against the wall, one foot propped up on the wall. He glanced at her and smiled.

Jordan's pace slowed to a walk and she gave a toss of her head in the door's direction. "How are they?"

"Angry and disenfranchised," he said with a smirk. "But they are decently behaved for their ranks and expectations. They are fed and watered, though I am careful of the amount of liquid they have access to so they cannot Draw Down and Light Up all willy-nilly."

"Good," Jordan nodded. "Good. May I—"

"What? Take a look-see?"

She nodded again.

"I don't see why not. They constantly seem to be looking for you. They ask after the Conductor nearly every day."

Her brow furrowed at the thought. "Whatever for?"

"They only wish well for the Stormbringer," he said with a smile.

"Oh. Ohhh. They think I'm the Stormbringer? Well, as flattering as that might be, they are most certainly wrong."

Stache squinted at her and turned to the door, brandishing a key. "If you say so. Only, don't say that to them—they'll likely rip you to shreds."

Jordan cleared her throat. "Then perhaps—just this once—I should continue on my way ..."

"No one would say such a thing was wrong of you," he assured. "If I was you," Stache said gruffly, "I'd be try'n find your little sister first."

Jordan paused, but rather than correct him, she simply went on her way.

# Chapter Thirteen

A man ain't got no right to be a public man,

unless he meets the public views.

—CHARLES DICKENS

*Philadelphia*

"I will not reveal my agenda to you," Catrina hissed at her uncle. "It is for Rowen and Rowen alone to know."

"Catrina," Rowen warned. "Damn it." He reached out and smashed a lamp resting nearby.

"Clumsy boy!" Catrina giggled.

"You're insane," Rowen said, finally having regained her attention.

"Perhaps I might help," her uncle insisted. "One never knows what sort of person may be useful in an uprising."

"Wh—what?" Catrina fluttered her eyelashes innocently, and shot a look at Jack, the stranger.

Jack pocketed the money she had handed him and kept a wary watch on Rowen.

"Tell Rowen what you've planned."

"Stop it," she said, shooting him a glare.

"Tell him how you'll fix things for your kind."

"Stop it, stop it, *stop it*!" she shouted, stamping her foot so the sound of her heels rioted through the room.

"Maybe, if you tell him, he'll stay."

Catrina's face stretched in fear and she gaped at Rowen.

"Look at him carefully, precious," her uncle said. "As a man who wants nothing but to leave you, I know what it looks like when someone feels the same way."

"No," she whispered.

"Tell it true, Rowen," her uncle said. "You aren't interested in staying, are you?" He reached toward the wall and pulled a chair away from it, slumping into it to watch.

"Nothing she can say can make me stay," Rowen said through clamped teeth.

"Oh, no, Rowen," she begged, placing her hands on his forearm.

Her uncle nodded. "Do at least listen to her before you go. Hers is such an intriguing idea. And tell her what it is you've been too much a gentleman to say. One good turn deserves another," he added. "She should know what's in your heart."

"None of that matters," she said. "He was put in my custody by this good fellow—Jack. He is mine. I paid the reward money."

"And you paid that because Jack delivered me to you. The money does, in no way, guarantee I will stay." Rowen unrolled the poster. "See? *Delivery to.*" He held it out before her so the paper brushed the tip of her nose. "I do not have to stay. And I won't, Catrina."

She grabbed the poster and pulled it down and out of his grasp, hurling it onto the floor. "You don't have to stay if you don't want to," she agreed, chin quivering. "Only give me a chance to explain."

Rowen and Jack exchanged a glance.

Jack shrugged.

"It is entertaining," her uncle goaded.

"Go," Rowen said.

"I wanted to keep you nearby—that is no secret," she said. "I never before felt the way I do about you. But my motivation goes beyond that, Rowen. I have plans to change the world—to make it better. To be rid of the ranks that keep us all separated."

Rowen's eyebrows rose. "You? Get rid of the ranks?"

"Yes, of course! Ranks are such an old-fashioned notion. We are centuries (and an entire ocean) removed from true knights, fiefs, barons, and things of that sort. They are very much why people used ranks—to show their connection to the crown. But we have no crown, so should we not be ranked according to our capabilities and not by simple ancestry?"

Rowen squinted at her. "Your capabilities ... ?"

"Everyone's capabilities! Imagine if the slaves were allowed to exhibit their skills—what art or science might we see that we are currently crushing? What if we encouraged other sorts of energy to be developed so we didn't need to use the Weather Witches' skills. Yes, let them keep their airships and fly wherever they like—"

"You do not know what it's like to be a Weather Witch, do you?" Rowen whispered, dread in his voice. "My god, no wonder ..."

"What is there to understand? They are taken, educated, and given ships."

"Educate her, Rowen," her uncle whispered. "I see the understanding in your eyes. Perhaps now is the time to pass along that light to someone very much—very *tragically*—in the dark."

"What are you talking about?" Catrina growled.

"Yes," Rowen whispered. "I think we must ..." He glanced about. "But where? I have no ship to show her the truth of things ..."

Every light in the room dimmed a moment and Rowen said, "Close your eyes," just as the Pulse came, shooting out from the city's Hub like fingers of lightning and racing through wires, humming, to recharge all the stormcell crystals at once. There was a flare of white light strong enough to blind if one was caught off guard, and the light receded, returning to its normal ambience.

"Ah. The Hub," Catrina's uncle said. "I think it's time we took a family outing to the Hub. An educational trip of sorts, yes?"

His jaw set, Rowen nodded. "Yes."

"You are both so frustrating," Catrina exclaimed.

"The carriage for the first leg and then walk it in?" Rowen suggested.

"Indeed. Come, dear niece," her uncle said, rising. "Come and see how bitter reality truly is."

They trundled her off to the stables, where her uncle took the lead, getting the guard to let him past and enticing a stable boy to hook up the family horses to the carriage that more frequently rested under cover than traveled the streets. He climbed into the driver's seat himself, driving their steeds out onto the herringbone patio. He paused there and let them get situated.

"Jack," Rowen said, watching the way Catrina's uncle slumped in the seat, "Perhaps you should help him drive?"

"Yes, Jack," Catrina agreed with a bat of her lashes, "Do help Uncle Gerald with the driving so we do not spill on our way down the Hill and die a most ignoble death."

Jack grimaced at her, but climbed out the window, clambering up beside her uncle and taking the reins.

Catrina waved her fan before her face. "Rowen, if you wished to get me alone, all you needed to do was ask ..." She peered at him over the edge of her fan, fluttering her eyelashes.

"For years people accused me of being clueless, Catrina. Clueless, vapid, egocentric, self obsessed ..."

She hissed.

"They believed that the way I obsessed over my clothes and hair showed that I cared little for anything else—they felt that I did not have the capacity for anything more than dressing well and looking a part—a part I was unworthy to play."

"Ugly people often think that way," Catrina said. "Pay such talk no mind. They are jealous."

"No, Catrina. They were right. I was a vainglorious sot. I had no true value in society except as a window dressing."

"Oh, Rowen, do not be so hard on yourself! You are a handsome, handsome man."

He rubbed his forehead, and, shaking his head, just stared at her. "But even as clueless as I was, I still had a more realistic view of the world than you do," he whispered. "I knew that Jordan would need rescue from the fate of being a Weather Witch. So I went to find her."

Catrina returned to fanning herself. She stared out the window, watching the fine houses of the Hill disappear as they descended into Philadelphia's Below and neared the Hub. "Yes, yes," she murmured, "truly a hero's quest."

"It was," he insisted. "Even though I arrived too late."

Catrina returned her attention to him then, watching him with renewed interest. "You arrived too late, you say?"

"Yes. Jordan was being loaded onto an airship, I was on horse in the courtyard below ... I have been told it was not meant to be."

She smacked her fan shut on his knee. "And I would agree with whoever it was that told you that. It was surely not meant to be if you arrived too late."

The carriage came to a halt.

He swept her fan off of his knee and stared at her coldly.

"Besides," she continued. "What horrendous fate were you truly rescuing her from?"

"I fear you are soon to find out," he said, exiting the carriage and reaching back in to grab her by the arm and tow her (less than courteously) out.

"Not far from here, my lambs," the uncle said with a grim laugh. "Not long until your questions are answered, your nerves are rattled, and your conscience, dear niece," he specified, tweaking the tip of her nose, "is given a hellish shake."

They tied the horses to a post and, Catrina's uncle leading the way, they followed in a silent single file line. Before a building bristling with metal poles and wires of varying thicknesses stood a pair of dour-looking guards.

Gerald swept his arms back to keep the group of them behind him. He put a finger to his lips and said around it, "No need to disrupt them from their duty. There is another way inside." He signaled them around the side of the building and they shadowed some shrubs that softened the austere image of the Hub. Around the building's side was a smaller door, this one unguarded, poorly lit, and with nothing but an unremarkable doorframe, bowed metal handle, and hinges to mark it as a door. Simple and obscure, it was the entrance they needed. Gerald loped across the break between bushes and wall, and leaning against the wall, waved them forward as he turned to open the door.

They slinked inside, bumping into one another as they closed the door tight behind them.

"This is quite unsavory," Catrina whispered.

Rowen shushed her and, realizing her hands were on him yet again, peeled her off and held her wrists in his hand.

She seemed not to mind.

He thrust her hands away and jabbed a finger toward the dimly lit area ahead of them.

All around them water sounded. Water, running in thin rivulets along the seams of the building, glimmering in strands at all the places where walls met floor. Water, dripping down walls in shimmering threads of moisture. Water, hanging far above from the ceiling, illuminated by stormcell crystals wedged in the rock walls, and waiting to plunge to the floor where it spattered to bits or became one with a puddle.

Water made their footsteps louder and their words carry, echoing in the dark, dank building. Water hung in air so thick Rowen imagined it might be pierced with blade or bullet. They tiptoed down a slender corridor, Catrina's dress making a soft whooshing noise as its hem wicked up moisture and its broad skirt rubbed along the walls.

Her uncle led the way, Catrina behind him and obviously unimpressed, Rowen following her and wary enough for them all. Jack brought up the group's rear.

Rowen may have visited the Below many times, but not even he had come to the Hub.

Her uncle stopped and Catrina sucked in a breath in surprise. Peering over both of their heads, Rowen could see ... something.

Long lines like strings—no, heavier, like rope; no, slicker than the fiber of ropes ... cables. Cables ran like snakes from holes in the ceiling and down the only wall Rowen could easily see, then hung in a giant web-work that seemed to focus on the room's center—a spot just out of sight ...

Rowen adjusted his position, pushing against the wall to peer around the corner. He barely stopped himself from gasping at what he saw there, in the room's center, hanging from the coalescing cables.

Suspended, his bare feet inches from the floor, was a man. His shirt and pants stuck to his thin frame with the damp and his thin gray hair was plastered to a head bowed so deeply his bearded chin rested, wet, against his chest.

They all jumped when he spoke, in a strangely dry voice considering his surroundings. "Step forward," he said, lifting his head the slightest bit so his eyes, squinting against the dark, met theirs.

They stood even more still than before, hearing his command.

"Step forward," he repeated. "You had the gall to come here, have the guts to see your choice through. Come. Get a good look. See what magick brings!"

Gerald looked at Rowen and took a long step forward, staying with his back nearly to the wall. Catrina looked at Rowen, her mouth agape.

He put his hands on her shoulders long enough to march her forward.

"Ah," the hanging man whispered. "And what has brought you here this"—he rolled his head on his neck and closed his eyes

—"evening? Were there no grand galas on the Hill to attend? No soirees?"

They stood silent, dumb.

"Answer me. You can at least do me that one small kindness as you gawk at me, displayed here to feed your every need with the power I call down from the heavens."

Rowen cleared his throat. "It is important she—" He swallowed. "Important we all know ..."

"Is it then?" the man wondered aloud. "And when did it become important that the higher ranks know what Witches do? How we ... live?" His voice cracked on the last word and he coughed and then fell into a fit of laughter, his cables swishing in midair and rattling against the walls.

"It became important when I realized my friend was going to be one of you," Rowen admitted.

"Ah. Yes. Another's plight never really matters unless it impacts you directly. Predictable," he scoffed, and let his head hang again. "Go. Take a look. Stare, giggle, and wonder. I shall educate you as I do others."

They continued to stare dumbly.

"Ask me my name," he challenged.

Rowen stuttered out the words: "What is your name?"

"I am *the Hub*. My given name ceased to be important when I was connected here—absorbed here. Now I am nothing but the energy I provide. Nothing but the location that possesses me. Ask me another question," he demanded.

Jack spoke up. "Why the cables?"

"Ah. They've become clever here—more efficient. The Hub used to require two Witches, most often the most rare of all kinds —a mated pair. The energy had to be more than just one type. It had to be complementary."

Rowen choked at the thought. "A mated pair," he repeated lamely. "Witches who were husband and wife?"

The Hub laughed, a dry sound like autumn leaves rattling in a slow spin. "Two Witches may not marry. It is not permitted."

"Like being a priest," Gerald muttered.

"A Witch might only marry if the ceremony is performed before he or she is discovered to be a Witch," the Hub clarified.

"So they were—"

"Lovers."

Jack shook his head.

"But lovers, especially young lovers, are volatile things. After a few ..." the Hub paused, his eyes rolling up as he searched for the word, " ... incidents, mated pairs were found to be too dangerous. So key members of the Grounded learned to more efficiently milk the power from individual Witches through the cables. We breathe, we expend energy. It flows out of us like our breath. And now it all is collected. A Conductor must think about his or her ship nearly every minute of every day. They must focus to keep a ship aloft. But now—I eat, I sleep, it matters not what I do because the power is all leached away from me regardless."

A cable attached to the side of his head swayed, a rat slowly bouncing its way across the line toward the man's head. The Hub did not even twitch but watched them watching him. "Now go home, go back up the Hill and forget again."

"No," Rowen whispered. "How could we forget?"

"The same way all the others do."

*Aboard the Artemesia*

Down the hall Jordan went, scouring behind each unlocked door, inside every armoire and trunk, and beneath each bed until she was nearly at the end of the hallway. She rested a hand on the wall and yawned, only then realizing how her exhaustion at lack of sleep had been building in steady increments. She sighed, wishing in part the game was over, but wishing even harder she'd found her two companions.

It was then that the ship whispered to her.

She straightened, craning her neck and focusing her ears to catch the strange noise. Perhaps it wasn't the ship at all but ...

Meggie?

As if a scene floated before her, Jordan saw the child crouched behind a stack of trunks in a different room than any she'd searched. A bigger, grander room. And, perhaps strangest of all, she felt a single word fill her brain: up. She shook her head to clear it. Up? That would mean Meggie had taken the elevator. But that was nearly impossible as she had been told quite firmly to stay on tis single floor.

So Jordan ignored the strange and nagging sensation and checked the remaining rooms.

Oddly, she was not surprised when she failed to find Meggie in any of them. Frowning, she headed for the elevator. Stepping inside, she was faced with the bank of buttons. She chewed her lip, staring at them. She wanted to be done with this game—to be done with all games. And then she saw it. A faint glow emanating from the number five.

She pressed it and felt the elevator lurch its way to her unplanned destination. The doors opened and, stepping out, Jordan had the distinct feeling she should turn right. So she did.

She found herself pausing outside one particular door after trying none of the others. Placing her hand on its knob, she gave it a twist and stepped inside. There in the corner where three traveling trunks were stacked one atop another, and shaking her head, she lunged around the back of them.

Meggie shrieked in a mix of surprise and delight, hopping up and down on her feet and exclaiming, "You found me! You found me!"

Jordan merely nodded, perplexed, and grasped the child's hand. "Shall we find that troublemaker Caleb?" she teased.

"Oh, yes!" Meggie squealed merrily.

This time Jordan paused, wishing the game was over and that Caleb was found just as fervently as she had wished the same with

Meggie. But there was no image in answer, no sensation to point her on her way.

It only worked with Meggie.

The next twenty minutes were full of tedium that Meggie evidently felt none of, bounding as she did from door to door and jumping into each and every room to shout, "Surprise! We have found you!" with the same fervor she'd shown the first time.

Finally, having exhausted all the rooms on the floor, the pair stood staring at each other.

And then they heard it.

The sound of music being played.

On a pianoforte somewhere on the floor above.

Could no one follow her instructions?

"Caleb!" Jordan shouted, grabbing Meggie's hand again and towing her to the elevator. They bounced up a single floor and, stepping out, were surrounded by the lively sounds of a intricate tune just right for dancing. They followed the sound to its source —a grand cabin with a divan, a padded chair, a low and ornately carved mahogany table, wide bed, and a pianoforte—being played more passionately than it had probably ever been played before.

Caleb rose off the bench—playing the whole time—and exclaimed somewhat apologetically, "I got tired of waiting to be found! I decided perhaps I might speed the process ..." He winked at them.

Jordan grinned. "It is a most welcomed way to end a game of hide-and-seek," she admitted. "Although neither of you remained on the same floor as I requested."

They did her the courtesy of briefly looking ashamed.

"This is a grand apartment," Jordan added, and then her heart sank, realizing where she was. Hate bleeding from her eyes, she turned on him. "These are his apartments, are they not?"

The music stopped. He nodded. "He is dead, darling girl," he said as if it was assurance enough. "You must know that. In your heart. He is dead and gone, Jordan."

That did not stop her knees from turning to water and letting her crumple to the floor.

Caleb rushed to her, joining her on the floor even through she flailed her arms at him, hissing. And Meggie dropped to her knees—doing the only thing she could to help. She dropped Somebunny and wrapped her tiny arms around Jordan, hugging her so fiercely Jordan felt her strength and hope biting through the haze of pain and betrayal.

Philadelphia

The Hub laughed. "Do you think you are the first to come through that door in the back? Do you believe it was just luck—an oversight—that it was not locked? It is all design, boy, all part of a grand and wicked design. You are not the first to see the human heart of the Hub—you are not even the first tonight!" he hissed. "You won't remember. You can't."

The rat paused by his ear before boldly climbing up the dome of his bald head where it rested, sniffing the air, its hairy, segmented tail sweeping down across his forehead and cheek before it turned to face the group of them.

"Yes, yes, I can remember," Rowen snapped, stepping forward. "Because I can do something about this. Then I'll remember," he promised, stepping closer, "and *they'll* remember," he dragged a crate over, "and you," he grabbed a cable, "will *certainly* remember."

The rat screeched, scurrying away as Rowen gave the cable a twist. There was a popping noise and the cable fell loose, slapping against the wet floor and slithering back toward the wall. Rowen barely paused, noting with satisfaction that the man did not bleed but tried to drag himself away from Rowen by grasping the other cables.

The Hub hissed, "Stop," his eyes wide and fearful.

"No," Rowen insisted, his hands making short work of the

cables connected the man's head like some strange corona. "You are frightened—understandable." He barely paused at the two thicker lines that coiled out from the man's temples like the horns of some mythological ram. He stripped his legs next, letting the seams along the outside of his trousers fall closed against his thighs and calves once more. The man lowered inch by inch as the cables and tubes holding him aloft fell limp. He whispered to Rowen, his voice strained and frightened, urging him, begging him, to stop, to consider the repercussions ...

The lights in the room dimmed, pulsed, and began to flicker. "Stop," he whispered, his voice fierce. He thrashed against Rowen, but Rowen held his ground.

Jack said, "Rowen ... mayhaps he's right. Mayhaps you'd best stop ..."

A few tubes and cables remained, connected to the sides of his ribs, and Rowen lifted the mildewed shirt and pulled them free as well.

"Ro ... wen," Jack repeated, the word emerging slowly, the syllables so far apart it seemed they were two words instead of one.

The glow of the lights pulsated again.

The last cables ran in a line along the outside of the man's arms, running from triceps to forearms. Rowen flung an arm around his waist and pulled the rest of the lines free.

"No!" the Hub shrieked, falling out of the tangle of cords and to the wet floor with a slap. Shaking, his hands ran the length of his arms, feeling the flaps in his flesh where the cables had been inserted.

The lights fluttered like the wings of a dying bird, and he screamed, "You do not understand the repercussions ...

"You will kill them all," he gasped, staggering to his feet and reaching for the cords that hung, limp and lifeless, near him.

"What, kill who ... ?" Rowen hissed, grasping the wobbling man.

His hand was slapped away, but Jack slipped onto his own

knees beside him, throwing an arm under him for support. With a grunt, he hefted the Hub to his own knees.

"Them," the Hub hissed, pointing. "God, for the naïvety of youth and wealth," he whispered, snatching at the cables before he collapsed again in Jack's grip, cables slipping free from his trembling hands. "My legs, nothing works," he whispered, terror in his voice.

He was as useful as some child's discarded rag doll, his skin resting on bone and veins, much of his muscle mass gone from hanging inert for so long. "You will be the death of them all," he cried, stretching with one arm to sweep a hand toward the cables that remained dangling overhead. They were all out of his reach.

Rowen followed his crooked and shaking finger to a group of mildewing newspaper pages hanging on the wall. Each featured a headline reading something like: "Girl Loses Hand in Steam Explosion" or "Baby Rushed to Hospital After Illegal Steam Power Experiment Goes Wrong." But the largest article was about a child named Wally who was horribly burned—his face disfigured beyond recognition—while playing with a steam-powered toy cat.

"They are hospitalized ..." the Hub whispered, reaching out to Catrina for help. For compassion. "It is my power—my energy —that keeps them alive ... Help me ..."

Catrina stepped back, jaw hanging slack. She shook her head, disgusted.

"I would let you all rot in darkness," the Hub spat. "Every one of you," he admitted, "except for *them*. How can I wish children and babies dead?"

Rowen stood frozen.

Gerald rushed forward and joined Jack, bending awkwardly down to loop the Hub's arm across his shoulders. With a groan, he looked to Jack, then Rowen, and he began to lift.

The lights wavered again.

"Hurry," the Hub begged. "Reconnect me. Help me keep them alive."

"Rowen, goddammit. Help us here," Jack snapped.

Rowen blinked and rushed forward, taking the man's weight so that the uncle could slip free. He stumbled along the room's edge, looking for something. "Uh," he muttered, grabbing the wooden crate and towing it back underneath where he needed to be suspended. "Up. Get up on this," he instructed, grabbing one of the man's legs and lifting.

Together they hoisted him up, and the man reached out and snatched a cable, shoved back the fabric of his sleeve and tugged back the skin of his forearm with equal disinterest.

Rowen looked away as the first of the multitude of cables was inserted. The Hub snared another, and another, Jack reaching up and out to help, watching and matching his actions, twisting each into the sockets cut in his flesh until the lights steadied and they were all connected once again.

Rowen grabbed the final cable, hooking it into the Hub's wrist.

His hand flexed, curling closed and opening again.

And yet, Rowen thought, it was not true movement. He would never truly move—never truly live again.

Spread eagle once again, his limbs pulled wide and wires, cables, and tubes making up his wings, he leaned back in the nest of wires, threw back his head, and gave the most satisfied sigh Rowen had ever heard. The lights glowed on again, growing stronger and brighter with every breath the reconnected Witch took.

There was a rattle behind the Hub and they drew back, slipping back the way they'd come as the front door opened and the guards stomped their way inside, growling out questions:

"What the bloody 'ell's 'appening back 'ere?"

"Damned lights flickered off and were out citywide for nary a full minute. That cannot stand ..."

"People'll start to complain, they will, and blame us. Why'd you not fix the Hub when you reckoned there was a problem, they'll ask."

They came to stand in front of him, not noticing Rowen and his crew standing so close in the shadows and trying so hard to keep their breath light and their presences concealed.

"Fix 'im," one chuckled. "Aye, but we did," he added, swinging a staff at the Hub's groin. "Right when we knew there was a problem—a distraction, was she not?—fixed 'im but good."

Rowen's jaw went slack, realizing.

The guard's staff poked at the Hub's groin again. "Make sure you do not again let the power or lights slip, you fool," he warned.

The Hub only pulled his head back up straight, regarding them with indifferent eyes.

They began to leave, but the other guard paused, noticing the misplaced crate. "Damned rich kids," he muttered, kicking the crate back to the wall again. "I think we'd best lock the back door now we know they're getting so bold. It's the rich 'uns are willing to come in poking and prodding, what might happen if some crazy hears and gives it a go? Might try and kill him."

The other guard nodded. "Or free 'im."

"Worse yet. I'll go around and lock the stupid thing," he said, jingling the ring of keys on his belt.

They marched back toward the building's front, the door closing behind them.

Jack grabbed Rowen, tugging him toward the back door and escape.

In a minute they'd be locked in.

But Rowen went the other direction. Toward the Hub.

"Rowen," Jack growled.

It was to no avail.

Rowen addressed the Hub again. "Your distraction ... you were part of a mated pair but ..." he whispered, brow furrowing. "Their fix ... And then the cables ..." He shook his head.

The Hub smiled at him, a pained, but honest smile. "Young lovers are the most difficult," he whispered sadly. "And the most passionate and powerful."

Rowen raked a hand through his hair.

Jack reached out and grabbed his elbow, yanking on him. "We must go now."

But the Hub's words made them all pause once more. "Perhaps you will remember, after all. Perhaps this once you will remember."

They turned, running back the way they had first come, the Hub laughing behind them. Down the dark hall they went, Gerald leading, then Jack, Rowen, and Catrina, her heels clomping on the stone floor.

Gerald pulled up short at the door, signaling them all to silence, and they skidded and bumped into each other. Gerald tried the door, but instead of a rush of cool night air greeting them as the door opened to freedom, the temperature seemed to rise, the compressed humidity making the hair on the back of Rowen's neck sticky, and he watched as Gerald's shoulders slumped. He turned back to the lot of them, his expression drawn.

"My sincerest apologies, lads. It seems we've been locked in."

Jack smacked the heel of his hand into his forehead. "And now?" he asked Rowen. "Now we've tried to educate the lass, but it seems we're about to be schooled. How do you suggest we make our escape?"

Rowen ran his hands through his hair and groaned.

"I'd suggest out the front, were I not in the company of a wanted criminal," Gerald said, shooting a look at Rowen.

Rowen just sighed. "You're right. We can't go out the front. Because they will surely notice me."

"Hush," Catrina said, straightening and brushing off her cloak. She tugged the hood up onto her head so that its hem rested on the crown, the hood falling slack on either side of her face. "You may be highly noticeable, dear boy, but you are in the presence of far more memorable people now." She glanced at Gerald. "Surely you and I can get the lot of us out by distracting two highly uninterested and overworked guards."

Gerald snorted, his eyebrows rising. "We are, most certainly, far more memorable than two shabbily dressed men who slouch more often than they stand up straight.”

Rowen straightened so fast it was as if Gerald had spoken in his mother’s voice.

Gerald’s mouth rolled up on one end, curling into an uneven smile. “Slouching is a good thing in this case,” he corrected Rowen. “Though, in consideration of your future posture, I would suggest that once we are safely in the carriage and safely away that you endeavor to never slouch again.” He turned back to address his niece. “So how shall we do this? Me, weaving and inebriated—”

“—it is always best to act out what is your natural state,” Catrina said with a sniff as she smoothed the leather of her gloves.

“So you will play a harping shrew?” Gerald asked without skipping a beat.

Catrina’s lips puckered. “I will be the beautiful diva who is less than impressed by the social inadequacies of her family,” she corrected.

Gerald sniggered. “Well said, child. Well said. What a pair we make.” He pushed past Catrina and led the way, waving a hand over his shoulder toward the rest of them. “Remember, lads, slouch and stay quiet and in the shadows.”

Jack shoved Rowen. “Wonderful idea this was,” he muttered. “Wonderful way to teach someone a lesson. What lesson have you learned tonight, eh?” he prodded.

“That you talk too much,” Rowen retorted, rolling his shoulders forward and slumping enough that he began to feel it in his lower back nearly immediately.

Past the Hub they went again, slinking along the way the guards had gone. Down a hall studded with stormcell-lit pierced tin lanterns, their spotty glow dotting the trespassers and casting strange shadows on the opposite wall.

They came to the building’s front, a pair of broad wood and ironwork doors marking the main egress. Gerald placed his hands on the door, looked over his shoulder, and whispered, “Here we go, lads—" and he shoved the doors open with the most hideously accurate caterwaul of drunken confusion Rowen could imagine. "Ohhhhh," he cried, stumbling out of the doorway. Turning around to face Catrina, he flailed his arms wildly and nearly fell. "You thought it'd be a bloody good time seeing that hanging man and saying that I'll—" he stuck a finger up in the air as if telling her to wait, and stretched his mouth wide to await a belch, but only a hiccup came out instead and he continued, "—damn, I thought that would be far more impressive ..."

"Is that not what that girl you've been courting says about most everything you do?" Catrina scoffed, pushing past him. She placed a hand on his shoulder and made a move as if to push him over, but the guards stepped forward.

"Eh! You there! What are you doing inside the Hub?"

Catrina's face wrinkled in a clear show of disgust at being addressed by someone so obviously below her station, and Jack and Rowen slipped quietly by while Catrina and Gerald made enough noise for more than the four of them. "What were we doing? What do our kind do at the Hub? We come in the back, we snoop around, we joke, we poke the Witch, and then we go home. Back up the Hill."

Gerald was laughing so hard, he nearly toppled over. "Oh, lads, I daresay you'd best not tangle with a Fourth of the Nine! Not with Miss Catrina Hollindale! She will have your hides to make her new heeled boots!" he laughed.

The guards exchanged a look.

"Fourth of the Nine," Catrina said with a snap of her gloved fingers.

Standing in the shadows of the high hedgerow, Rowen thought hers was a move that would have made most men act like the dogs Catrina likely thought they were.

The guards stepped back, one even politely closing the door behind the mismatched pair of wealthy guests and muttering, "Begging your pardon, milady."

The other was not so gentle. "Look here, you. You tell your

little friends up on the Hill that the freak show at the Hub is now closed. None of your type need risk themselves in the Below to take a poke and a gander at the Hub. Tell them if they have questions about the things what happen here they best go ask their mum and dad—same as they would 'bout the birds and the bees. No need to come snoopin' no more. The fun is over."

Catrina pouted, tapping the toe of her shoe on the flagstone entryway.

"Over," the man repeated, rolling the word out with a menacing growl at its end. "Now get yerselves gone." He waved a hand at them and Gerald broke into a rolling giggle that would surely make anyone in earshot think he was either completely skunked or insane.

Catrina's hand snapped out and snagged his arm, dragging him along. He took a few weaving steps, swatting at her to free himself. Straightening, he pulled at his coat (only dragging it further from straight) and tugged at his cravat, letting it flop loose.

He stumbled after his niece, and the group of them disappeared beyond the boundary the high hedgerow marked and together they raced to the waiting carriage. Gerald bounded up to the driver's seat, snatching the reins up as if he'd never done anything but drive a carriage.

The rest of them barely seated inside, the door still hanging partly open, the carriage jolted forward and the horses pulled it toward the crest of the Hill.

Rowen looked from Jack to Catrina and back again before he and Jack burst out laughing.

# Chapter Fourteen

How glorious,

and yet ofttimes how painful,

it is to be an exception!

—ALFRED DE MUSSET

*Philadelphia*

"You must admit," Jack choked, "the Hub was correct. We will all most surely remember that experience—every bit of it!" He rolled back in the soft seat, laughing. "You," he said to Catrina. "Brilliant. He may not like you, and I may not like what you did to Jordan, but that—that I liked."

Catrina smiled and tilted her head in a rare show of modesty. "And what did *you* think, Rowen? You who he says do not even like me?" she asked. "Are you glad that I saved you from capture and imprisonment—perhaps even death?"

Rowen leaned back, stretching an arm across the back of his seat, and appraised her levelly. "Yes, I am glad—I am thankful that I am free. Because it means I can soon return to the *Artemesia*."

"And Jordan," Catrina concluded.

"Yes," Rowen agreed. "And Jordan."

"And is Jack right?" she whispered, her eyes narrowing as she observed Rowen. "Do you truly not even like me?"

But he refused to grant her an answer, instead turning his face to the window and, as they sped past in a blur of stormlights and vague memories, stared out at the spots of the city of Philadelphia he was far more familiar with than a young man of his rank should have been.

Back at the Hollindale estate, the carriage and horses hidden, Rowen confronted Catrina one more time. "I will not stay here, Catrina. I do not love you. I … I love Jordan."

"You dumb ass," she hissed. "You need not say that—do you think I do not know that now?"

"Then you must let me go."

"I am as ready to do that as you are ready to let Jordan go," she muttered.

"That I will never do."

She stomped and screamed at the floor, throwing her arms into the air in a sudden fit. Catching her breath she smoothed back a few stray wisps of golden hair back into place and fixed her eyes again on Rowen. "Exactly. I will not give up on you either, Rowen. Do you know why?"

He rolled his eyes. "It certainly is not because I have sent mixed signals regarding my intentions …"

"Because I know people change, Rowen."

"I will not change."

"A couple is made of two people, Rowen. It only takes one of them to change their mind, changing things for both. Has Jordan not changed?"

Jack jerked away, thrusting his thumbs into his belt and studying the house's architecture with sudden fascination.

Catrina's eyes darted after him and she smiled what Rowen thought had to be the most wicked smile he had ever seen. "She has changed," she whispered. "A great deal, I take it."

"Because of what you threw her into," Rowen hissed, feeling

the way his lips curled, pulling back from his teeth. It was surely an unattractive look, but he hoped it was equally threatening. "You threw her to the wolves, Catrina. You are what nearly killed her. You," he stressed. "Without you she would have never been hauled away to Holgate. Without you the Maker would have never gotten to hit her, strike her, cut her.

"Give her money back—I want no part of anything she has touched," he said, glaring at the floor.

Jack hesitated, the money still clutched in his hands, and Rowen slapped the pouches, sending them flying so they hit the floor and skid, spilling bills, coins rolling loose to wobble and roll in awkward circles before collapsing flat with a final rattle.

Catrina dropped to her knees with a whine, scooping the money up and pressing it back into the open mouths of the bags.

"Do you understand now, Catrina? No matter how Jordan has changed, no matter how difficult things are between her and I, no matter how our story ends—whether together or apart, whether comedy or tragedy," he assured—"I will never feel differently about you than I do right now." He shook his head and Jack stepped up to him, resting a hand on his shoulder. He shook it off. "I do not love you. I cannot like you ... I hate you, Catrina. I *hate* you. For what you did to Jordan and, selfishly, because of what hurting her did to me."

Catrina tightened the cords running through the bags' necks, and stood, quivering. She stepped up to him, her hands reaching out for his own shaking arms, reaching out imploringly for his hands, now balled into fists.

Jack stepped between them, warning, "Do not. We should go." He wedged himself between them, placing his back to Catrina. "We must go. *Now.*"

Rowen nodded. "Yes," he said from between clenched teeth. "*Now.*" He was first to turn toward the exit. He led the way to the door, hearing Jack close behind. He reached for the doorknob, but Catrina's voice stopped him as his fingers closed on the cool brass handle.

"Rowen."

He stiffened at the sound of his name, and straighting, he slowly turned back to face her, the hurried noise of her heels clattering their way across the marble floor as she raced toward him.

She held the pouches out to him. "Take the money. Just take it," she insisted. "Hate me all you want." She shook her head. "I cannot change what I did nor how you feel. But in this cause—abolition—we are united. I want to see slaves of all colors and kinds freed. It is the way the world shoud be. The way it *must* be. So take the money. Let me help people. Let me show that, whether you are mine or hers, that I do want to be a person who helps others. That I am a person who wants to change the world. For the better."

Rowen grunted and watched darkly as Jack crossed the distance to where Catrina stood, her eyes holding the ghost of hope.

*Aboard the Artemesia*

That night the nightmares were worse, like something of the captain lingered on Jordan even though he was dead—even though she felt no sense of him in his rooms or on any belongings. He was dead everywhere else in her nightmares.

She ran, he chased her. She was cornered, he found her. He grabbed her wrist even as she tried to slap him, holding her hand before her eyes, useless. And then she noticed how her fingers flickered when she stared at them—flickered and changed in number. She had four fingers, then seven, then a bushelful ...

Something inside her shifted. Woke. This was not reality and not memory. This was only a dream. *Her* dream. She focused on her ever-changing fingers and held the fact in her mind. This was merely a dream. And the captain, who had no power in the waking world, should have no power here either.

Suddenly free of his grip, she gave a shout, and hit him. Hard.

He flew backwards and she took a step, out of the corner he had driven her into, and into the light. She raised her hand again. Around her feet a breeze grew and played, making soft sounds. Amid her flickering fingers she felt lightning flutter and course. And then the world flashed white and hot and the only thing left of the captain was a mark where a small but of ash smoldered and smoked before being whisked away by the singing breeze.

She had evaporated him.

Eradicated him.

She stood on the *Artemesia's* deck having destroyed the last bit of him holding sway over her by using the very power he thought made her a slave.

She woke.

For a while she listened to her own breathing; she concentrated on the feel of the bed beneath her and the soft and normal noises of a ship groaning and whispering—singing in its peculiar way—in flight.

*Her* ship in flight.

Her stomach growled and she sat straight up in bed, her hand on her rumbling tummy, and she realized that, although she was certain she had been hungry since being aboard the *Artemesia,* this was the first time she had *felt* the hunger. This was the first time she wanted to eat. The first time she truly wanted to go on. To go forward. To fight for something more than simple, desperate survival. Untangling herself from her bedsheets, she jumped into her dress and raced Topside to satisfy the rumbling like thunder in her gut, grinning like an absolute dolt the entire time.

An absolute dolt just beginning to live again.

*Philadelphia*

Jack nodded as they slunk out of the shadows along the tall wall, recognizing the way they had come. "This is it," he whispered, the words coming out more question than fact. Rowen clenched his jaw and led the way, slipping through the gate, around the end of the massive home and into the expansive backyard. Jack prepared to lope across the garden to the pod, but Rowen grabbed his shoulder and held him back, squinting at the rambling house, part fieldstone and part brick. "I must see someone inside," he apologized.

"You must be joking," Jack muttered, examining the house himself. "This is the Astraea estate, aye?"

"Yes."

"Are you certain they actually remain on the premises? They were found Harboring, so would they not ..."

Rowen shrugged. "Old Morgan Astraea was of decent rank but he was of even finer finances. He would not leave the family home unless he had lost far more than rank."

"And you must talk to *him*?"

"No," Rowen said, "most certainly not. But I must talk to his wife. Reassure Jordan's mother."

Jack rubbed his brow. "The woman who brought him down?"

"It was not like that," Rowen grumbled. "Jordan was Morgan's offspring as sure as a sizzling summer day is long. And ... I am not sure it should matter if she was not. They have been husband and wife forever. And he certainly has not always been an easy man to live with."

Jack sputtered. "So if Jordan is not Astraea's he should still keep the wife?"

Rowen groaned. "I do not know. I know decidedly little about everything right now," he admitted, glowering. "I only know keeping Jordan will always be what I choose over losing Jordan."

"You are a stronger man than I."

Rowen shrugged. "I am merely a man in love. There is more strength in that—in love—than I ever expected."

"So you must see her mother."

"Yes. Jordan will ask after her. And she should know her daughter lives."

"You did not want to see your own mother ..."

"The fact you question that decision only proves you have never met the woman," he concluded softly. "Distance is best for now, I think."

Jack sighed. "If I knew my mother, I would want to see her—know her," he mused. "But she wanted none of me, so..." He shrugged.

"I am truly sorry for that," Rowen said.

"Eh, it is no great loss," Jack claimed. "Men grow up without mothers or fathers—or in my case without mothers and fathers—all the time. We still turn out well enough if we put our minds to it."

Rowen nodded agreement. "Shall we?"

Jack shrugged. "If you think we will be welcome ..."

"Lady Astraea is one of the most gracious hostesses in all of Philadelphia. She would even welcome the Pope!"

"Bold words. Lead on!"

They were not far inside when a maid spotted them and ran the opposite direction.

"You know her?" Jack asked, fingers flexing at his side.

"No. And her reaction is not a good sign ..."

"You think not?" Jack quipped.

"We had best hasten our way to Lady Astraea. She will straighten things out." Rowen jogged down the hall, ducking his head into open doorways as he went, Jack behind him.

They found Lady Cynthia Astraea as the staff found them.

"Interesting," she drawled, draped across a delicately embroidered divan. "Rowen. And you've brought a friend."

"Lady Astraea?" Rowen asked, realizing she looked like Jordan's mother—well, very nearly—but the way she sat and spoke ... It was as if he faced a stranger.

"If memory serves," she rested a hand on her chest and her

eyes flickered and seemed to change a moment, "there is a substantial reward offered to whoever turns you in …"

Together Jack and Rowen took a long step back.

Lady Astraea raised her hands over her head and slapped them together. "Gather them up!" she called.

But a young woman stepped forward, saying, "No, milady." Her eyes nervously darted to Rowen as if she sent him some message with the glance. "I am sorry, but I do believe it is your bedtime …"

A broad-shouldered older African man with salt-and-pepper curls shoved his way through the group and, looking at Jack and Rowen, shouted, "Go! Go now!" and he leaped onto Lady Astraea, covering her mouth with a rag.

Her eyes rolled back in her head and with a shudder they closed, and she sank down on the divan, unconscious.

Rowen and Jack spun on their heels, running back the way they had come. Out the mansion's back, past the well-manicured gardens and into the hedgemaze. With determination born of desperation they turned their pod around, shoved it to the slate stairs at the edge of the great granite hill on which the Astraea property sat and, jumping in, had just enough time to snap their buckles before the pod tipped nose-first down the staircase with a horrible grating noise and spread its wings, gliding over the rooftops of the Below and searching out an eddy to carry it higher.

# Chapter Fifteen

Take the whole range of imaginative literature,

and we are all wholesale borrowers.

—WENDELL PHILLIPS

*Aboard the Artemesia*

Tsu complained, "I thought we were going Topside."

"And we shall, lovely girl, so we shall," the Wandering Wallace assured. "But first I need to procure a few pleasant distractions for our friends upstairs. We will be in Philadelphia soon and must look the part, yes?"

She nodded.

They wandered down the hallway, Tsu following obediently as the Wandering Wallace tested cabin doors, popping them open and sticking his head inside. He scanned each room, looking for the little details that told him this was a prime spot to hunt. A beautiful trunk, an elegant pair of shoes, a well-cared-for carpetbag... He stepped all the way inside, opening the door wide to encourage Tsu to follow.

"Here," he said. "This is a good spot to try...." He immediately went to a trunk setting at the foot of the room's cot. It was nicely painted, with very few scratches or dents in its wood. The leather handles retained a subtle suppleness to them that was often lost with time, and the locking mechanism was highly polished brass. "Lovely, lovely ..."

"What are you doing, Wallace?"

"Shopping," he said, glancing over his shoulder at her. He crouched before the chest and tried the lid. "Hmmm. Only good things are kept inside locked trunks, do you not agree?"

She smiled and headed to the cot. Pressing down on its thin mattress with her palms, she tested it for give. Then she sat and crossed her legs, allowing one knee to peek out of her silk robe.

The move did not go unnoticed. He winked at her. "Lovely, lovely," he agreed. "But there is no time for such niceties," he complained, "not so near revolution."

He reached into his sleeve and withdrew one of the many small tools he regularly carried. He slipped the tip of it into the lock's hole and wiggled it, listening. The tumblers clicked and the lock popped, releasing, and allowing him to open the lid wide.

"Ah, ah, ahhhhh," he said, pulling out a shawl. And another. And one more. He unfolded each, laying them across the foot of the cot to display their fine designs. Flowers, birds, and frippery. Next came fans, each of elegant design. He snapped them open then hopped to his feet and made a show of fanning her. "Adjust your kimono, dear pet, or I will be constantly fanning us both—the sight of you warms me so I might start to steam."

She giggled and rolled her legs onto the cot, coming onto her knees. "Kiss me," she whispered, leaning toward him.

But thinking of the fox in the other room—the fox that had been far more than a fox—he pulled away. "Come, come," he commanded, scooping the shawls into his arms and closing a fan to tap her teasingly on the tip of her nose. "We must prepare our friends for this most amazing journey into Philadelphia. They will need guidance, surely, and I will need you, dearest, to stop tempting me into other things."

Pouting, she murmured, "Of course."

"Beautiful girl, there is much to be done—an entire world to conquer." He winked, and exited, certain she would follow shortly.

It only took a moment before he heard her feet hit the floor and she was beside him.

They emerged Topside, he with an arm looped around her. "Look, look, look," the Wandering Wallace proclaimed. He strode immediately to Meggie, who sat at her normal place on the Topside dais—not so close to Jordan as to get accidentally stepped on, but not so far away from her to not be able to see and hear precisely what she was doing. She glanced up at him, a smile spreading across her face immediately.

She set down the jacks and ball.

"Look what we have returned with!" the Wandering Wallace shouted, whipping the shawls out before him, their fabrics dancing as if they had lives of their own. He rushed to Meggie and dragged one around her neck so that she giggled and snatched it from his hand, and then he tossed one across Jordan's shoulders and threw another high into the air before it drifted down, settling on Maude's lap.

Behind him walked Miyakitsu.

Bran pulled up short and squinted. She still seemed somehow different from the Wandering Wallace's companion he had thought he had grown used to seeing. Somehow odd. Yes, her outfit was the same, from her kimono down to her shoes and socks—Maude smacked his arm, seeing him watching Miyakitsu —perhaps it was just the jewels. But her body language was slightly ... stiffer? As if she had not truly stretched for a very long time, or as if her muscles remained cold and tight even on such a warm day.

"You are staring at her. Again," Maude hissed.

He widened his eyes and scooted closer to her on the deck.

Slipping his arm around her waist, he pulled her tight to his side, moving so that his lips nearly brushed her ear as he said, "There is something different about her—don't you see? Something strange …"

She reached up and placed a hand flat on his face, playfully pushing him a few inches away.

But only a few inches.

She puckered her lips and rolled her eyes. "There is something strange about you," she teased.

He winked at her but he dropped his volume, going more and insisted, "I am serious. There is something wrong with her. Something about her makes me uneasy."

The Wandering Wallace was fanning Meggie as she chased him around the dais, the child laughing more and more with every step she took. As he teased her he also instructed. "There is a language to fans," he called, dodging her grasping hands. "Your fan may speak for you when you would rather not say a proper word."

"Like a secret language?"

"Very much like," he agreed.

"Show me, show me!" she shouted, grabbing for the fan again.

"No, no imp, this one is mine," he said. "Is it not magnificent? Here," he added. "This is an appropriate fan for such a grabby little monkey...." He handed her a far more simple-looking fan.

Meggie pursed her rosebud lips in disappointment, watching the Wandering Wallace's fan with a hunger in her bright eyes.

"Now," the Wandering Wallace said, demonstrating. "Rest the fan on your right cheek...."

Meggie did so.

"That means *yes*." He switched the side of his face that he set the fan on and said, "And this is *no*."

Meggie mimicked his moves, utterly serious.

Bran's attention wavered from the two of them, noting how Maude subtly copied the moves as well. He had never seen her sporting a fan. As a previous member of Holgate's staff, he would have wagered that she fanned herself with her hand or anything else that was nearby. Or perhaps she adjusted the neckline on her blouse ...

His eyes drifted to her bosom, and he swallowed hard, imagining Maude dappled with sweat and soft and warm beneath his touch ...

He tore his eyes away and whistled a sloppy and nervous tune before refocusing his attention on Meggie and the Wandering Wallace.

"Cover your left ear ... That tells your friend not to tell your secret."

Meggie nodded solemnly.

"Ah." The Wandering Wallace turned his attention to Bran and Maude a moment and adjusted his fan so that it half-opened across his face. "*We are being watched.*"

Meggie copied the move, turning briefly to peer at her parents before she spun back to the Wandering Wallace.

"Or," the Wandering Wallace said, "twirl it in your left hand and you say the same thing. *We are being watched.* And we still are," he added with a laugh.

Even Jordan had paused at the ship's helm to watch the Wandering Wallace and her favorite passenger.

"I see you staring at my marvelous fan," the Wandering Wallace teased. "Keep your monkey paws off it," he said, giving a derisive snort.

Meggie growled, declaring, "I am no monkey!"

"No, that is true—you seem much less monkey-like when you growl ... More like a troll," he mused. "And trolls may not touch my fan either."

Bran's opened his mouth to comment, but Maude touched his arm in a way that said, *Wait.*

The Wandering Wallace snapped his fan shut. "That is one you should know," he said. "It means, *I'm jealous!*"

"I am *not* jealous," Meggie said, stomping a foot.

"Then perhaps you'd rather learn to say, *I wish to be rid of you!*" He closed the fan and touched the tip of it with one finger.

Meggie snarled and stomped again, her eyes never leaving his fan.

A breeze stirred around her tiny feet, making the hem of her dainty dress wiggle.

"Or," the Wandering Wallace drew the fan through his hand whispering coolly, "*I hate you?*"

The breeze grew, wind twirling around her and pulling her wispy pale hair up and out on her head.

"Or," he opened and closed the fan quickly, "*you are mean!*"

Maude's hand tightened on Bran's arm.

The bag that was never far from him, the bag with Sybil's tiny skull inside, began to twitch.

This was a test.

Bran shifted, ready to stand and stop whatever the Wandering Wallace was attempting, but Maude held him.

"Let it play out," she urged.

A snarl rose out of Meggie, merging with the wind and then, with a rumble, the wind reached out and tore the fan from the Wandering Wallace's clever hands and thrust it into Meggie's hand, beside the smaller, less elegant one.

Meggie gasped, looking from it to the Wandering Wallace and back again.

The bag grew still as the skull inside it should have always been and Bran felt Maude's body pressed to his, muscles tight in anticipation and wonder.

By the ship's wheel, Jordan Astraea, Stormbringer, frowned and turned her back to them all. She ran a hand through her short dark hair and stood for a moment as if stuck in thought. Then she seemed to shake it off and reached out to the ship's large wooden wheel, and adjusted it.

But inside the Wandering Wallace's mask's mouth, Bran glimpsed the curl of a smile, and his gut grew heavy as his heart fell into it.

There would be no hiding Meggie's powers until she learned some self-control.

Aboard the Artemesia

No message birds came that day but Jordan assuaged the crew's fears by pointing out the depth of the cloud cover she'd cast. Sorry to deceive them, all she had to do to get past the sorrow was remember how delighted the Wandering Wallace looked when he realized Meggie's abilities.

No one should go through what she had, of that Jordan was certain. Surely not a child. So she had edged them away from the course the Wandering Wallace wanted and kept the clouds thick and the wind at their back strong.

They would arrive at another port soon—one away from Philadelphia and any risk of the Maker being recognized. One where the Maker, his lover Maude, and little Meggie might start fresh. Then Jordan promised herself she would turn the ship southeast.

And go to war.

With Meggie hidden among the Grounded population.

It was as she sat with them, dining—tasting everything—that the clouds ripped apart.

The pod was not as graceful landing aboard the liner as it had been leaving the other one, Jack and Rowen scraping a long stretch of the deck. Jordan minded not a bit how gouged the wood looked—it could be repaired. But seeing Rowen emerge— she stopped eating (which seemed to surprise Caleb and the others as much as when she'd ravenously started).

She wiped her fingers on a linen and stood.

Not a word got past her lips before Jack burst from the pod, shouting, "Why the hell are you so far west? Have you decided Pittsburgh is the way to go rather than Philadelphia?"

Jordan froze, her heart stampeding in circles through her chest.

She set down the napkin.

The Wandering Wallace leaped to his feet, chair falling back with a clatter, and he stared at them both in equal shock.

"Oh, shite," Jack whispered, "she's taken you off course without you knowing."

The Wandering Wallace leaped across the table, grabbing a knife and a Weather Worker's lead and shouting, "Correct our course!" as he grabbed for her.

She knocked him back with a sharp wind, lightning menacing in the clouds above so brightly it seemed the ship sat directly beneath the noonday sun.

The Wandering Wallace paused then, watching her.

She licked her lips, glaring at him and daring him to stop her.

Rowen asked, "Why?"

Jordan faced him, words at the ready.

But the Wandering Wallace jumped and got the collar around her neck. A clasp clicked shut by her jaw and the world fell away from her. Standing dazed, knees weak, vision blurred, her skeleton seemed only as strong as a thick pudding.

The lightning overhead flickered and failed. The world tumbled in to crush them in darkness and for a moment everything was still. Everything was hushed.

Then the clouds peeled away from them and sunlight speared through and illuminated the awful truth: they were falling.

Everyone grabbed for a railing, a post, the ship's wheel, even the chair still bolted grimly to the deck—anything to keep from flying free from the deck.

The Wandering Wallace wrapped his legs around the post holding the ship's huge crystal heart in place and held tight to Jordan's lead.

"Evie!" Rowen shouted.

Evie, one arm wrapped around a railing, flung out her other its fingers flaring out, and her head bent back as she called clouds to the falling ship.

To *both* of the falling ships.

Struggling against the natural desires of gravity she slowed them.

Jordan blinked, everything before her in muted colors, movement slow, the world wobbling. Even so, she knew slowing two falling airships was much different than *flying* them.

"I cannot. Not both!" Evie cried, her eyes wide.

"Cut the *Tempest* free!" the Wandering Wallace shouted.

But, her hat gone and her red hair flying up like a fiery tornado, Evie shrieked, "Never!"

Meggie, strangely calm in Maude's heavy arms, looked at Jordan, pinning the ship's Conductor down with her brilliant eyes. Somebunny clutched tight, its ears waving wildly by her own, Meggie said to the Wandering Wallace, "Let Jordan go."

Evie screamed her agreement. "If you intend to make Philadelphia—if you intend to *live*—unleash her!"

"Damn it!" the Wandering Wallace shouted, "The child, Meggie ... dear poppet," he tried. "You could ..."

Jordan managed one word from her thick-feeling tongue: "No."

The Wandering Wallace screamed, too, frustration ripping the words into meaningless syllables. There was a click and the collar fell away from her neck again.

She was solid, she was whole, and she was angry.

Thrusting both her hands up, Jordan clamped down on the drifting clouds and threw them under the bellies of both ships. There was a whine and a booming groan shook the heavens and the *Artemesia* and *Tempest* shuddered to a stop, slapping the rest of them against the deck before the ships hung in midair, like the most pregnant of pauses.

Jordan looked at each of their startled faces. "The child," she began, her voice shaking. "And the Maker and his woman—they should not go into Philadelphia. He will be recognized. She will be taken ..." Words failed and furrowing her brow she looked down at the pitted and scarred deck. She laced her fingers together before her and stared at them, her lips pressing together before she worked the last of her explanation between them, "I cannot let that happen."

Bran pulled Meggie and Maude to him. Tilting his head, he squinted at Jordan. "You would risk the success of the revolution —for us?"

"For *her*," Jordan clarified, looking at Meggie. "I am no captain in this revolution. Revolution will come when it must, my involvement changes nothing."

The Wandering Wallace shook his head but Jordan put her hand up.

"But as the captain of this ship I can change a few lives."

Rowen grunted. "You do not give yourself enough credit. Leave them aboard the *Artemesia* under heavy guard. We will make sure they are safe."

She studied his face, the faint worry line between his eyebrows that was a recent addition, the promise in the set of his jaw. She nodded. "I trust you."

Something flashed in his eyes and she looked away.

The next word caught in her throat. "Philadelphia?" she asked softly.

"Philadelphia," came the stern reply from the Wandering Wallace.

With a grunt she shoved past him. "You will not take the city as yours alone," she hissed. "You will share power."

"Yes," he said.

"You heard him. You all heard him," she said. "Hold him to it." She stepped to her dais, adjusted the ship's wheel, and announced, "To Philadelphia."

*Aboard the Artemesia*

The next day the birds again found them at noon.

It was as they soared just outside Philadelphia, Jack and Rowen reworking their pod and rebuilding a few of the smaller lightships that had attacked them a week ago, that the Wandering Wallace let loose with a lengthy string of curses that ruffled the feathers of the nearest birds.

Miyakitsu was immediately at his side, her necklace and bracelets sparkling.

"What is it?" Jordan asked, seeing he held a slip of parchment in his hands. The government supported news stories.

He shoved it into her hands.

"Young Terrence Malloy was found burned nearly to death as the result of playing with a steam-controlled cat. His house a complete loss, both parents dead, the boy is doomed to be a social pariah with scarring covering both face and body ..." Jordan swallowed hard. "Poor boy," she whispered. "Do you know him?"

The Wandering Wallace shook his head. "After a fashion," he whispered. "I would wager there is no Terrence Malloy."

"What?"

Rowen and Jack set aside their tools, and the rest set down their diversions, too, to see what the fuss was all about.

"Ten years ago I *was* that boy. Only it was not the cat's fault. It was the man who came to collect the cat. By force. He set everything on fire as my parents slept upstairs. I lost everything. Everything," he repeated. "And now they are recycling the story to keep the populace in fear ..."

Rowen cleared his throat. "It is not so simple."

The Wandering Wallace asked, "What do you mean?"

"Does it say anything else?" Rowen asked Jordan.

"Due to the heroic efforts of doctors and nurses at the hospital, the boy lives, powered by stormcell mechanisms."

Rowen looked down. Then he began to explain the Hub and his motivation to keep powering the city, all for the sake of suffering fictional children.

This time when the Wandering Wallace let loose with obscenities, he included words in languages Jordan had never heard.

Perhaps because sometimes there were not the right curses in just one, she supposed.

Watching him storm away, Miyakitsu at his side, the others drifted back to what they had been doing before until Jack announced, "I think it's time we train everyone in more advanced fighting."

There were nods all around, and Jack and Evie spent the next twenty minutes working with everyone Topside.

And then, getting more serious yet, Jack called for Stache to run them through additional moves.

# Chapter Sixteen

*Aboard the Artemesia*

They stood there a long moment, hands on the rails of the *Artemesia*'s bow, looking down on the city of Philadelphia as they tested their masks, slipping them on and adjusting the ribbons that held them in place.

To Bran they looked more like the attendees of some slightly out-of-fashion soirée than the instigators of revolution, but perhaps on the eve of the Boston Tea Party someone had had a similar thought. And that had all turned out well.

Except for one man who was knocked unconscious.

And except for King George becoming so outraged he passed the Coercive Acts.

Which led to the War for Independence.

In which approximately 100,000 men between both sides wound up either dead or wounded ...

Yes. Bran drew down a breath.

Yes. That had all turned out *very* well ...

The sun was lowering over the western hills and lights were beginning to rise in the homes and storefronts all the way from the docks, where wary fisherman and warehouse workers unloading lumber ships prepared to work late into the night, through the sprawling Below, where soon raucous laughter and drunkenness would spark parties, and up the Hill that sparkled like a carefully coiffed and classically constructed beacon to high society.

"For all its faults," Jordan whispered, "this is my city. Be gentle with it," she implored the Wandering Wallace.

But Bran could see his eyes were fixed on a spot near the foot of the large hill—on a building draped with wires and cables and crowned with more wires and tall metal posts than any other.

The Hub.

"This is how it begins," the Wandering Wallace said, his voice softening.

"Yes, and it must be now," Jordan specified, removing her mask once more. She pointed to the clouds gathering at nearly the same altitude as their ships to begin the scheduled city rains. "As in most large cities, rain is scheduled. We are graced with cloud cover."

"Are not modern sensibilities wonderful?" Marion rolled his eyes.

"There were advantages to knowing when rain would fall," Rowen murmured. "No romantic strolls were ever ruined."

Maude shook her head. "Did you never get caught in spring rain with a lover?" she asked. "Or surprised by the booming of thunder which made your heart skip?"

Rowen shook his head.

"Jumped in puddles as a child?"

They all looked at her.

"Or kissed in a summer rain burst?"

They were mute, watching her.

She laughed at them. "Was I the only one raised near the

Fringe—where weather did not abide anyone's wishes or act according to any man's design?"

Bran took her hand, enjoying the warmth of her touching him. For a moment he was transported—no longer standing Topside on the brink of revolution—he was somewhere even grander, and she was all he saw. This was it, he realized, this was being moved by emotion—being lifted by love. "You must show me all of that," he said.

She beamed at him and squeezed his hand.

"Take me to him," the Wandering Wallace said, his voice thin.

Miyakitsu slipped an arm around his waist and leaned her head on his shoulder, cooing.

"Take me to the Hub," the Wandering Wallace insisted. "We will start this revolution with a strong dose of truth."

Jordan nodded. "A novel idea. So we will dock; you will ride to the Hub with Stache, Miyakitsu, Evie, and Marion; Rowen and Jack will fly ahead then meet the human allies as the army of mechs marches from the landing point," she took a breath and then added, "the Maker, Maude, and Meggie will remain under guard here; and Caleb and I will keep the home fires burning?"

The Wandering Wallace nodded. "Until I call for you. We will march as one to the Council. And your parents will be there."

Jordan raised her head, surprise in her eyes.

Rowen reached out and rested a hand on her shoulder. Not Caleb. Rowen. And she let his hand stay and reached her own up, capping his with it. She held his hand that way, so tightly her fingers ached.

Nearby, Caleb smiled.

"Do we need our fans and finery yet?" the small voice of Meggie asked.

The raven's head turned to her. "Not yet, darling child. Once we secure the city, make things right with the Wildkin, and are safe ... Then we shall have a grand celebration," he assured, leaning over to tweak her nose so that she tittered with laughter. "And you ladies will need fans, finery, and fabulously feathered hats."

"And you men?" she squealed.

"We shall dress in our most colorful waistcoats, our sleekest jackets, and tallest hats. We will polish our boots and pocket watches and practice our dancing."

"And I may attend?" Meggie asked.

"Of course! You and Somebunny will receive a beautifully handcut invitation," he assured. "Everyone who has helped shall attend!"

Meggie cupped her hand around her mouth and whispered, "But I have an early bedtime."

"Perhaps, this once," the Wandering Wallace said, "your mama and papa would allow you to stay up—overthrowing an unjust government is cause for later bedtimes."

Bran lowered his head, preferring the view of the city sparkling below to the man spinning out tales for his daughter's delight. "Count not your chickens before they are hatched."

"These chickens will not only hatch but they will fly like eagles," the Wandering Wallace promised.

Jordan pulled the clouds together, stitched them up tight, and brought the ships in to land under the cover of falling darkness, knowing the city lay blind on this night with rain so regularly scheduled.

*Aboard the Artemesia*

After the others disappeared belowdecks to ready for attack, Jordan remained Topside, easing the ships closer to a docking point. She stood at the bow of the ship, looking over its edge and down onto the city through a narrow hole she'd pierced in the cloud cover.

Nearly as blind to the city as it was to her approach with the press of dark storm clouds between them, Jordan proceeded forward by feel, feeling the tallest spires and rooflines brush her cloud cover as a cat might identify its surroundings with its whiskers.

Clock towers, bell towers, the tips of turret rooms and high-set balconies, her most outlying clouds teased past them all, and combed through the Hub's lower stormclouds. She felt each teasing touch and knew each place the way water learned a building's architecture by raining over it and dripping into every crack and crevice.

She shivered as they burst through the heavy veil of her clouds, screeching, wings churning the air with a sound like thunder. And Jordan knew them instantly, feather by feather. She swallowed and approached the perching owls, her jaw set, stride determined. Reaching out to each and, slipping the key ring off her hip, she opened the canisters attached to their legs and withdrew the messages.

Holding the curling paper stacked between her fingers and thumbs, she read them, then read them again.

And again.

This was not good.

She tucked the slips of paper up her sleeve and unwrapped a ribbon from around her head. Easing back to the owls, she wrapped the ribbon around the rail and threaded it through their leg bands. Knotting the ribbon, she securely tethered the trio.

They would not carry their message any further, instead she would carry it to the Wandering Wallace.

She ran a hand over the nearest owl's head and made her way to the elevator. With a stomp, she summoned it and rode it down to the Wandering Wallace's level.

He came to his door, masked again, now a raven, black and iridescent feathers and purple, black, and blue ribbons trained back from his brow and trailing down onto his shoulders and into a thick, short cape.

Perhaps not masked again, but still. Perhaps he was always masked.

"What?" he asked, inserting his fingers into the eyeholes to rub the bridge of his nose.

"Owls have landed Topside."

"Owls."

"The Wildkin are making their way north. An army of them," she whispered. "It's war."

"We are so close ... But war ..."

"We dare not wait any longer. We must make our move now. March now. The Council will still be in their chambers. They do not dismiss on rain days until the skies clear and the downpour stops. They would not risk their outfits getting damp."

"Gather the troops, don the masks," he agreed. "We do this *now*."

*Aboard the Artemesia*

The Artemesia had turned madhouse as the final frantic preparations for revolution were made. Still, in the thick of things, Rowen paused before her, goggles hanging around his neck like some heavy, exotic necklace, the pod he and Jack had taken before into Philadelphia modified with an open cockpit and sitting with its nose hanging off the edge of the deck, a gun bolted to a swivel post inside.

Jack was buckling up, but Rowen—he was watching Jordan with a focus that made her shift her weight from foot to foot. "We will land and unite our human troops with the mechs and march on the Council. I will not see you again for ..."

" ... a while," she agreed. "Perhaps at the Council. Perhaps north of here. When at war," she added. She blinked and put words to the fear she felt. "Perhaps not again."

"No," he insisted. "We may not see each other for a while, but we will see each other again. I will not lose you again and you will never be free of me," he promised, stepping forward. His boot brushed the side of her foot and he slowly reached his hands out to her and rested them lightly on her waist.

The weight of his hands, the size of them, the warmth of them—she felt it even through the fabric of her dress. It was a touch and a moment so intimate it made what she could feel through her clouds pale in comparison. Her heart hammered in her chest and, licking her lips, she looked away from those changeable eyes of his, focusing instead on his broad shoulders. "You will find me again?" she asked so softly he leaned in to better hear.

"Yes. And I will not wait nearly as long as this time." He pulled her a hairsbreadth closer to him, but even such a small move—in a presence so large as Rowen's—made it hard for her to breathe. "But you must promise me something as well ..."

Jack cleared his throat.

"What would you have me promise?" she asked, slipping her hands up to rest on his shoulders. She peered up at him from beneath her eyelashes.

His voice deeper, thicker, he said, "That you stay smart and stay safe. As you once told me, take no unnecessary risks. Do nothing in which the cost outweighs the reward."

"Is that all you require? That on the eve of revolution I look out for myself more than for others?"

He groaned and his hands walked around her waist until they rested on the small of her back. "I am a selfish man, Jordan. A needy man. And no, that is not all I need of you before I go. There is one last thing, Jordan Astraea of the grand airship *Artemesia*."

She could not help herself but the edge of her mouth curled up, cutting into her cheek to create a dimpled smile. "And what would that be?"

Jack cleared his throat again. More loudly.

Out of the corner of her eyes, Jordan spotted Evie moving toward the pod and Jack. She paused by the open cockpit, watching him with a soft smile on her face.

"Just one, little thing," Rowen guaranteed.

Jack cleared his throat so loudly it seemed he'd swallowed a growling dog. But the sound was squelched when Evie leaned into the cockpit and kissed him. Hard.

Jordan blinked and returned her gaze to Rowen, her eyes resting on his chin. "What?" she whispered, feeling the answer deep inside her. Her stomach somersaulted and her toes flexed against the cool wooden boards of the deck.

And when he kissed her she only rebelled for half a heartbeat, fighting the swell of panic with the authority of logic. This was Rowen. Rowen who had done his best to defend even the memory of her honor. Rowen who had journeyed to free her and in the process lost his best friend since childhood. Rowen, her far too willing but always too late hero.

Opening her eyes, she let Rowen's image push back the ghost of a far lesser man like sunlight forcing back shadow. And she kissed him back, melting against the firm press of his lips and running her fingers up his neck to slide into his thick blond hair.

She let him pull her closer so her body crushed against his and she struggled to catch her breath, and finally pulled back, watching Rowen's half-closed and glittering eyes.

Evie had stepped back from Jack, and Jordan realized that all eyes on Topside were pinned to her.

Everyone was smiling.

She blushed fiercely, stammering out, "You had better go. And now." Her fingers slipped back down his neck, and he shivered. Her hand rested on his chest, palm flat, and she was reassured as his heart thudded as rapidly as hers.

"Yes," he rasped. He took her hand in his and swept it to his lips, giving it a gentle kiss before releasing it. "I will see you again. And soon. I swear it."

Then he loped across the deck, slipped into the cockpit, and buckled the belts around his body. He pulled his goggles into place before reaching out to the swivel gun mounted above Jack's headrest.

Stache, Marion, and the Wandering Wallace stepped over to the pod's back and, counting to three, shoved it overboard. For a moment it whistled, shooting straight down, and then the noise of the wings popping open reached Topside and Jordan breathed again.

Topside on the *Artemesia* began to empty as many of the rebels vaulted over the makeshift crosswalk to the *Tempest*. When the last of that crew was aboard the two ships separated, Evie taking back her command to land the smaller ship and release the army of automatons waiting inside it.

*Aboard the Tempest*

There was a dull crunch as Evie set the *Tempest* down near the Western Tower. She winced and ran a soothing hand over the ship's rail. "I'll make sure you're all patched up and right as rain," she assured it. "Soon."

The mechs waited at the bottom of the ship, just inside the doors and standing in neat rows, their arms at their sides, their eyes glowing nearly as strongly as the soul stones in their chests.

The ship's door opened with a groan, slapping against the wet grass beneath it and under cover of graying and drizzling skies, the mechs marched forward, their orders clear. They would meet Jack, Rowen, and his friends at the crest of the Hill. Not far from the Astraea estate.

*Philadelphia*

The mechs making their slow and steady progress toward the Council, the Wandering Wallace's small band headed for the Hub. With no sense of ceremony, Stache kicked down the back door and the group of them pressed into the hallway, rushing forward to face the hanging man.

"What are you doing here?" the Hub cried.

"Delivering the first of many doses of truth," the Wandering Wallace said from behind Stache, Evie, Marion, and Tsu.

"No one is to be here anymore," the Hub growled. "Leave before I summon the guards."

But Stache and Marion moved aside and Evie leaned tight against a wall, allowing the Wandering Wallace to step between them and forward, into the spotlight. Such as it was.

Evie and Tsu lingered in the hallway, Stache and Marion skirting the Hub and moving down the hall behind him to secure the other door. Or deal with the guards more directly. It did not truly matter.

"You are free," the Wandering Wallace announced. "The Council, the newspapers—they have lied to keep you and your kind enslaved. But that time is at an end." He reached up to cut one of the man's many hanging cords.

"No, you mustn't," the Hub cried. "No, not again ... the children ..."

"There are no children," the Wandering Wallace soothed, "there haven't been in years."

"No," the Hub insisted, whimpering. "The newspapers ... the boy was so badly scarred ..."

"Yes," the Wandering Wallace agreed. "He was scarred in a purposefully set fire more than a decade ago. And he survived—in part to the lights and power your kind kept lit. But not the aid of proper doctors or nurses. The lights that saved him led him into the Night Market where a beautiful violinist took him in, healed him, and made him her son. But that boy is grown. And he is ready to change the world and free the Witches."

"No," the Hub insisted, his eyes sparkling. "The stories ... ?"

"Are recycled," the Wandering Wallace said.

"And the boy?"

"Stands here before you," the Wandering Wallace stated, slipping off his mask and hood to reveal his damaged face, "a man scarred but well. Very much alive. A man who has come to release you from slavery." He gave the first cord a twist and popped it free, then he slipped his arm around the waist of the dangling man.

"You are he the child in the old paper—Wallace?"

"Yes." He undid the next cord, and the next, accepting more and more of the older man's weight as his own as more of his supports—and his tethers—were pulled loose.

"Stop," the Hub still insisted, and the Wandering Wallace paused, looking into his lined and weary face.

"Why?"

"Leave me hang here," he said, shifting away and grappling with the remaining coils and chords. He wrapped one arm around a section of them and reclaimed some of his weight from the Wandering Wallace. "Let me leave in my own way. Let me make them deal with what's left of me."

"And what will you ... ?"

"Let me go. Step away and cover your eyes," the Hub commanded, and the Wandering Wallace knew from his tone that now was not the time to question. He covered his eyes but the blast of white light shooting free of the Hub's flesh bled through the narrow spaces between the Wandering Wallace's fingers, making him hiss and hunch against the biting glare.

A *boom* shook the small building and hundreds of small popping noises blended together inside and out like a mad chorus of crickets.

The lights throughout the grand city of Philadelphia winked out and, taking his hands away from his face, the Wandering Wallace knew the Hub was dead.

And Philadelphia was utterly blind and drenched on the night of his revolution.

The Wandering Wallace slid a small light free of his sleeve, one of few dozen he had Jordan fill with enough power to light one's path. Evie held another, as did Stache, Marion, and Tsu. The enemy might be kept in the dark, but the Wandering Wallace's people were prepared for anything.

He hoped.

He tugged the hood back on, adjusting the eyeholes in the mask so his vision was clear and sharp—the way any good revolutionary's vision should be on the night he'd change the world.



They left the Hub quickly, the guards unconscious, the doors wide open, and a third of the cords that connected the man who had given the Hub its life and power cut so no one else could quickly and easily take his place.

They ran until they found a carriage and, when they could not persuade the driver to hand over the reins peaceably, they hit him and left him curled by the road. Such were the sacrifices made during revolution.

One of Jordan's special lights hitched to the front of the horse's harness, they pressed hard for the Hill and the Council's chambers, the rain a veil, the air thick with the tangy scent of minerals. Behind them the sound of confused voices rose and spread as people realized there was no regular stormlight left glowing in the city.

The Wandering Wallace pressed the beak of his raven's mask to the nearest of the carriage's windows and peered out at the dark streets, only the gloss of rain-slicked cobbles and bricks reflecting light back at them. The carriage slowed, Marion picking his away along roads he wandered as a child—roads, much different in the dark. The Wandering Wallace curled his hand around the Grounding bar hanging above the windows and chanted, "Faster, faster," as if that was all that was required to get them to the Council's chambers.

Tsu leaned against his back, combing her fingers through the feathers and ribbons adorning his hood.

He closed his eyes and tried to relax beneath her gentle touch —tried not to think of the fox lying asleep in his cabin—the fox who was his Wildkin wife in every way but the legal ones. The fox who would likely never return to her human form and would never be able to act as his intermediary with the Wildkin who were now amassing their forces and swimming north along the coast.

The fox named Miyakitsu who held his heart and had been the beginnings of the doppelgänger who now rested against him, more comfortable than he felt he would ever be in her presence. She was, in nearly every way, an exact replica of Miyakitsu. Except for her memories and her knowledge of how she came into existence. Sometimes lies were the fairest tales to tell, he thought.

They turned up the sloping road that wound around the face of the Hill, and the buildings spread out, thin alleys first and then narrow swatches of yard and grass between them. Water pelted the windows and pulled the images of buildings down in long, tearful streaks, and he sighed.

The carriage faltered by the graveyard, grinding nearly to a halt before he heard the rattle of reins and the muttering of Marion. The wheels hissed through thin puddles and the carriage picked up speed, horses trotting, as if either Marion knew this road best of all or as if something dogged their heels. The Wandering Wallace sat up and listened. No noise of another carriage or cart came from the road behind them, no sound of more horses' hooves or men shouting at the realization revolution had arrived.

He switched seats, moving to the padded bench across the aisle from Tsu, and peered out the windows on the carriage's other side, looking down the hill and into the Below.

Down the Hill and toward the waterfront and the glinting waves beyond.

Although there were no stormlights, it seemed the Below was coming to life with torches—smudges of orange light glowed on his running window.

The Below was not legally connected to the Hub's power. The Below did not legally have access to city light and power.

But few things in the Below happened legally.

And the people living there were often the first to know when something had gone wrong.

And the first to speak out against anything that seemed a slight.

They were his mob-in-the-making. The flesh, bone, and very vocal backup for his mech army. If all went according to plan they would march on the Hill and be encountered by Rowen, his friends, and the mechs.

Jordan would make her presence known and, believing the Stormbringer prophecy, they would unite beneath her.

He hoped.

If they didn't all kill each other first, they would march on the Council and meet him shortly after he had persuaded the Councilmen to step down.

Without bloodshed.

He hung his head, resting it in his hands. So much depended on complete strangers—people he had never met and surely did not trust.

But he did not trust anyone easily.

"Soon," Tsu assured, leaning across the aisle to wrap her slender fingers around his wrist.

He pulled back from the window and clapped his hands around both of hers, letting his gaze travel up her body and land on the mask obscuring her face. The ornate lace mask she had fashioned—like those she'd made for each of the other women and even one for little Meggie—made her features seem even more foreign—even more beautifully mysterious. He sighed. "I believe it is time to set the next stage of our plan into motion."

He pulled a small box out of the waistcoat he had decided to wear on this most special of evenings. It was said one should dress to impress and he had taken every related precaution. He would most certainly leave a lasting impression on the Councilmen.

And the entire city of Philadelphia.

At the very least.

He opened the box and withdrew a finely wrought pocket

watch etched with curling vines and flowers. He attached the chain to one of his mother-of-pearl buttons and, holding it between he and Tsu, he opened it.

It was no ordinary pocket watch.

As he was no ordinary revolutionary.

If there could be such a thing.

The center of the clock's face was set with a large, flat ruby and the brass hands issuing from it lay still on the clock's face, awaiting his command. He pulled in a deep breath and, winding the watch tight, he set the hands and pressed down on the knob once, twice, three times.

He let out his breath, unaware he'd been holding it.

The carriage leveled out and he glanced through the window, shifting from one side of the carriage to the other as they made a final turn toward the Council.

A mile at most was left before his mettle would be tested. He watched the houses all along the final leg of their journey, waiting to see a door open. Waiting to see an important and well-dressed woman exiting ...

Two blocks from the Council's chambers he saw the first one and he leaned back in his seat with relief. A door had opened and, in the wet and the darkness, a woman stepped out, shambling down the stairs of her expensive home, a butler shouting behind her, following her with a parasol to shield her from the rain.

But she was impervious.

Focused only on finding her way promptly to her designated destination, she ignored the man, staring straight ahead, her path lit by the glow of the ruby ring on her finger.

More doors opened, more red pinpricks of light glinted in the dim of evening, and more women tottered out, making their way to the same place the Wandering Wallace's carriage was headed.

"Never have the ladies of Philadelphia looked more beautiful." His gaze dropped to something glimmering in the hand of a nearby woman who staggered along the road's edge. "Or so well prepared for winning a political debate."

The carriage pulled around to the back of the Council's chambers and Marion opened their door, his jaw set, face grim.

The Wandering Wallace hadn't noticed the heavy shadows under his eyes before. His eyes seemed sunken behind his mask.

Leaping down, the Wandering Wallace extended a hand to Tsu. She stepped daintily down the carriage's steps, smiled. She pulled out her fan and adjusted her kimono and hair.

Evie looked up and down the alleyway and adjusted her sword and guns.

"Perfection," the Wandering Wallace remarked in the direction of both of the women.

Marion looked at the Wandering Wallace as Evie and Stache stepped away to secure the door. "Ready?"

"Can we ever be?" He shrugged. "Take us in."

Marion nodded and followed after Evie, Tsu and the Wandering Wallace trailing them. There was the noise of a scuffle and the heavy clunk of something like crockery hitting cobblestones.

They stepped around the bodies of two Council mechs, the command stones popped out of their chests. Evie tossed them up into the air and caught them again. "Clear as day," she remarked. "Not a soul to them." She leaned over and opened the door with a grin and a bow, "After you," she said.

Inside, Marion waited for them, his breathing fast and shallow, his eyes on the room that opened up just ahead of them, his hand out behind him to stop them. Evie slipped around them to join him, and the Wandering Wallace listened, calming his own breathing to hear what was said just beyond his view.

"But why the devil are they here?" someone snapped.

Indistinct grumbling met the question and the Wandering Wallace's heart raced. He tapped Marion's shoulder and mouthed, "Who?"

Marion leaned forward and pulled back, whispering, "There is a line of mostly ladies ... and more keep coming."

"Excellent," the Wandering Wallace said, barely stopping himself from clapping his hands together. "That then is our cue, good friends." He dropped Tsu's hand, straightened his spine, threw his shoulders back and tipped up his chin.

Heart pounding, he stepped out into the large room, spared a glance to the ladies and two young men standing fine as ducks in a row, and he cleared his throat, saying, "I do think the appearance of such special guests would merit some explanation."

Councilman Loftkin stood behind the long Council table and, slapping his hand on its surface shouted, "Guards!"

But, no matter how long he was willing to wait, the Wandering Wallace knew no guards would answer the call.

His eyes wide in panic, Councilman Loftkin shouted to one of his peers, "Fetch Gregor Burchette and have him rally his men." Before Evie could reach him, the man had slipped out the door and begun a hard sprint down the street.

Evie spun to face the Wandering Wallace, but he raised a hand. "There is no need to chase him. Things are well in hand."

The Council's faces were a mix of stunned expressions, jaws hanging loose, eyes wide.

Clapping his hands together before him, the Wandering Wallace began to explain how things were about to change in Philadelphia.

# Chapter Seventeen

If one advances confidently in the direction of his dreams, and endeavors to live the life which

he has imagined, he will meet with a success unexpected in common hours.

—HENRY DAVID THOREAU

Aboard the Artemesia

"Right then," Jordan reported, swaying up and back on her feet where she stood, peering over the bowsprit and into the city far below. "The ship's in good order," she said more to herself than to Bran, Meggie, Maude, or Jeremiah, and more as a question than a statement— "Caleb and I shall join the others in the city." She knelt before a very worried-looking Meggie. "I'll be gone for a few hours."

The child pouted, her eyes large and moist, her grip on Somebunny fierce. "I do not understand why I cannot go," Meggie complained. "I have learned the same fighting moves that Stache taught the rest of you ..."

Jordan nodded. "I know," she said. "But I have a far more important job for you, dear one."

Curiosity bloomed in the child's face. "What?"

"A moment please, as I set things to accommodate my absence." She stalked to the ship's wheel, gave it a nudge to prove it was locked, adjusted the lever that controlled the position of the wings, and stood a moment, her eyes closing as her mind rolled in on itself and her thoughts became wind, not words.

The ship quivered beneath her feet in response and the cloud bank pulled in about them, thickening.

The stormlights on the corner posts glowed even more in contrast, casting a warm and steady glow across the glossy deck boards. Jordan nodded, seeing it was all well done, and leaned over Meggie who, with Somebunny at her side, had watched every movement the Conductor had made. "Will you watch my ship while I step away for a while?" Jordan asked, gently tweaking the child's plump cheek.

Meggie nodded, a look of great seriousness coloring her doll-like features. "Of course," she said. "I will watch her and take great care with her. And ... If ever I need you—"

"Oh, I do not think that you will," Jordan interrupted.

But Meggie shook her head. "If ever I need you—" she began again.

"All you need do is call," Jordan assured, pointing back to the ship's communications array and then tapping the thing she wore strapped to her wrist.

A thing Jack had devised to ease mobile communication over distances. It was heavy, but nearly as pretty as a bracelet.

Meggie nodded and Jordan tousled her hair, smiled at the ever-present Maude, and, going with Caleb to one of the light-ships Jack had fixed, she stepped aboard.

Caleb started the craft, and Jordan wrapped her arms around his waist and smiled as they launched in the direction of destiny.

*Philadelphia*

The angry sounds of men and women on the march were music to Rowen's ears. He saw the blaze of torches minutes later and looked at his friend, Kenneth Lorrington. "I expect this moment is best suited to your talents," Rowen said.

Kenneth nodded and moved forward to address the crowd that had stopped, grumbling and pointing to the long line of mech soldiers. Mech soldiers stacked five deep.

"My good people," Lorrington shouted, waving his hands for quiet. "We are gathered here to greet you as our brothers and sisters."

"Brothers and sisters?" someone shouted. "You treat us like bastards, you rank-riddled skunks!"

Rowen winced at the words and rested his hand on his sword's pommel.

"Not true, my dear friends ..."

"Friends?" another voice called. "How are we friends when you built this city on our bent backs? On our sweat and struggles? Tell us how we are now friends!"

The bodies in the crowd shifted and the grumbling became louder. Angrier.

"Shite," Rowen whispered. This was not going as planned. Or even well. And if Kenneth, who was known for his eloquence, could not quell a murderous crowd and convince them to join their cause ...

This called for drastic measures.

Like honesty.

Rowen stepped around him and gave a shout, "You are right!" he shouted. "You are absolutely and unequivocally correct! You have been stepped on, you have been used and abused, and it is because those of great rank do not respect or even understand the contribution of your work."

The crowd quieted, torches hissing in the rain that had turned to a drizzle now, smoke trailing up from the flames. From the back of the mass of people someone said, "Who the hell is that? I've heard that voice afore ..."

And, "Is that Rowen Burchette?"

"Damn my eyes—did they not catch him after he killed that

prick, Lord Edwards?"

The volume of muttering rose.

"Damn fine service he did us, ridding us of that pompous ass," someone else declared.

Another in the crowd turned on them, warning, "Treason—Lord Edwards was of rank! Burchette was caught dueling."

"I heard he was drunk."

Rowen sighed, but held his ground and widened his stance.

"I've drunk more'n me share with Rowen Burchette!" a deep-voiced man said with a laugh. "He's a good man—for a ranking man!"

Rowen began to open his mouth and begin again—there were few better introductions when facing down such a crowd as that, but before he could get words out someone else had shouted, "I was there! He got into the duel because he was defending a Witch!"

The crowd grew so quiet the only noise Rowen heard was the pounding of his pulse in his ears.

He closed his eyes for half a heartbeat and, gathering his courage, squeaked out, "Yes." He cleared his throat. "Yes," he said more firmly. "Yes, I defended the reputation of a dear friend. A dear friend accused of Witchery."

The crowd was expressionless, waiting.

"And I would do it again!" he shouted. "For as much as you have been crushed beneath the heels of the Philadelphia Council, the slaves—African and Weather Witches both—have been used even more cruelly! They slave with no hope for a better life, with no rest but death itself! I have been to Holgate where the Conductors are Made. I have seen the scars marking their bodies and seen the pain in their eyes—the pain in their souls ... And I know that, as much as your situation, must change! We must abolish not only slavery, but also the rank system! We must make Philadelphia as they once said, *A city upon the Hill*! We must abolish inequality—and that is why we are here tonight my friends, my brothers, because the change must start with us. Here.

Now. We must be brave. We must rise up. We have a chance like no other. Now. But only if you join us! We can only succeed if we stand united!"

It was as if the crowd had stopped breathing and, his speech at an end, Rowen caught his breath, his eyes scanning the crowd for some sign of emotion, for some clue as to what they thought.

Kenneth had slunk back toward the mech army, watching as fiercely as Rowen did.

"How do we know we will win— How do we know you won't screw us?" someone sneered, "Like the rest of your rank is wont to do?"

Rowen again began to speak, but he clapped his mouth shut, hearing the hum of a familiar engine in the cloud-pocked air above. He pointed, a smile dragging up the edges of his mouth.

The crowd turned its eyes to the sky, watching a small light-ship descend.

Steering it was a much-scarred young man who Rowen had come to respect, if not quite fully trust. He was still too handsome to be fully trustworthy, he thought with a silent groan. But behind Caleb stood the most beautiful woman in the world.

Straddling the craft was Jordan of House Astraea.

She sparkled, her short hair standing up like a sparking crown of thorns, her fingers snapping out lines of lightning far superior to any fireworks display ever seen. A black lace mask covered the upper two thirds of her face but did nothing to cover her wild and shining beauty.

The craft circled the crowd, Jordan bending down over the small ship's side to brush her fingers with the ones reaching up from the crowd for just a touch of her potent power.

The clouds trailed her like a dark and glittering bridal train, their edges deckled like fine lace. And she was all at once the most beautiful and most terrifying thing Rowen had ever seen.

That was how he again knew it was love he felt. Because only real love was as lovely and as terrifying—as awesome in the most truly traditional sense of the word—as what he felt at the sight of her.

And Rowen raised his fist into the air, feeling the ship zip nearby and, opening his fingers, he too felt the warm and promising brush of hers, and he shouted, "How do you know we shall not fail? Because we have the Stormbringer on our side!"

It started as a rumble, and Rowen caught his breath, the sound new to him as it grew in volume and became a roar.

Rowen stumbled back, his eyes searching the crowd and finding—acceptance? Enthusiasm. "Holy shite," he said under his breath, realizing he'd stirred and inspired the crowd needed to carry them forward with mere words—words that focused them on the task at hand and made it inevitable that their cause would win the night.

And change the world.

Revolution was as difficult as he had feared.

But he would make it work.

Just as he readied the words he needed, the most beautiful and vexing of womankind spoke above the roar of the crowd, above the purr of the engine and the distant rumble of thunder, and proclaimed, "This man," she pointed to Rowen, "defended my honor when no other would. This man searched for me, fought for me, believed in me when I could not believe in myself—when I was too broken to believe in anyone or anything. This man is my hero and tonight I will loan you my most handsome and steadfast hero and he and his men will lead us to victory! Tonight we will change the face of Philadelphia. We will begin down the hard road to true equality! Tonight we join as a family should! Tonight we band together with no rank to blind us from each other's abilities and we march on the Council to support our forces there and our voices will be heard!"

And the roar of the crowd became deafening.

The man burst in on them, his Council robes flowing, his face red and out of puff. "Lord Gregor," he hissed between breaths, bending at the waist. "Come quickly—raise the troops ... The Council ... Rebellion ..." He was wheezing now, words failing, so he pointed weakly toward the door.

Their city lights had gone out some time ago, but Gregor, being a clever military man, had maintained a few stormcells in reserve. Unruffled by it all, he mentioned it was all likely just the result of Councilman Loftkin having some sort of tantrum.

Again.

Lord Gregor Burchette got to his feet, his dining companion, Lord Morgan Astraea, rising as well. The two men exchanged a glance and said, "Rebellion?"

The Councilman nodded frantically.

"Hats and coats, I suppose," Gregor snapped at a staff member.

"And canes," Morgan added. "I have not known a rebellion where someone later did not regret a poor choice of clothing and accessories."

"Indeed."

Together they headed for the door, grabbing the items they requested as they rushed outside.

"Will you raise the guard?" Morgan asked.

Gregor shook his head. "You know as well as I do that rebellion is warranted. Frankly, we should have arranged it ourselves."

"Rebellion is a young man's game. Even prearranged rain makes my joints ache now," Morgan muttered. "The thought of organizing a rebellion would send my back into spasms."

Gregor seated his hat firmly on his head with a nod of agreement. They pulled themselves into a waiting carriage that was both well-guarded and well-horsed and, one of the few perks of being the city's military leader, and therefore at the Council's beck and call. Gregor smacked his cane's head on the ceiling. "To the Council. And swiftly." As the carriage took off, he looked at his friend of many years and smiled.

"Just who do you think is behind all this?" Morgan asked, peering out the carriage windows at the dark city beyond.

"I cannot be sure. But if it is well-planned and well-organized, I do hope our children have stepped up to take a part in it. Perhaps this is something they might excel at—something besides looking smashing and throwing lavish parties."

"I have reason to believe there is hope that Jordan at least is involved. And you are correct. They have long needed something more suitable to spend their time doing," Lord Morgan said. "The number of times I wasted good staff watching them *sneak away* into the Below ... God. I do hope if they are involved they have arranged all this more carefully than their supposedly secret rendezvous."

"Let us hope for that as well as their safety, regardless," Gregor said.

"Amen," came Morgan's stalwart reply.

*Philadelphia*

In the Council's chambers, the Wandering Wallace paced in a long, slow oval before the Councilmen's table.

"I firmly believe it is in your best interest to do as I say," the Wandering Wallace said.

"What?"

The Councilmen looked from one to the other, but then their eyes returned to their wives, well-dressed women standing unnaturally rigid, their faces turned straight ahead and slack—devoid of stress, fear, or pain—devoid of any expression at all.

"They will do whatever I tell them to—of this have no doubt. If I wish ..." He made a dramatic flourish with one hand, ending the gesture pointing to the line of stoic women. "Ladies, your knives? Please produce them."

Out from the folds of each lady's gown she drew a gleaming dagger and held it lightly in her fingers, showing it as playfully as if displaying a recent acquisition of jewelry to a friend.

An automaton-like stance was taken by all wearing the bright ruby rings the Wandering Wallace had secretly sent as seemingly harmless gifts, whether the Councilmen's wives or a handful of others, including a single Wraith and Lady Catrina Hollindale. In sharp contrast to their body language, not far from the Councilmen and leaning like recalcitrant schoolboys, stood Mikah Vanmoer and a second sleeper in a body also not her own.

Lady Marsham peered out through Lady Astraea's eyes, her body language, with her lounging attitude and the brazen tilt of her hips far different than that of Jordan's mother. Marsham slowly dug the tip of a narrow stiletto beneath the nail of her index finger, whistling a tune with disinterest as she worked out the dirt she'd somehow gotten under her nails.

"My friends," the Wandering Wallace addressed the stiff line of people, placing his hands behind him and going up on the balls of his feet to sway back and forth a moment, "prick your finger."

Without a moment's hesitation, they did as he bade, blood welling up on delicate fingertips like perfect beads of red.

The Councilmen straightened, eyes wide or very narrow, but either way, the Wandering Wallace knew he had all of their attention focused on him.

"What do you want?" one councilman grated out, taking a slow step forward.

"A changing of the guard, so to speak. I want to make a difference by fixing this broken beast you call government. It is very near one hundred years since we declared our independence from England and yet can we truly say we are any better than when we were firmly under old George's thumb? We subjugate others—the Indians, the Africans, the Witches—and each time a new set of immigrants comes pouring onto our shores, hopeful as they are. We are a country built on lies and you perpetuate them!"

The Councilmen stood as still as their statuesque wives, but now all their eyes were narrowed. Wary.

"You would replace us," Loftkin hissed.

"Of course! We would be mad not to."

"Then wait for election results. Let this go peaceably and without incident. Elections are the proper way to make such changes. If the majority agrees with you."

"Ha!" The Wandering Wallace chortled, the sound sharp and short. "You own these people, body and mind! You lie to them through newspapers and headlines read over airship communication arrays. The idea of me convincing such obedient citizens to *vote* you out is preposterous!" He shook his head. "My power has its limits so I will do this my way. The risk is one I accept. As are the rewards.

"My friends," he said firmly, "knife points at your wrists ..."

Marion and Evie stepped forward, aghast, but Tsu stayed still and the Wandering Wallace raised his hand.

"All these good men need do is step down. Abdicate their thrones, so to speak. Then no one will be hurt. But sometimes greedy men need additional convincing."

The room filled further as Jordan, Caleb, and Rowen came in through the side door and Lord Gregor and Lord Morgan pushed their way in through the front, Stache following them, watching and waiting for fresh orders.

There was an uneasy moment as more eyes scanned bodies, faces, and weapons, the situation newly assessed.

Loftkin nearly shouted with joy, seeing Gregor Burchette. "Tell them to drop their weapons!"

"Yes," Jordan agreed, looking at the Wandering Wallace and the people standing stiffly behind him. "Instruct them to drop their knives."

Gregor shook his head at Loftkin. "I daresay this man's concern is a valid one. And this Council is long in need of a significant change."

"What?" Loftkin roared.

"Step down. I will rally no troops—good men all—to your defense. Not any longer."

Tsu drifted to the long table, unrolling papers and setting them before each outraged man.

The Wandering Wallace pointed his raven's beak at the papers. "Sign those and go home. Let them serve as your most noble of resignations."

The men looked at the hostages, and the host of others crowding the chamber, and picking up the provided pens, they set to signing.

*Philadelphia*

"Truly?" A woman's voice suddenly asked. Lady Marsham stepped forward in Lady Astraea's occupied body, her hips swaying and her eyes cold. "You call this a rebellion—a coup? Will this give you the revenge we are all due?"

Jordan's gaze found her mother, as did the gaze of her father. "Mother—"

Marsham leapt behind Catrina, disarmed her neatly and pressed her own stiletto to Catrina's throat. "In every life a little rain must fall, in every rebellion a little blood must spill ..."

"Do *not*," Jordan stepped forward.

Rowen's hand grasped her arm. "She is not ..."

"She is not my mother," Jordan agreed.

"Marsham," the Wandering Wallace said calmly. "Let the girl go. There is no need for violence."

In silent agreement, Marion shifted his weight.

"*Marsham*?" Jordan asked, her eyes narrowing.

The woman ignored Jordan, and rolling her eyes hissed, "Oh, I think there is. Let me gut just one little fishy—this most trouble-some one. She has been a thorn in the side to everyone. I can see it in the deepest bits of my hostess's brain. I see it—I see it all. This girl is the reason Jordan was taken and Made. She was the wedge between Jordan and Rowen's blossoming relationship and I doubt anyone will truly miss her ..." She pressed the blade more firmly to the flesh of Catrina's throat.

"Drop the blade," Jordan commanded, fingers flexing at her side as she tasted the air in the room—tested it. "Or I will ..."

"Or you will what?" Marsham snapped, whipping the weapon straight for her head.

"Miss Jordan!" came the deep and booming warning from John, the freed slave who worked for the Astraeas because of their reputation for generosity.

It seemed word of revolution had spread to all.

A rogue wind caught the knife and held it, halting it inches from the eye of its intended target.

The remaining knives were wrenched free of ruby ring adorned fingers and hurled at Jordan with equal spite.

They, too, stopped and hung before Jordan, quivering in the air. With a snort and a wave of her hand she cast them to the floor, sticking their points two inches deep into the broad wood boards.

"You must teach them all respect, Wallace!" Marsham shrieked. "Lay them low so they understand true power!"

Jordan watched the Wandering Wallace, her eyes wide as she pulled every bit of moisture out of the goblets and tankards in the room, broke it apart and forced it to reshape ...

A wet wind delivered a stinging backhand to the woman wearing Lady Astraea's face, knocking her away from Catrina with a yelp, and onto her rump.

The Wandering Wallace rushed past Jordan, tugging a knife from midair and he leaped onto Marsham, growling, "I should not have brought you back ..." And he dug the blade into her flesh.

"The stone!" John shouted. "Here ..." He tossed something that sparkled with light and life, the Wandering Wallace catching it with a deft hand before his strong sense of decency made John look away.

The Wandering Wallace dug one soul stone out, throwing it

wide of Marsham's grasping hands as the woman beneath him shuddered and died.

Again.

The body convulsed even as he slipped the fresh gemstone into the hole in her chest and pressed the wound closed with his hand.

She was still.

He jumped back from her and looked to Jordan. "*You* must bring her back. Call lightning in a pulse and restart her heart ..."

Jordan's breath ragged, she reached for lightning, but found nothing. She flexed her fingers, thought with spite of Catrina lying so close, of her mother, replaced callously by the Wandering Wallace's political desires ...

Betrayal surrounded her.

Her breath caught, her eyes blurred and the fire in her soul— that bit that connected to whirling weather and simmering storms was snuffed.

Smothered.

Dead as her mother.

"Quickly now ..."

She tried again, but there was nothing left to draw from anymore—she was filled only with sorrow, made hollow by exhaustion.

She felt someone else's fingers fill the spaces between hers and Rowen's lips brushed her ear and he began to sing, to fill her head with hope. "Your courage is the key—"

She lost herself in the notes of his voice and choked out the words, "—to freeing yourself—" and light burst from the fingers of her free hand, and finding her mother's body, it lit her like a freshly falling star.

She sat up, hand over her heart—over her soul stone—and Jordan and Morgan rushed to embrace her, but not before Morgan used the metal tip of his cane to crush the wayward crystal that had once possessed her.

Kneeling and wrapping his arms around his wife he whispered. "I knew it wasn't you ... I knew the truth all along—deep inside—but I am such a dense, proud old man. God," he said, "how glad I am to have you back!"


*Philadelphia*


The Wandering Wallace adjusted a pocket watch he held in his hand, and all who had stood so stiffly moments before relaxed, the light fading from their ruby rings as a new light—that of independence—returned to their eyes.

Jordan stood and took a long step back. "This evening I learned the Wildkin are swimming for the north. Gathering their forces and leaders. The War has reached a head and we all risk more lives being lost," she said solemnly to the crowd. "But there is hope! This war is a contrived military exercise—a way the Council diverted our attention from real issues—issues that would have changed your lots in life—improved your stations. Now is the time to rally and end this war—make a peace with the Wildkin and allow us to focus on the things that matter—the things that will improve our lives here and now."

Gregor pointed to the Councilmen and shouted, "Take them into custody for crimes against their own people!"

Though there were no guards, people in the crowd moved swiftly and the Councilmen were dragged from the room, Gregor Burchette following and sparing only a glance for his son. And a smile.


*Aboard the Artemesia*


"What a fine, fine job you have done keeping my ship so well," Jordan proclaimed when she and most of the others returned to the *Artemesia*. The Wandering Wallace, Marion, Stache, and Miyakitsu remained behind to work on things of government import, and the greater part of the army (now mixed human and mech) had returned to the *Tempest,* readying to meet the Wildkin, peaceably if possible.

Meggie beamed up at her.

"It went well?" Bran asked.

"Amazingly well," Jordan admitted. "Miraculously well!" She swept the clouds back around them and closed her eyes, raising the *Artemesia* into a sky that was only now beginning to lighten.

Not far away, Evie, Jack at her side, was again raising the *Tempest.*

"North," Jordan said.

At her feet, Rowen sat by Caleb and together the three of them sang their way north to intercept the Wildkin and end a war that never should have been.

Philadelphia

It was shortly after the Wandering Wallace welcomed Morgan Astrea back onto the Council and appointed Gregor Burchette, and Marion Kruse as well, that he traveled to the menacing and medieval looking Eastern State Penitentiary to speak to past-Councilman Yokum.

It only required a brief conversation seated in the skylit solitary confinement cell for the Wandering Wallace to make his decision as to Yokum's future.

Seeing him freed, and seeing that other substantial changes were already in the works, the mood in Philadelphia quickly became one of celebration. It was merely two evenings after the bloodless coup that, as the Wandering Wallace worked late on Philadelphia policy, he heard the sweet sounds of a violin encouraging the singing of a crowd somewhere outside the Council Chambers.

Setting down his pen, he replaced his favorite and most fearsome mask—that of a dragon—and he stepped out onto the street and was immediately swept up by the raucous crowd, bumped along until he was nearly face-to-face with the musician.

She bent and swayed in time to the music, just one more part of a living, breathing song. Until she saw the masked man before her. The bow scraped across the violin's strings, delivering an unholy noise, and she dropped her arms, staring at him, her mouth agape. "Is it you?" she asked, stepping down from a wooden crate. A small dog took her place, dancing around on its hind legs. "Come, Zeeke," she instructed, and the dog stopped and cocked its head in curiosity. "Wallace," she whispered, "my son, is it truly you?"

He nodded, and grinning at him, she thumped the bow against her chest, giving a whoop of joy.

"I have searched for you—but it seems I am never where you are when you are! Oh, my beautiful, beautiful boy!" she exclaimed. "And you are the one who did this?" she asked, swinging her bow out over the heads of the crowd. "You have set straight this city?"

"With help from the finest of friends," he nodded, suddenly shy.

"Oh, I knew you were clever. I knew you were good!" She wrapped her arms around his neck. "But do prove it to me," she begged. "Take off the mask you wear and let me see my sweet son's face!"

He hesitated, but she said, "What man who is proud of the person he has become—of the things he has done—and who owns up to his past mistakes and looks to a better future for all should go about masked? We all have scars," she reminded solemnly.

With a nod and a racing heart, he removed the dragon's scaled and glittering head and hood and stood there, scarred and bare to the gawking crowd. But his mother screamed in joy again, and, reaching out, grabbed his face and covered it in kisses.

The crowd roared their approval. And it was then he knew that as this new man, this bold and honest man, he would need to have a bold and honest talk with Tsu about her origin. And their future.

And he realized he finally owed his friends beautiful handcut invitations to quite a celebration.

*Maine*

They were amassing in the waters far below when Jordan cleared the clouds away. Finding the spot that teemed with the greatest volume of Merrow, she set the *Artemesia* down on an island thick with trees. The *Tempest* followed suit.

They tempted fate still more by making their way to the water's edge, past scraggly wild blueberry bushes, Jordan wearing a cloud like a cloak to keep her raw power ready. She had been unable to convince the Maker, Maude, and especially little Meggie to stay aboard the Artemesia, so she let her frustration spark out in tiny bursts off lightning. At the lapping water's edge Jordan gathered her courage, pushed down her memory of the one Merrow attack she had witnessed, and announced, "We wish to speak to a representative of your people."

The water thrashed in response. She cocked her head and corrected her perception. Not precisely the water, but something within it and something—no, Jordan thought—*someone* rose from the water.

Droplets cascaded down the Merrow's long hair and skin like thousands of silver beads and dripping diamonds danced in starlight, and she remained calf-deep in the waters just offshore, her body supple and shimmering and so very close to human that Jordan's breath caught in her throat.

Close to human, but not so heavy. Not so hairy nor so apelike.

Beautiful.

As horrifying as the other Merrow had been, so equally gorgeous was this one.

Jordan found herself strangely jealous of the creature, who seemed more than human with her glittering and glistening scales and muted facial features, which were more like Miyakitsu's than anyone else's. Where Jordan had hair, this creature had long strands of stuff that at first glance seemed to be different varieties of seaweed, as if a section of the ocean floor had grown into her scalp allowing plants to root and join with her. Spines flashed like silver needles along her sleek back, and she rustled like a porcupine, perhaps deciding if she greeted friend or foe.

Where Jordan had hands, she had webbing that ran between long slender fingers, giving her something akin to fins at the end of each well-muscled arm. Where Jordan had legs, she had a long and curving tail that held her upright in the slowly rolling surf but twisted like a serpent's end, coiling in the water and changing into a fluke that seemed almost tattered. But Jordan stared at the appendage and saw the edge was not tattered at all but deckled like the edge of an elegant paper. Along its edge pearls glittered, piercing her tail's fluke alongside silver and gold rings large enough to be bracelets.

This was no simple soldier Merrow.

This was nothing like the Merrow who attacked the horses on Jordan's way to Holgate.

This Wildkin sported no gaping mouth with rows of sharp and protruding teeth or eyes set in the sides of her head rather than the front ... All across her shimmering skin designs seemed delicately etched—flowers and grasses and tree leaves—things of the land decorated her flesh, sparkling over her skin and scales like they were as ephemeral as tracery drawn in the morning dew.

This was a creature that evaded Jordan's ability to describe her. She stood before them all, commanding their attention. And—

—their awe.

Throughout the surf, slipping in and out of waves like serpents, other Merrow swam, fleshy snakes undulating barely below the surface of the water.

Jordan only caught glimpses of them—of faces and fins as they split the surface and dove below again. She thought among the spines and skins she also saw the tips of spears—of weaponry crafted of black volcanic rock and shattered sea shells strapped to narwhal horns.

They were so utterly amazing.

So foreign.

So deadly.

So wickedly and wondrously primitive.

Jordan lowered her hands, letting sparks of lightning fall and smolder in the damp grass by her feet. This was the moment then —the reason she and the rest of them had disembarked from their ships—in hopes a leader might be reasoned with.

That through words rather than war understanding might be reached.

Her eyes narrow, she assessed them, remembering how fast Merrow could surge over land using their tails like coiled springs to propel them. She shivered at the memory of flying Merrow, gnashing teeth, the screams of horses and the shouts of men. They had seemed so savage then. So cruel.

But now they were ... she cocked her head.

Still wild.

There was no doubt about that. But, even swimming as they did, they seemed somehow at peace.

The queen raised her hands and opened her mouth to speak. Great fluted gills shivered along the sides of her ribcage, fluttering as she spoke.

Transfixed by her voice—it was an entire minute before Jordan realized she could understand no part of what was being said.

Except for Jack's, "Shite. How do we arrive at peace if we cannot understand each other's words?"

Meggie stepped forward, and standing beside Jordan, took her hand.

Bran was not far behind, a bag hanging from his shoulder.

"Papa," Meggie whispered. "She is calling me ..." She squeezed Jordan's fingers so tightly Jordan winced, but she looked down on the towheaded angel.

"Who?" Bran asked, his voice snaring in his throat.

Jordan saw how his eyes went from Meggie to the queen and back, but Meggie's attention had fallen on the bag slung over his shoulder.

"Sybil," she said. "Sybil is calling, Papa ..."

"Do not answer her," he whispered, his voice a desperate plea. "Do not let her back into your head, dear little dove," he begged. "She is here only for an ending—to find final peace."

"No, Papa," Meggie insisted. Her hand went limp in Jordan's hand, and now it was Jordan who gripped her tight to hold her at her side. "I must answer. Sybil says ..." She tilted her head and the wind tousled her pale curls. "She says we are connected. That water makes us and hems us in and rushes through us, connecting us all together ..." Her eyes flashed and she yanked her hand free of Jordan's. "Give me the skull, Papa."

"What? No," he said, taking a step back and pressing the bag against his side.

But Jordan saw how the bag at his side—with the skull inside it—vibrated—hummed.

Up the hill, the army watched and waited, Rowen at its head.

Suddenly butterflies rose up from the wild blueberry bushes, surrounding Bran, a swirling mass of beating wings coloring and thickening the air around him. They spun in a whirlwind only inches from his flesh, wings flashing, Bran shouting and trying not to slap at them, trying to focus on keeping the skull in his bag from doing whatever it seemed intent upon.

Then Meggie was directly before him, her hands out expectantly, and the butterflies peeled away from Bran, a colorful cloud dividing and going off in different directions as quickly as they had come. He gaped at his daughter.

"Papa," she whispered. "Trust me."

He blinked, then dug into his bag and relinquished the skull.

The child held it, cradled it.

Meggie raised the skull high, rolled her head forward, and closed her eyes. Out of the water rose another form, one fashioned of a rainbow of droplets. A form mirroring Meggie's own.

The water around the Merrow Queen stilled, and as Meggie spoke in a voice not quite her own, her watery form shimmered, making ripples that raced to the queen, caressing the spot her calves and feet should have been.

"Great Queen," Meggie began, "we humbly beseech you to set aside this war, to join instead with us in peace. Our government has been replaced. The men who wronged you will be punished according to our laws."

The water rushed back to them, sparkling, and Meggie answered in a slightly more melodious voice, "We have only sought peace since our discovery that the death of our prince so long ago was murder by our own kind. But every time we reach out in peace, you return our offer by redoubling the war."

"No longer," Meggie assured. "We wish for full and lasting peace. Search my soul. Reach through us and see the truth in our words. Will you give this peace to our people? And grant it to your own as well?"

The waters around the queen stirred, waves choppy and agitated, but she raised her arms and made the water grow flat as glass, saying, "Yes. We are one as the water is one in our desire for peace. But know this: as each ripple and drop is felt by the ocean, so is each action and intent felt by all the peoples of the earth. Tread carefully and mayhaps someday we shall see each other as kin once more." Then she burst fully from the water, twisted and turned back in a dramatic flip, and disappeared into the water leaving not even a splash behind.

*Maine*

Jordan looked at the land, at the great pond leading out to the sea, and the solid beauty of the earth on which the *Artemesia* now rested while its crew again readied for flight. Having come down the slope to join her, Rowen slipped an arm around her waist, his eyes on her as if he waited for her to say some grand thing—to make some wise political statement about equality or peace or love ... But all the statements had been made through action. The slaves had been freed—what they made of their newfound freedom was beyond her control and certainly not for her to judge. Peace had been agreed upon—whether it would hold or not depended on the ones who had brokered the deal and on the people they represented. Jordan could do nothing more about that, either.

Rowen tightened his grip on her.

Most everything had been set as right as she and her companions could make it.

And what of the feelings she felt for Rowen?

What of love? Well, it was something she was just now beginning to discover and understand herself—surely she was not one to preach or advise on something as desperately powerful as love ...

She pondered a moment, looking toward Meggie, who stood between Bran and Maude and looked as expectant as Rowen did. Letting loose a long sigh, Jordan Astraea broke free of Rowen's grasp to lean down and say, "It seems to me it is time to set someone to rest ..."

Meggie nodded and held out the skull.

"You have done you and your kind proudly," Jordan whispered to the skull. She reached into her dress and pulled out the soul stone she had found in her cell at Holgate, a soul stone she had carried with her frequently since. "I believe this, too, is part of you, dear child, and so, it too should have peace." She reached for Rowen's sword and, setting the soul stone on a nearby rock, she smashed it with the pommel.

Sparks flew into the air, flying up like tiny butterflies before evaporating into the bright sky above.

They buried the skull where the blueberry bushes were

thinnest and marked it with a modest cross, and then they made their way back to Topside on the *Artemesia.* Jordan paused there, leaning out over the bowsprit and examining the earth below.

Making her decision, she turned and looked at Meggie, her smile soft. "I tried to protect you by turning this ship away from Philadelphia and conflict once—to let you hide from your powers and grow up just like everyone else. But I think, having seen the hero inside you speak up so boldly, perhaps that is not your destiny." Jordan shrugged. "Perhaps falling into shadow is not fit for one with a heart so bright and bold." She licked her lips, considering. "So I have a question for you." She paused. "Will you watch my ship while I step away for a while?" Jordan gently pinched Meggie's sun-kissed cheek, noticing the spray of freckles across the bridge of her tiny nose. No longer would a Conductor or captain be fated to live out their lives beneath dark storm clouds.

There were better ways to live than in darkness, after all.

Meggie nodded, a look of great seriousness changing her inno-cent features into those of the determined and capable young woman Jordan felt sure was only a few years in the child's future. "Of course," she said. "I will watch her and take great care with her. And if ever I need you—"

Jordan chuckled, brushing a stray curl back from Meggie's forehead. "Oh, I do not think that you will," she interrupted, flashing a savage smile.

Still Meggie shook her head. "If ever I need you—" she began again.

"All you need do is call," Jordan assured, pointing back to the ship's communication device.

Meggie nodded and Jordan tousled her hair, smiling at both Bran and Maude and knowing they would be well kept by their daughter, and she, Jordan Astraea of House Astraea, once fallen and once famed, could now retire into anonymity with Rowen— at least anonymity here, on the beautiful island not far from the coastline where true magick—the magick of peace and under-standing—had finally shown itself.

What more could any hero in any story ask but all she'd been granted?

"Farewell," Jordan whispered, kissing the child's forehead.

Meggie smiled, saying, "Farewell—"

"—*Stormbringer*," they concluded in unison.

That day, and for many after, the weather did precisely as it wished, with neither a push nor a pull from the Witch that shouldn't have ever been. And that was precisely as Jordan Astraea felt it should be.

# Afterword

Sleep not, dream not; this bright day

Will not, cannot last for aye;

Bliss like thine is bought by years

Dark with torment and with tears.

—EMILY BRONTË

I would like to tell you that Jordan Astraea and Rowen Burchette went on to live their lives in the peaceful anonymity that Jordan so desperately desired. I would like to tell you that they married in a proper ceremony and that everyone who was anyone (as well as a grand selection of nobodies) were there and that they had a lovely (if merely comfortable) home and children that were as pretty and clever as both of their parents (and as bad at processing cucumbers as their father) and that both Rowen and Jordan lived to see grandchildren and great-grandchildren who never knew war, famine, or disease, and that, finally, with their time here on earth done, their lives fulfilled, that they died together in their sleep and that where they were buried two trees were planted which, in time, grew together as a sublime demonstration of the power of their love lasting even beyond the grave.

I would like to tell you all that.

But that would be a lie.

Because, as you and I both know, dear reader, the journey to freedom and equality is not something that is made in a single bound. Many people, though technically free, are enslaved. By background, by circumstance, by their own desires ... And a peace that comes quickly is seldom lasting and true. People have their reasons for wanting, making, and continuing war—whether it be a war between friends or lovers, or between colleagues or countries. Most times the reasons are petty and shortsighted, but they are, technically, reasons.

So to guarantee you that no one ever came calling to again ask the aid of Jordan and Rowen would be naïve—good people are always needed and sometimes most often needed where they seem unwanted. And to leave you believing that they and theirs never wanted for anything—never suffered? Well, that seems highly unrealistic in fiction as well as in fact.

Yes, there might be Weather Witches, Wraiths, and Wardens (and frequent capitalization that irks some critics) but a time without want or need? A time free of suffering?

Let me be clear: This book should never be shelved under "Utopian."

Fine, fine, you concede. Slavery isn't cleared up as easily as a breakout of acne, and peace may or may not last depending on the selfish motives of leaders.

But what about love?

Ah, love. That—*that* I will grant you because whereas I may not believe in the possibility of everlasting peace or absolute equality, I do believe *absolutely* in the power of love.

So yes, readers, friends, fans ... Jordan and Rowen do have a love that will last. Is it an easy love? No. Real love takes time, energy, work, and frequently requires forgiveness. Will the next few years be simple for our lovebirds? Likely not. She will suffer sleepless nights as a result of all she's faced. He will feel guilt and possibly fall into depression because he didn't reach and rescue her before so many awful things happened to her. She will have trouble trusting people and he will likely never let another female close to him other than Jordan.

They will argue and fight. She will stomp her feet and storm clouds will appear and he will stomp his feet and ...

... he'll stomp his feet some more, I guess, and probably raise his voice.

But they'll fight in a healthy way. They'll never be petty or vicious. She'll never call him a mama's boy (though she may think it) and he'll never say she's stupid or ugly or bring up the fact she was once so out of control that she cut herself to feel like she did have control over *something*. They won't dredge up the past or lay their hands on one another. They will never abuse each other—not verbally or physically.

Because they love each other.

And as imperfect as people and relationships are, love ... well, love is about as perfect as things get here on earth, and I figure they've fought through so much that was far less than perfect that they'll fight with a strength to rival any paranormal anything to maintain something that *is* perfect.

And, in short, that's what I want for Rowen and Jordan—a love that lasts. And, as this is my series and these characters (messes that they are) are *my* creations, I get to play god and say, "You two—love one another" and it's all good.

And frankly, that's what I want most of all for me and mine and you and yours, dear reader—love—a love that's worth the struggle and the sacrifice.

Love that lasts.

Forever and always.

Thank you for joining us all—my original team at St. Martin's Press, my family, beta readers, and dear friends who saw this series through—on this amazing and tumultuous journey—this book, this series, my *career* is dedicated to each and every one of you who has given my books a chance to grow in your hearts.

# WEATHER WITCH

Watch for the new edition of the Weather Witch series—coming in late 2026—and packed with even more action and adventure!

## Weather Witch
## Stormbringer
## Thunderstruck

Some fled the Old World to avoid war, and some fled to leave behind magick. Yet even the fiercely regulated and stormpowered New World cannot staunch the power that wells up in certain people, influencing the weather and calling down storms. Hunted, the Weather Witches are forced to power the rest of the population's ships, as well as their every necessity, and luxury, in a time when steam power is repressed.

Jordan Astraea of Philadelphia hails from a background with no taint of magick, but on her seventeenth birthday she is accused of summoning an unscheduled storm. Taken from her family, Jordan is destined to be enslaved as a Conductor — an airliner's living battery. Her beau, Rowen, finds himself forced aboard a different airliner — manned by a dangerous crew and carrying a cargo so treasonous, it will herald a storm of revolution for the still young United States.

# BEASTLY BABES
## Nine Classic Tales of Female Vampires

Long before Dracula haunted the pages of literature, readers devoured tales of the vixens of vampirism: Carmilla, Lamia, Clarimonde, and others! Nine classic Hell's belles of horror fill the pages of this curated, edited, and annotated volume of traditional vampire tales written by literary greats including Poe, Kipling, and Goethe—giving readers a murderous mix of fabulous femmes fatales!

Edited and annotated for Wolf Print Press, LLC by award-winning author Shannon Delany to include: Notes following each story, biographical information about the author and his life, Book Club Questions, and more.

**Carmilla** by Joseph Sheridan Le Fanu
**Lamia** by John Keats
**Berenice** by Edgar Allan Poe
**Christabel** by Samuel Taylor Coleridge
**Wake Not the Dead** by Ernst Raupach
**The Vampire** by Madison Julius Cawein
**Clarimonde** by Théophile Gautier (translated by Lafcadio Hearn)
**The Vampire** by Rudyard Kipling
**The Bride of Corinth** by Johann Wolfgang von Goethe (translated by E. A. Bowring and translated by Aytoun and Martin).

# 13 to LIFE SERIES

*The new edition of the series which was published by St. Martin's Press in 2010 is now greatly expanded and packed with even more action, adventure, romance, and angst!*

## 13 to Life
## Secrets and Shadows
## Bargains and Betrayals
## Destiny and Deception
## Rivals and Retribution

After the sudden death of her mother, all Jessie Gillmansen wants is to deal with the loss in her own time, avoiding any more life-altering changes and regaining some sense of control. Living in the slow-moving town of Junction and focusing on school and the strangeness surrounding the wolf attack in a nearby city may be her best bet—

—until Pietr Rusakova moves in.

Pietr is more than good looks and a fascinating accent—he's a guy with a dangerous secret whose mysterious past is about to catch up to him and turn Jessie's life upside down all over again, threatening everything she thinks she knows about life and the world she lives in.

With secrets coming to light and danger closing in from all sides, time's running out for Pietr and Jessie, and it seems change is one thing Jessie definitely can't avoid.

## Teenage love, loss, and oh, yeah...
## ...werewolves!

# About the Author

Since she was a child Shannon Delany has written stories, beginning writing in earnest when her grandmother fell unexpectedly ill. Previously a teacher and now a farmer raising heritage livestock, Shannon lives and writes in Upstate New York and enjoys traveling to talk to people about most anything.

To find out more about Shannon Delany's books, her writing and publishing journey, and the myriad things (and people) included in it, hop over to her website at:

**ShannonDelany.com**

Sign up for her **"Frequently Infrequent"** newsletter at:

Shannon can also be found on a wide variety of social media platforms where she is frequently encouraging other writers and authors, and welcomes many readers.

www.ingramcontent.com/pod-product-compliance
Lightning Source LLC
Chambersburg PA
CBHW070437300726
48975CB00007B/1955